NEXT YEAR PERHAPS

Next Year Perhaps is Chris Clinton's first novel. It is a consequence of many years of adventures in Saskatchewan, Canada's northern wilderness. Sometimes alone, sometimes with friends, many times with high school teenagers.

Chris Clinton was born, raised and educated in the UK, moved to Canada forty years ago to be a teacher, and with his wife, raised their family of two sons. They now have three grandchildren.

He still resides in Saskatchewan, but spends many months of the year travelling to different parts of the world, Ethiopia in particular, seeking further adventure and writing opportunities.

NEXT YEAR PERHAPS

Chris Clinton

NEXT YEAR PERHAPS

For Keith

Olympia Publishers

www.olympiapublishers.com
OLYMPIA PAPERBACK EDITION

A CIP catalogue record for this title is
available from the British Library.

ISBN: 978-1-84897-045-8

First Published in 2010

Olympia Publishers
60 Cannon Street
London
EC4N 6NP

Printed in Great Britain

Dedication

For my family, friends and students who accompanied me on
many canoeing adventures on the rivers and lakes of
Saskatchwan's northern wilderness. Together we faced the
elements that challenge the mind, body and soul.

Acknowledgements

This Book could not have been written without the encouragement and help of many people. Thanks to Rob Clarke, teacher of English, who read my first rough draft of the opening forty or fifty pages. His positive vibes were all I needed to continue writing (I resisted his recommendation to add a villainous Mendoza to liven up the characters!). My thanks go to three people who were instrumental in editing the final draft: Rae Benson, a school librarian, Roxane Poulin, my daughter-in-law, and Lilian Donahue, a canoeing partner on many trips. Thank you for your time, patience and support as this story slowly came to fruition.

I also wish to thank the many students who patiently listened to my readings at the campfire circle while canoeing through areas encountered in the novel, and who pleasantly surprised me by requesting more on subsequent evenings. There is no better tonic to keep one feeling young and invigorated than to take on an adventure in the Canadian wilderness with a group of teenagers.

Many thanks to Vinh Tran, my publishing coordinator, and to the staff at Olympia Publishing in London, England, for your faith and cooperation while I was travelling overseas.

Before this novel was written, several books were important for research and inspirational purposes. Among these, I wish to mention *The Lonely Land* by Sigurd Olson; *Company of Adventures* and *Ceasars of the Wilderness* by Peter C. Newman; *Lost in the Barrens* by Farley Mowat; and *The North West Company* by Marjorie Campbell.

The novel is based on countless canoeing experiences; nonetheless, it is a work of fiction, and all characters and events are pure fiction. Although many landmarks on the Churchill River are recognizable to fellow adventurers and are correctly named, some have been slightly altered to fit the shape of the story.

NEXT YEAR PERHAPS

Moonlight silvers the treetops but fails to penetrate the evergreen canopy. The undergrowth, in funereal black, is deathly silent yet voraciously alive: herbivorous ants march, a ragged column scuttling from a harvesting operation to their log home; a predatory spider weaves a death-net, its tiger-striped legs meticulously suturing silken threads; mosquitoes dip proboscises into nectar-filled flower-cups and inadvertently become flora sexual intermediaries; and microbes forage, clean-up, multiply.

The forest's creatures sense the timber wolf's arrival. Black-opal eyes flash when a moon-dart pierces the darkness. Alders and Labrador tea, pushed aside, bend as if genuflecting. Velvet feet crush last year's leaves, stirring up sweet aromatic decay. The beast pauses, ears probing. Damp air licks each black nostril. A tongue slips between fangs, hangs glistening.

Wolf-scents presage the *rendezvous*. The animal remembers: playful cubs, brawling adversaries, and the male sibling that challenged him last spring.

Squatting on a tuft of spiky grass, the wolf, head back, coat burnished blue-grey by moonlight, summons the pack, its howls reaching the stars. The deep-chested oratorio floods the valley, pinballs between cloistered trunks, sinks into mossy hollows and fades into the night. Creatures hearing that call take heed. Moose lift heavy-racked heads, alerted to their destiny; ravens savour easy pickings; owls remember scuffles in red-stained snow.

Seven adults arrive, singly or in pairs, males and females, each in deference – tails between their legs and lips peeled back in conciliatory grins. A female leads in four grown, tail-wagging pups. Excitement erupts into a welcoming fracas of circling, wrestling, and curious noses nuzzling warm genitals.

Alpha-male sits apart, stately remote.

The scrimmaging languishes and the wolves slump to the sand, lick and scratch. One, a lone grey male, tongues an angry groin wound.

The initiates' mother struts across the knoll in front of her mate and enters the trees. Alpha-male rises, stretches and follows. Meeting him at the treeline, she prances lightly with bowed head, whines softly. Coming together, she reaches up and licks his muzzle, nibbles his cheek until he arches and drops his head; his stomach convulses and disgorges feathered remains. A spruce grouse? She avidly consumes his gift. They disappear into the forest, licking mouths, gamboling on their front legs. The pack, inured to foreplay, ignores the exit.

The copulants return as dawn paints her colours; she summits the knoll and howl-barks the sinking moon; he lopes toward, and scatters the recumbents into the pines. At his mate's side, he dedicates two lugubrious cries soaked with passion and hunger, a lament for the ailments of the wild, cries of defiance to humanity. Without a backward glance, he vanishes into the forest, followed by eleven disciples.

The grey limps in pursuit, resolved to betray, to usurp command.

ONE

A heavily laden canoe edges steadfastly across the lake named *Nipew,* a Cree word meaning *Dead Lake.* The name, Indian or white man's, evokes a pall of despair, overshadowing the spectacular landscape. Decades ago, the Cree inhabiting these rock-encrusted shores, hunting in the boreal forest and fishing the clear icy waters, were devastated by smallpox and starvation. The canoeist knows *Nipew's* history, and on every crossing, bizarre pictures escape from the dungeon of his memory. This time, his head aches, as though a native calling-drum is relentlessly pounding in his skull. The misshapen Tilley hat covering his grey, cropped hair seems to offer no protection from the unusually hot July sun. His journey only three days old and already he's questioning the sanity of his decision.

"The lab results aren't good, Mr. Jordan."

The prognosis harks back and ricochets in his mind, triggers a sweat down his back. Few words said, yet sufficient to kill a ten-year dream.

Peter Jordan shakes his head, mulls over the chain of events that has brought him to *Nipew.* It began on a Wednesday afternoon, overcast, snow barely melted, sitting in the doctor's office, hands white-knuckled on the chair arms, his eyes glued to the man's bronzed face.

The doctor, seemingly too young to even be qualified, three months in Canada with his family from blood-soaked South Africa, had ordered tests – blood, X-ray, colonoscopy. The results, hidden in a tally of numbers on a sheet of paper, stared at him.

"Give me the verdict," Peter Jordan had demanded vehemently, fearfully, scared his sentence would match the one that had shattered his life two years ago, that had taken Danika from him.

"There's a tumour on your colon. Fortunately, quite small. With an operation it can be removed. I've booked you into University Hospital next Monday. Of course, you'll miss the rest of the school year." The doctor's velvety voice and unexpected accent, softened by the lilt of the African veldt, made the news surreal – cruel justice presented on a silver platter.

"And if I don't?"

"Hard to say. Gives you a year, maybe six months. The worst scenario... three months. But if it ruptures, you may have only a few days. Four max. Much depends on you. Diet, attitude, how you look after yourself. You see, what will happen..."

"I'm canoeing to the Arctic this summer," Peter announced bluntly, as if accusing the man of sabotage.

"That's a long way, isn't it?" Peter gave one sharp nod. "Not such a good idea. Have the operation, Mr. Jordan, then go next year," the doctor had suggested with an endearing smile.

Peter had sat for several moments, concentrating furiously on his fingernails, conscious of the white shirt sticking to his skin, his bowel tightly knotted. The man's wrong! He's African. A witch doctor, godammit!

"What will happen... if I go on my trip, that is?" he said, loosening his tie and unbuttoning his collar.

"This type of cancer usually grows like a napkin ring around the large intestine, eventually blocking it," the doctor said, making an O with his thumb and forefinger, then squeezing them together into a fist. "You won't be able to eat or drink. The pain will be excruciating – worse than a kick in the testicles. It's likely the cancer will metastasise, invade your liver and kidneys."

"What about painkillers?"

"Only morphine will help."

Why me? Why not Arthur Sinclair, a lousy teacher in the same math department? Heavy drinker, overweight, a miserable bastard to his wife and kids, and mean to his students. Suddenly resentful, angered by the doctor's tapping pen, Peter stood, kicking back the chair.

"Give me three month's supply." The doctor, with a shrug, slid a prescription pad across the desk and scribbled.

"I'll tell you Friday – about the operation. Otherwise, I'll fill this," he'd said, waving the prescription as he went out the door.

At home, Peter had slumped into his armchair. When daylight faded, he stirred, and, with resolve hardening his face, had fallen into bed, eyes red from staring at a framed photograph. The family portrait. Taken nine years ago, it had celebrated in part his twentieth wedding anniversary. He'd married relatively late, at twenty-six, and Danika, younger by three years, had entered his life fresh from university. Their daughter, Sarah, was delivered by Caesarian two years after the big, Ukrainian-styled wedding. Danika's voice entered his head, encouraging at first and then alarming, reminding him of the pain she'd suffered and the relief of death, and questioning him on Sarah's whereabouts, questions he couldn't answer, didn't want to contemplate.

She jogged his memory. The crazy Arctic notion had taken root beside an evening campfire while canoeing on Saskatchewan's Churchill River.

"How about, one day, when we're good at this canoeing game," he'd mused, "tracing Alexander McKenzie's route to Inuvik?"

The brainchild that night had set them speculating, glibly discussing distances and supplies, rapids and portages, and how long such a venture would take. Subsequent trips would see the idea ferment, their conversations harping on the challenge. When Danika died, Peter adopted the Arctic expedition as a symbolic journey of their love, a celebration of their lives.

Now what? Fulfil the dream, or risk the knife. Go! And have surgery upon his return. Why not? The speed of the tumour's growth was as unpredictable as next week's weather. He'd read of cancer going into remission with a recipe of fresh air, a diet of staples, and a mind-filling challenge. I can beat this, he'd determined.

He skipped the appointment. Had told no one; his closest friends, colleagues, not even his daughter, Sarah. Two months later, with supplies packed and cache points arranged, he'd driven north to Missinipe and the Churchill River.

And now here he is, on *Nipew,* his five-seven body crunched into a canoe, his transportation for the next three months, his mind-set lodged in the early nineteenth century.

A band of Chipewyans, trading completed – beaver pelts for beads, and blankets, and steel knives – drunk on gut-burning Jamaican rum, had plundered a small community of white families infected with smallpox. Feverishly they'd donned the settlers' clothes and, unwittingly, precipitated the contagion of the disease. It over-ran the indigenes like fireweed. Indians perished by the thousands: Woodland Cree of the Boreal, Chipewyan from the Barrens, and the Sioux of the Great Plains. Unknowing, they believed that somehow they had angered the spirits: lumps became festering sores, pustules erupted – harbingers of death. Without natural immunity, they rapidly succumbed to the variola virus. Pits and scars marked the few survivors.

Medicine healers, wizened old men or women, had tried their usual remedies, their herbal concoctions; broth of willow bark, tea of crowberry, a wash from choke cherry, *Prunus virginiana,* that contained cyanide. But nothing stopped the persistent itching, the suffering, and the dying.

The tribe that had summer-camped along these north Saskatchewan shores had been decimated to thirty souls, and from that time the lake was dubbed *Nipew*, place of the dead. Even the animals; moose, wolf, wood bison, and deer had disappeared. Later generations hunted elsewhere, had avoided this lake – 'like the plague', Peter reflects with a bitter smile. On days like today, stifling with blistering heat and blistering flesh, had they, the Knisteneaux tribe, just lain in their teepees, or taken to the Churchill in birch canoes, like himself, in search of release? He'd read somewhere that many braves, overwrought with pain and loss of their machismo, had submerged themselves in the lake until they drowned. My fate could be the same, he meditates bleakly.

Peter dips the glistening paddle, catches the water on the blade, and with a fluid pull, pause, and outward curl perfects another J-stroke. Then another. And again. A monotonous rhythm. His lithe motion as he paddles shows upper body strength, surprising flexibility, and an expertise honed over many years. A necklace of gems hangs momentarily between blade and water. The sand-coloured fibreglass canoe cuts the water with a bow wave that extends V-shaped until it laps a distant shore. Peter estimates, thin blue eyes squinting, the distance to an island that hovers mirage-like on the skyline. To his left, south, he searches for a distinguishing shoreline feature. Two high outcrops, bare rock against a backdrop of green, enclose a narrow bay. Eyes drop to the waterproofed map, pinpoint his location and confirm that the island is three kilometres away. A half-hour, he figures, to shelter from the mid-day heat, a bite to eat, and to hopefully clear his head.

A sudden breeze caresses his shoulder, touches his bare leg, and goes on to corrugate the water fifty feet ahead. Peter instinctively glances behind, half-expecting cumulus clouds fluffing up on the horizon, but the sky is clear. Possibly an approaching change in the weather, or a native soul still not at rest, he muses.

Peter drifts a few yards from the rocky island, caught off guard by a choir of songbirds welcoming, as it were, this unexpected visitor to their roost. Tremolo chirps from several chipping sparrows provide a background pizzicato; a clear high whistle from a white-throated sparrow is singing *Oh Can, Canada, Canada, Canada,* and for harmony, the sweet notes of a yellow warbler join in. A red-winged blackbird's attempts to add its two cents worth are angelic, but after each promising start, it ends with a gurgling *tee-err.* Peter leans on his paddle across the gunwales, hardly breathing. His shoulders relax, his eyes light up his smile.

Strong strokes take him round a rocky point and into the shade of the island. Sculling sideways to shore, he stows the paddle between a weathered Duluth bag and the side of the canoe. Grasping the gunwales, he lifts his weight off the seat. Then, like unfolding a paper clip, painfully coaxes cramped legs from underneath him, grimacing as he straightens each limb in turn. Gingerly he stands, balances, places a foot firmly onto a rock, and slowly adds weight to it. It's dry. In early canoeing days, his first foothold, carelessly planted, had often sent him crashing, arms wind-milling, reaching for anything – overhanging branches, a friend's hand, the air even. Spread-eagled across the canoe, or up to his waist in water, he'd sworn, then laughed at himself because he hadn't noticed the rock's slimy veneer.

Peter Jordan arches backwards, stretching cramps, relishing the strength in his fifty-five-year old muscles. Compact with broad shoulders, he's upheld its square proportions by a lifetime of exercise; hiking, biking, and weekly visits to the gym. His stomach, however, once a hard knot, shows recent history – a lackadaisical diet triggered by the death of Danika, then rectified drastically two months ago.

Grabbing the bow, Peter hoists the canoe from the water. No bigger than a baseball diamond, the island is dense with trees; trembling aspen, black spruce, paper birch; and shrubs, red-osier dogwood, pincherry, red willow. The underbrush, a veritable lush carpet, includes Labrador tea, prickly hawthorn, and thick spongy moss.

He drifts over to the mossy bed where he had camped eight years earlier. The island had become a favourite call on Churchill trips. His face brightens. He remembers that first time, chuckles; squirrels had spent the better part of the night quarrelling outside the tent, keeping him and Danika awake. Exasperated, he'd eventually crawled out. The reason for the ruckus lay in tatters. The pesky animals had chewed his new synthetic-chamois towel to shreds. Hearing a squirrel high up in the black spruce, Peter is certain that it has inherited a nest with an orange-coloured lining.

Pushing his way into the bushes to urinate, he's surprised to find the old aspen that had been toppled prior to his first visit is in leaf. With half its roots still wedged into bedrock, the rest are sky-reaching, sapless claws, tinder brown and twisted. A spider's web hangs to ambush flying insects. Dried cadavers of flies bear evidence that the trap is lethal. With a toehold, he reflects rhetorically, a hand on his stomach, one can cling to life indeterminately.

Back at the canoe, Peter grabs his daypack from behind the seat, pulls out a plastic bag, and from it extracts a fist-sized piece of fresh bannock. Sitting in a handy hollow by the water, he chews the sweet, heavy bread.

As soon as he's finished, he lays back, pulls his hat over his eyes. Gone are the enjoyable catnaps after lunch the last few years, usually stretched out in a not-too-comfortable staff-room chair. Now, rather than women's chatter, bird-song rings in his ears, accompanied by the rustle of trembling leaves, the drone of a myriad flying insects, and the occasional rasping from an ill-tempered squirrel. Soon he sleeps, snoring softly.

He dreams. There's Sam and Emily, neighbours and canoeing companions for years, wishing him "a good trip" as he left home four days ago. They're unaware he might not return. Sam's tending his garden, mowing the lawns, and collecting his mail.

Colleagues flash to mind, coming at him like ghosts on a television screen. He tries to censure, to shelve them under 'Oblivion' where they belong, not wanting to hear their farewells. "See you when you get back." "When you come through Edmonton, phone me! Give us a couple of hours warning. Tidy the house. Right?"

Peter Jordan had retired with five others from a Saskatoon high school, each having poured their lives into a lethargic river, a thankless flow of Saskatoon's young. One hundred and eighty collective years of service, lifetimes of tempering young minds, or, depending on who you ask, tampering with them.

Countless students had passed through Mr. Jordan's classroom, faces remembered but names forgotten. In the early years, he had loved to teach, was devoted to his young charges, but changes over the last decade had left him disgruntled, resentful of self-serving, political mishandling. He yearned for a fresh opportunity. Canoeing, his passion, would open up new horizons, lead him to rarely travelled lakes and rivers of the Canadian shield, and carry him along the ancient highway that had pushed back Canada's boundaries two hundred years earlier.

Of course, there had been the requisite farewell banquets and parties organised by teachers, the school board, and other well-meaning friends, but Peter had quickly become exhausted by the hollow accolades, sickened by the mushy rhetoric, bored by the cards wishing good luck for the future. Future? Huh!

The doctor's again, but different. Danika sits beside him. She's given a year. Despite his prayers to a re-found God, in less than six months, six excruciating months, she'd shriveled into a yellow corpse. His care, his devotion, proved futile in the face of the merciless disease. He had tried to get her to quit, alternately pestering and scolding, pleading and demanding, but she continued smoking, stubbing out her last cigarette when the ambulance had taken her to the hospital.

Her face suddenly dances into his head, wasted, ashen eyes sunk into darkened skin, tufts of thinning hair. Words spew silently from lips tight over yellowed teeth, a wolfish grin. What's she saying? What's she telling him? Is it… a warning?

The cackling effigy shrinks, diminishing to a distant speck. Then, suddenly, it envelops him, even less human, racing down a mercurial river on a gurney. As it passes, a claw rises and gives a royal wave. A wave of farewell or a genuflection to mock his God? Close behind, wild hair flying, three Indians are giving chase in a birch-bark canoe. Two are paddling furiously, and the third, a medicine healer kneeling in the centre, is shaking a dark leather gourd and mouthing a chant. They catch up with her as she and her contraption are sinking. The healer leans over and grabs a clump of hair. The head rises, cascading water, but suddenly the hair comes out by the roots, like a scalp grabbed by a triumphant warrior. Peter clearly sees Danika's face, now beautiful beyond reason, as he remembers it on the day they met. She's thrashing the water beside the canoe, trying to stay afloat. Peter reaches out, reaches... The water covers her mouth, her nose. Her eyes open wide, bulging against eyelids as water washes over. A desperate move lifts her clear and she calls "Pet...er.r.r... So.ooo.n," then sinks. The lake becomes crystal smooth.

Peter's eyes flash open. A groan grates in his throat. His stomach churns. Tears well up and run hot down his cheek. He swipes them away with the back of an angry hand, knocking his hat off. Damn it! He draws a deep breath. The head-drum returns. Fists clench. His red shirt darkens, like blood, from sweat, not from the heat, but from a well of pain that is so deep, only in dreams, nightmares, does it surface.

He turns onto his side, slaps the Tilley hat onto his head. Leaning on his elbow, he watches two squirrels race from his daypack. His violent awakening had interrupted their thievery. They scamper across the rocks, towards the nearest black spruce. One with a chunk of bannock wedged in its mouth, the other giving chase. Peter can't help laughing as they scratch their spiral path up the trunk, bushy tails a quiver.

Realising that's all the napping he's likely to get, Peter jumps up, seals his pack, stows it, and within minutes, pushes off. Despite his fears, he'll press on, will follow his heroes, experience their drive for adventure, seek new lands that few eyes have witnessed; Peter Pond, Alexander Mackenzie, and John Franklin, who, prior to his ill-fated search for the North West Passage, had snowshoed this way in mid-winter from Cumberland House to Lake Athabasca.

Ahead, a dip in the horizon foretells where the river flows into *Nipew*. The afternoon promises more challenges than the morning. He'll face Churchill's current as it gushes out of Mountney Lake. Peter tingles with excitement, increases his tempo. His favourite section approaches; a series of turbulent rapids that test the best canoeists, that attract visitors – present-day voyageurs – from around the world. He has run them many times, gaily plunging downstream, purposely bouncing off the biggest waves to give his bow-partner a cold dousing.

However, this time will be different. He's alone and heading *up*stream, fighting the current, scrimmaging for every inch. Like recent years of teaching, he reflects ruefully, or, indeed, life itself.

Peter cocks his head. The murmur of tumbling water triggers a grin – rapids electrify more than lakes. The sound surges and fades like ocean waves sucking at a pebble beach. He drives firmly into the current, favouring eddies where possible, pushing the canoe between high, aspen-lined banks. Rounding a bend, his eyes light up like blue pearly buttons and excitement shimmies through his veins.

He has encountered many: rapids that are mere riffles, rapids that are a mass of white foam plunging over malignant rocks with frighteningly tight, twisting routes, on week-long trips in loaded canoes, on summer weekends with friends, joy-riding empty, exploiting their own wet-and-wild playgrounds. No matter their difficulty, all excite him, terrify him. He loves the anticipation – the void in his stomach, the hammering in his chest. They test his mettle as he threads a course. His reactions, slick and immediate, are faster than an epéeist. All too quickly the run is over and he's catching his breath, licking dry lips. When he becomes blasé, the river retaliates and bucks him unceremoniously into the foaming brew.

Bouncing over waves, Peter cuts across the current using short, shallow strokes and slips into a bay on the right-hand shore. Carefully he climbs out and stands wide-legged, neoprene sailboard booties gripping the rock-strewn ground, and figures out a route.

Afternoon sunlight glares off the water. A spotted sandpiper skims across the torrent, wings beating in a shallow arc, missing the wavetops by inches to land on a flat rock on the opposite shore. It teeters delicately, darts on spindly legs like a ballerina on her points, and sends urgent *peet-weets* to an invisible mate. Behind him, from silvery-green wolf willows, a white-throated sparrow scolds, its lyrical cry reverberating sharply against the thundering water.

The air smells sharply clean. Seen and unseen, the landscape teems with life: insects run from spiders, green frogs sit motionless, sedges compete for space with herbs and horsetails and mushrooms, birds eat their weight in mosquitoes, trees shelter shrubs; each in complete harmony, one dependent on the other from time immemorial into the distant future. If man passes without stopping, all will be well, will remain wild.

Peter detests portages, so chooses to line his canoe. Through scrunched up eyes, he targets a large pink slab of rock that juts into the river like a breakwater. In between, slow moving water offers safe passage.

Peter shifts the packs towards the stern so that the bow floats higher. He grabs the front painter. The rope unravels as he skips ahead from stone to stone. A rock moves. His foot slips, jars his knee. On the table of granite he breathes safety, looks back. The canoe, some thirty feet downstream, is nosing from behind a wedge of grey gneiss. Leaning out over the rushing water three feet below, Peter gives the rope a tug. His arm yo-yos up and down. He topples forward, catches himself. The boat leaps from the eddy like a greyhound after a racetrack rabbit and surges into midstream. Peter's stomach heaves and his hands shake. The canoe clings broadside to the torrent, a wave climbing the side, foam-fingers reaching for the gunwale. The bow tugs. The rope, wrapped around Peter's hand, tightens, pinches viciously, cuts into his flesh. He envisions two outcomes. If he lets go, the canoe will race downstream and smash against a rock. If he pulls too hard, it will swamp and the weight will yank Peter into the river, jerking him over rocks, toss him around like Benjamin Franklin's kite.

He has only one choice. He has to hang on. He *must* hang on or lose everything. Desperately he leans backwards, feeling his arms ripping from his shoulders. A foot skids on grit towards the edge. Clings. Painstakingly he heaves on the rope. Slowly, oh so slowly, the river yields to the tug-o-war, and then, suddenly, capitulates, releasing the boat into the current. Caught off guard, the rope suddenly slack, Peter almost falls backwards off the rock. For an instant, he sees himself as Wile E. Coyote toenailed to the edge of a hundred-foot cliff, and almost laughs. Falling to his knees, sand grates the skin, forces out a sobbing breath. His face turns the colour of winter legs. It's insanity to want to go on. Thoughts paint his mind red, an art exhibit, a canvas that had made him cry, a desolate red canoe cast up on a beach, its owner, painter Tom Thomson, mysteriously drowned. Tears glaze his eyes again, fogging the image of his boat disdainfully dancing in midstream.

"You think you're so fucking smart," he wheezes angrily, "trying to escape like that. Don't you dare do it again. You scared the fucking daylights out of me!" Peter habitually blames his canoe for all *his* mistakes.

Ten minutes pass before Peter reels the rope into a heap at his feet. The canoe bounds through the waves bow high like a young colt entering a horse-trailer and into the eddy below. He drops into the water and grabs the bow before it grates onto a jagged rock.

Peter forges up the rapid, bracing against the water tugging at his legs, slipping on greasy rocks, battling the relentless current. The flow eases at the head where the river widens into a small lake. Dragging the canoe into the shallows, Peter coils the painter with shaking, bruised hands and tucks it under a shock-chord on the foredeck, and repositions the packs.

It hits Peter depressingly. Climbing the rapid had almost ended the trip. His heart thunders against a tight chest. A gloss of sweat darkens his shirt, trickles down his temples. He leans on the gunwale, closes his eyes, and sucks air. Doubts flood in, drowning his resolve to reach the Arctic.

He recalls another challenge, the class three years ago that had tested him; unruly, insolent, and intolerable. A group of misfits beyond control.

Remembering his own childhood, he'd changed tactics, revamped some ideas, and the group had survived the year and actually knew how to add, subtract, make change, and calculate their wages.

Peter strips, dropping his clothes on the rocks. He loves being naked, canoes that way sometimes with the sun burning fire into his bones. Wading into the lake, he slips and flops into the water. He swims to the middle with an untidy breaststroke, his legs kicking ineffectively. Turning onto his back, he sculls into deeper water, watery blue eyes gazing at the arching sky. He floats, and tension dissolves into the infinite blue. His feet slowly sink, toes stretching for the bottom. *Bomba, bomba, bomba* tolls in his head. He swivels, eyes wide, sees a shark-fin cutting towards him, then chants in a deep tone: "Bomba, bomba, bomba." Arms flailing, he races for shore, legs kicking up foam, a vision of '*Jaws*' chomping at his feet, water bloodied. In the shallows he laughs aloud, a touch light-headed, and slides along by hooking his fingers onto the slimy rocks, exploding clouds of algae. Fish fry dart among the floating morsels, indifferent to the giant. A crayfish, poised on a rock with its tiny claws raised like a boxer, scuttles backwards into a crevice.

Peter, still giggling, rises, water cascading from his muscular frame. Droplets cling to each sparse black hair, diamonds briefly in the sunlight, and evaporate. He dresses wet, wiping only his face with an open hand.

Squinting into the sun, he estimates the time at between three and four o'clock. His watch is at home, on the kitchen counter. After a lifetime of direction by school bells, he's decided the hands of a clock would no longer program his day. Eat when hungry, drink when thirsty, and sleep when tired – his new motto.

Peter heads for a low, rocky point. Rounding it, a second rapid greets him, a wide jumble of chattering boulders, like babbling school children at recess as the water effervesces between their crannies. Except for a groove in the centre, the water is ankle deep – known to canoeists as a boulder garden. Rather than the rope, he grabs the skittish pony by the bit, and splashes confidently up the channel. Fifteen minutes and the rapid is history and he's squeezed back into the boat.

Snaking through a labyrinth of narrow, black waterways, willows spilling from each bank, Peter enters Mountney Lake. Passing a wooded island, he pulls up sharp when a bald eagle lifts from the treetops, its outspread wings grasping at flight. With a pitifully harsh, creaky cackle, the king soars overhead and informs all nearby creatures that danger is amongst them. Peter ships his paddle, watches the bird on its seven-foot wings, primary feathers vibrating, its white head turning from side to side. He feels the yellow eyes watching him, piercing his soul. The bird veers off, apparently satisfied that the intruder means no harm to the chick in its untidy eyrie, and heads west in search of a hapless fish too close to the surface.

Peter stares ahead, follows the bird over azure water, between islands of green, and caresses the sun-gilt ramparts of a canyon that funnels the Churchill River from a major torrent. His mind leap-frogs to nine-eighty-four Windsor Street, a stuccoed bungalow, his home for twenty years, and perches in front of a photo on his study wall: a man, a woman, and a canoe, half submerged, are plunging into the waves at Rock Trout Rapids. The picture used to pull his eyes from marking assignments during winter nights, and, like the eagle, he would soar over waters wild beneath a cobalt sky. A cascade of memories: his first run; the late afternoon downpour that sent him and his companions running to their tents; a jigging teen reeling-in her first catch – a ten-pounder; his love for the venerable jack pine overlooking the rapid that had been boot high to the explorers when they passed by in their birch canoes and York boats. The seed that had grown into the Arctic quest had germinated here, at Rock Trout Rapids.

Peter lands at the portage a half-hour later. His shoulders sag as he wearily checks-off the load in the canoe: a bulging Duluth bag wedged between the gunwales leaving a foot-wide space for his knees; a green-painted box sitting lengthways in the back, its lid level with the thwarts; and between it and the seat, a daypack that had at one time carried schoolbooks, assignments, and test papers. Peter lugs everything to the top of the steep bank then drags the canoe from the water. He hoists the Duluth by side straps onto his knee, then onto his back. He staggers sideways, buckles under its weight. Grabbing his two paddles in one hand and fishing pole in the other, he strides along the narrow, root infested trail, thankful that it's no more than a hundred-yard hike. He's hungry. Maybe a fish for supper. Dying for a hot mug of tea. He'll sleep well tonight, have an early night. It's hot, even in the shade.

Fifty paces down the path he stops abruptly, frowns. He sniffs the air, roving his head like a foxhound. Infused with the sweet fragrance of pine needles, a trace of fresh wood-smoke piques his nostrils. Someone is here, has already made camp. Irritated, he swears sharply. Since leaving Missinipe, he's gorged on solitude, loving every minute. Distant fishing boats had passed by, outboards buzzing like bluebottle flies, spewing acrid fumes, their complement of beery fishermen with arms raised in salutation, then waves that rocked him. Otherwise, no one had crossed his path.

Fuming, he stamps, resumes his pace, ill at ease. The path emerges from the tunnel of trees into a park-like area of jack pine and trembling aspen. Expanses of ice-shaved quartzite, greyed by weather and lichens, are interspersed with warm green scatter rugs of low bush-cranberry, delicate wild lily-of-the-valley, pink-petaled prickly roses, and spongy moss. To his right, muffled by river alders, the roar of the rapid. He tastes the humidity in the air and, now and then, wood-smoke.

He pauses on a high point, searching through the trees for campers. A solitary green tent sits at the edge of the gorge. "Thank God," he mutters. The site isn't overrun with teenagers on a school outing. A plume of smoke draws Peter's eyes, and there, at its source, half-hidden by a tree, a body is hunched over a fireplace. Peter watches for a few minutes; a dark green shirt, long sleeves down, and black wind pants. The head is hidden inside an olive-green mosquito net. The figure is bending over the reluctant fire, shoulders rhythmically rising and falling.

Peter scans for others, listens for voices, an axe cutting into wood. Almost certain there's no one else, he approaches, his footsteps hidden by the boom of the river.

"Hi! Fire won't burn?" he says from ten feet.

The person catapults into the air, almost stumbles into the fireplace, and turns, mouth agape, eyes like marshmallows inside the net. The mushroom-shaped headpiece makes the recoil all the more comical, like an apiarist hopping about with bees swarming inside his pant-legs.

"Oh!" A gasp. A voice that's obviously not male. A long, thin hand plucking at a shirt collar, the neck. "I didn't hear you coming... with the rapids and... blowing," waving a hand towards the fire. The headgear is snatched off. Wide-open hazel eyes in a narrow, sun burnt face, stare at Peter.

"Sorry. I didn't mean to startle you," Peter apologises, genuinely surprised. "I thought you were a guy. I didn't expect to find a girl... I mean woman... here."

"Where did you come from?" she asks fearfully, backing away, putting the fireplace between them.

"Bottom of the portage."

"Oh." The woman catches her breath, her eyes flick to the rock-formed fireplace. A dismal pile of dead twigs lies on a grey bed of ash. Traces of smoke spiral up and are snatched by moist fingers rising from the waterfall.

"Not doing a good job, am I? Nearly had it going, but it died. Wood's wet. I want a smudge fire to drive off the blackflies." She looks at Peter, thin dark eyebrows arched, blinking back tears, tears from smoke, frustration, and, now, anxiety. Her accent's like the Queen's but with a twang Peter doesn't recognise, certainly not Beatle-ish. One of his mother's imperatives was to listen to the Queen's Christmas address, at first on the radio, and when they could afford one, on television.

"Bad, are they? Well, this *is* blackfly season. They live in running water until ready to fly. The females want your blood for their eggs. They're lousy flyers, though, so you should have made camp away from the river, over there, say," pointing to a clearing fifty feet into the bush. "Also you're dressed wrong. You're like a beacon. People don't realise that bright colours don't attract bugs as much."

Shifting from foot to foot, they stand, glancing at each other, skipping eye contact, one ill-tempered, the other apprehensive, neither sure of what to say. Peter suddenly slaps his bare leg, picks off the black speck.

"By yourself?" he asks, mushing the blackfly between his finger and thumb, like a piece of grit.

"Yes," she says uneasily, her eyebrows puckering together. "And you?"

"Yeah," he replies pointedly. "You won't mind if I camp here," and without waiting for a reply, heads up the slope to the clearing he'd just indicated.

The site is visibly popular: flat squares cut within the pines, tree trunks as benches frame a heap of blackened rocks, charred logs, burnt cans and crushed silver foil, ugly remnants of fleeting chefs. The ground is scuffed bare, littered with wood chips, candy wrappers, bag-ties, cigarette butts. Leaning his paddles and fishing pole against a tree, Peter shrugs off the Duluth, it thuds to the ground, ground that he's rooted to.

"We'll put the tent here. It's nice and flat."

"You set it up while I get a fire going. Kiss me first." They cuddled; clothes slid to the ground.

"I adore you," he whispered, and the forest quieted except for the distant murmur of Rocktrout and a pair of boreal chickadees that chattered overhead.

"You said you were going to make tea," said Danika when it was over, in a voice gritty from a dry throat.

"Uh, uh. I said I'd light the fire while you put the tent up."

"Get off me then," pushing his shoulders with two hands, slapping his backside with a cupped hand as he rolled off, a slap free of reprimand, yet with the sting of love.

Their clothes remained on the ground until dusk. Peter gathered them before entering the tent, before frenzied mosquitoes found their naked flesh, before they loved again and slept like Hanzel and Gretel.

"Is this where I should camp?"

Peter pivots. The woman is standing inside the circle of trees. He feels cornered, like the up-to-no-good youngster caught in the beam of a policeman's flashlight. How long has she been watching him, he wonders. Nosy bitch. But she looks bewildered, like a cast-out street-kid.

She backs away and crosses to the fireplace, bent as if she's carrying his anger on her shoulders. "I didn't see this earlier. You're right. There're no blackflies." She squats on a log, hands clasped between her knees.

He wishes she would go back to her own site, back to her cloud of bugs and smoke, but conventional courtesy compels him to ask, "You heading to Missinipe?"

"Yes. It's about three days from here, isn't it?"

"Two. Three if you take it slow. Where'd you put-in?"

"I've just come down the Paull River. Do you know it? I camped on an island on McIntosh Lake last night."

"Sure. I've done that trip several times. It's a pretty river." Peter snaps his fingers, drops onto a log opposite her.

"I know you." She stares wide-eyed at him, eyebrows raised. "You flew out four days ago, right?"

She nods. "In a seaplane. How can you possibly know me?"

Peter guffaws, smiles broadly at the advantage he has over her. "We were talking about you at the outfitter's before I left Monday. You rented a canoe and camping gear and bought food from Shorty Hayes. Right? You're from England; Kent, I think Shorty said. Fact is, he asked me to look out for you. I'd forgotten. He was a touch worried, but obviously you're okay."

"Except for Kent you're spot on. I live in Surrey. Woking, actually," she says, brightening, her body relaxing.

"It's not a seaplane," he interjects, chuckling, "We call them float-planes. We're thousands of miles from the sea." She colours slightly, drops her eyes.

"Woking, eh. Is that near Portsmouth?"

"Umm…" She hesitates. "Close to forty miles, I would think. Why?"

Peter smiles, blushes a little. "I was born there, during the war. Between air raids, my mother used to tell me. She called it Pompey. I've no idea why. Had a great soccer team, she said. Welcome to Canada," he adds quickly to shelve her interest in him, "especially the best part, right here on the Churchill."

"Thank you. You're very kind," she replies with a hint of a bow, a smile creasing her face, her forehead smooth. "I have family in Winnipeg. My mother's sister and brother-in-law. It was their idea that I come on this journey with my cousin, but business changed his plans. It's unbelievable how friendly everyone has been, so helpful. Unlike England."

"This is God's country, that's for sure," he says. He stands, looking down at her. "I'd better go and get the rest of my gear. You didn't give me your name."

"It's Sara Sutcliffe."

He grins. "Sarah, huh." The name of his daughter, mother of two grandsons. "With or without the 'h'?"

"Without."

Peter mentally alters the spelling and adds, "Ha. Nice. Very English. I'm Peter, Peter Jordan."

His step perks up as he hurries off. Unwittingly, they have links drawing them together; name and birthplace. For a few hours at the most.

She'll be gone tomorrow, travelling east, another face to fuse with others. He stops in mid-stride, a frown creasing his forehead, his heart suddenly heavy. Why hadn't I phoned Sarah? Bull-headed old coot! Oh well, no point dwelling on it now, he rationalises, and tramps on, shoulders drawn.

The Churchill River, or *Missinipi*, meaning "very big water", was the voyageurs' highway linking the Saskatchewan River to the north-western Barrens. Trading posts, forts and log cabins sprang up along its banks, serving *les hommes du nord* as they paddled and portaged back and forth from Montreal to the Arctic. Little remains from those heady days: rotting logs on fading foundations, overgrown graves, a clay pipe found high in a jack pine left there when the tree was a sapling. Surviving are names – islands and lakes and waterways branded by employees of the Hudson's Bay Company or the North West Company to commemorate explorers and company men, royalty and political hacks, and loved ones at home – mothers, wives, sisters. As well, scratched on the land by a myriad of moccasins, are portages that skirt the impassable rapids and falls.

With the wannigan strapped on his back, daypack against his chest, and canoe balanced on his shoulders, Peter slogs along the trail. Salt sweat stings his eyes.

Young Alexander Mackenzie, early twenties, in a black frock coat and white ruffled shirt buttoned-up under his chin, paces alongside him. His black eyebrows above searching eyes are set in a deep frown. He's lamenting, as if Peter were his clerk, the lack of progress despite their four o'clock start that morning. The men will lose their rum quota, he warns, if they don't hurry on the carrying-places. Mackenzie always drove his men to exhaustion, but he treated himself no less.

Peter emerges from the bush and heads towards the clearing. Glancing down the slope to the woman's site, he's astonished to see that she's changed into a white golf-shirt and tight fitting blue jeans and is dismantling her tent.

"What are you doing?" he hollers.

"Moving to your site. Isn't that what you suggested?"

"Yes, but... Oh, hang on a minute! I'll give you a hand," he answers sharply. He hadn't thought she would take his advice. Besides, he wants her to stay put.

Peter rolls the canoe off his shoulders and takes the pack to his tent site and the wannigan to the fireplace. He lopes down a path. One of three backpacks lying on the ground is spewing clothing, like Cornish hens bursting from a henhouse.

"Pull the pegs out," he instructs testily, standing at one end, "and we'll lift together." Holding the poles through the flysheet, arms wide, they raise the A-framed tent. Awkwardly they negotiate a path through the trees, the nylon billowing dangerously against snaggy branches.

"Over there," Sara says, nodding to the sunny side of the clearing. For an indecisive moment they stand, the tent between them, its ridge below Sara's chin, centred on Peter's chest. Sunshine slices through the upper pine branches. It has lost the hardness of the noonday sun. A shaft lights Sara's face pale amber.

"Thank you." Sara anchors the tent with the pegs wedged in her back pocket. "Thank you," she repeats, "I can manage now," dismissing him with a weak smile.

Peter crosses the twenty yards to the shade and his Duluth and extracts stuff sacks until a light blue one comes to hand. From it he erects a dome tent, like a blue igloo. He unzips the fly-screen door and tosses in his sleeping bag, a self-inflating mattress – his one luxury – and a bag of clothing.

He notices, through the corner of his eye, the woman's comings and goings with her packs, and eventual disappearance into her tent. Her presence still rankles, white shirt and blue jeans, city-wear, garish in his mind. He expected to meet canoeists on this busy stretch of the river, but not irksome women. His want is to emulate Mackenzie's 1783 journey as closely as possible with little human contact except when meeting Dene or when replenishing his supplies at pre-arranged locations. He wishes now that he hadn't told her he was going to camp here. Moving on now is impossible, awkward to explain, certainly not the 'Canadian way' he has led her to trust, that she has come to expect.

Peter unbuckles an axe from the side of the pack, pushes into the forest, wading through knee-high moss and fending off face-high lances of dead spruce branches. At a stand of birch he peels off a hand-size piece of bark. Back at the firepit, Peter ignites a redhead strike-anywhere match on a rock, sets it under the paper-thin material. It bursts into a yellow, smoky flame that defies extinction even when smothered by handfuls of loose pine and aspen twigs, followed by layers of axe-split logs hastily gathered.

"I wish I could light a fire that quick," Sara says as she leaves her tent and moves to the dancing flames, outstretched hands shielding the heat from her face.

Peter eyeballs the red hand-knitted sweater she's wearing, its colour contrasting vividly with shoulder length black hair; a trim waist and breasts like circumflex inflections. For a fleeting second Tom Thomson's canoe at Canoe Lake inundates his head. Red! Canvas-covered. Cedar-strip ribs.

"Like some tea?" he asks, uneasily dropping his eyes, startled by prickly warmth that's not due to the fire. He bends to the foodbox, turning his back on Sara. Have to use an extra tea bag, he thinks begrudgingly. The English love strong tea. His mother's recipe springs to mind – a spoonful of leaves per person plus one for the pot, steep five minutes. Bugger the pot, he reasons.

"That would be nice," she says eagerly, her smile exposing white even teeth. "Here, I'll get the water," she adds when Peter turns holding two blackened pots.

"Don't fall in." She shakes her head and wrinkles her nose like a rabbit and departs. He stares after her, striding down through the trees, pots swinging. Her perky step adds to Peter's perception that, although uneasy with him, she's pleased he has come along, that some unknown weight has lifted from her shoulders. She disappears down the steep bank at the water's edge.

While she's gone, Peter occupies himself with routine. He changes into well-worn, moosehide moccasins. Lacing them, he savours the smoky aroma of the soft leather that lingers despite their age. Five years ago, he had sat for half a day, drinking tea, reminiscing about the old-times, and watched a friend, Marie, a Dene woman with arthritic hands, bead a traditional pattern of red roses and green leaves onto the vamps.

He unclips a narrow grating from inside the lid of the wannigan and places it across the flames.

"I didn't drown," Sara gibes, as she returns, water slopping from each billy.

"Not this time. Thanks." He covers the pots and places them on the grate.From the box, Peter produces plastic containers of tea, sugar, dried milk, and a brown stained, hand-whittled wooden spoon. Closing the lid, he moves the wanigan to the smoke-free side of the fire and sits on it. He looks up, conscious of Sara's following stare.

"My favourite time of the day," he says, two hands slapping his knees like a car-dealer after selling the most beat-up wreck on the lot. "A hot cup of tea and a cookie after a hard day of paddling. Nothing better. Except maybe two cookies."

Sara laughs. "You certainly look at home. You must do this a lot."

"Yup. Tell us about your trip."

When the water boils, Peter makes tea. Sara relates how standing on a tiny beach after a thirty minute flight, surrounded by gear and her canoe, the only means of rejoining civilisation, had left her panic-stricken; how being infinitesimal in the vast wilderness is akin to a flea on a dog's back; and the excitement she'd thrilled to canoeing down the Paull River. "You're the first human I've seen in three days." Her account reminds him of his own trips on the river, of Tuck Falls and Stuart Rapids.

"You have a cup?"

Sara skips to her tent and returns with a shiny stainless steel one. Peter, plastic Tim Horton's mug already filled, pours her the remaining brew. She shakes her head to milk and sugar.

They sit opposite each other sipping tea, restless. Peter glances surreptitiously from fire to Sara and back, sees her face fluctuating as she fidgets, in soft purple shadow then washed beaten gold when the fire flares. It strikes him that he hasn't been alone with a woman since Danika's death. His eyes settle on a soft complexion beneath the delicate tan, skin enigmatically weathered by a gentle climate, yet her hazel irises are dull, albeit tempered somewhat by giddy clothes that highlight her hair more than her eyes. Beneath the cheery facade Peter suspects an individual that is out of place, maybe caught up in an adventure that's overwhelmed her, too fragile for this setting, like a Royal Doulton figurine in a hardware shop with a sign 'You break, you pay'. He could befriend this girl, but what's the point. She'll be gone in the morning… Suddenly he knows – like himself, she's fleeing from something, or someone who's caused abuse or grief.

He wants to distract her from her ghosts. "Did you run the rapids? There're some great ones," Peter asks.

"Three I think, the easy ones. I portaged the others. The rocks frighten me. I'm not that good. I've not done this sort of thing before."

Peter gapes. "You've *not*? Then this is your *first* trip?"

"Yes."

"But you must have canoed in England?" the pitch in Peter's voice rising, horrified that Sara is the complete novice he'd suspected.

"Well, no, not unless you count a rowboat on the Thames." She smiles weakly. Peter pictures a girl in a long white frilly dress, cushioned, her arm flung across the transom, and a boatered male poling a punt between water lilies and banks of weeping willows.

"What on earth are you doing out here by yourself? You must have rocks in your foolish head! You should've taken a guided trip."

"I've hiked and camped in the Lake District and the Cairngorms," she retorts indignantly. "I told you, my cousin was supposed to have come, but he had to cancel at the last moment. He said I could handle it. And besides, I had lessons at the Missinipe Outfitters."

"Oh sure! How to hold a paddle, go forward, go backwards, turn a corner," he sneers. "Did they tell you what to do when you capsize and lose your food and gear? How to survive with nothing?"

"No... They said take it easy, be careful, and I would be fine. Like I've been doing."

Peter scoffs. "Take it easy... Huh! I hope in hell's name you get to *tell* them how bloody easy," he says angrily, a crushed canoe snagged in his mind, a soggy red-sweatered body broached on a rock and raven-emptied eye sockets staring at the infinite blue, "for your sake as well as theirs."

Peter leaps up and stalks down to the river, snatching the empty cook-pot as he goes. What the hell was Shorty thinking? No wonder he had hinted that he look out for her. An experienced outfitter, he shouldn't have allowed her to take this trip alone? When they'd been chatting about her, Peter hadn't guessed at her lack of experience. Too many accidents happen due to poor decisions. Just that spring, three fishermen hadn't made it home, their lives snuffed out at Mosquito Rapids by hypothermia, *rigor mortis* in ten minutes. Shorty should have insisted on a trip closer to Missinippe, certainly one without dangerous rapids.

On the smooth rocks, Peter looks down at the churning water rushing by a few inches away, his emotions in a vortex of rage. He swallows the hot tea, relishing it scalding his mouth. On the other hand, he reflects with a smile, I tackled some hair-raising stunts in my younger days. Living in a prairie town can be worse than mundane: driving the streets looking for girls, drive-in movies on Fridays when the height of

39

excitement was squeezing four bodies in the car trunk, and reeling home drunk from the beer-parlour on a Saturday. You want life, do what the heart commands, tackle a wild river.

His very first run, here at Rocktrout, floods into his head. He grins, then chuckles as the memory unfolds. Muscles taut, adrenaline rushing, instructions yelled. First the impossible drop into the three-foot standing wave that catapulted them sky high, nerves shrapnelled. Frigid water landing in Sam's crotch, ejaculating hoots of laughter. Immediately, they made a sharp right turn, then left so as to align with the razor-thin vee, a needle's-eye in the middle of the second drop. Shoot! Missed... by inches! A giant curler, the dreaded rooster tail, had flipped them like hamburgers on a McDonald's grill. Heads surfaced gasping for air, hands reached for paddles and clawed water to swim clear of the upside-down canoe. Abuse filled the canyon, peeled rocks off the walls, pursued by an avalanche of laughter.

Missing the zigzag would have swept them under the cliff on the opposite side of the river, an overhang sculptured like a broken tooth, where, on one trip, he had discovered an aluminum canoe crumpled like a discarded beer can. He often pondered the fate of its late occupants. Had they survived? How had they reached home; had they been with a group, or terribly alone?

Peter scoops water into the pot and sits back on his haunches, drains his tea. It crosses his mind that he should guide Sara to Missinipe. Wasn't that what Shorty wanted? he figures quickly. That would set him six days behind. An admirable gesture, but one that would jeopardise the whole trip. Winter on the Canadian Shield doesn't wait. He dismisses the idea; somewhat regretfully, he's surprised to feel.

His temper mollified, Peter drags himself back to the campsite. Sara is squatting downfaced on his wannigan, chin in hand, the half-empty cup swinging in the other. The spectacle, her dull gaze matching the bed of embers, burns Peter with guilt, an emotion he's not encountered since losing Danika.

"Sorry!" Peter's apology is gruff. He never apologises.

Sara, her face like that of a scolded child, jumps up. "Oh dear, I've let the fire go out."

"I'm not angry at you, Sara. I'm furious with those bozos who should have known better than to send you out alone. If I ever... I mean... When I see Shorty Hayes, I'll give him such a piece of my mind... Not that it will do *you* much good." Peter, aware of the slip of his tongue, glances at Sara's face. It's blank.

"How about supper?" he tries, wanting to put Sara back at ease.

She tosses on wood, sending sparks dancing into the air. "You'll be glad to be rid of me tomorrow."

"What do you have to eat?" he asks, ignoring her prediction.

"I have packaged meals. Add boiling water, cook for ten minutes. *Et voilà*. They're not bad, except for what I had two nights ago. It tasted awful. I nearly choked! It said cous-cous on the packet."

"It's semolina. North African, I think. I don't like it either. We'll boil two pots of water."

They prepare their food together, cooking in separate pots but helping each other from time to time, stirring, sampling, stoking the fire. Sara is ready first, a seafood concoction in a white sauce that she ladles onto a shiny metal plate. Peter scoops his stew of lentils and noodles into a plastic bowl and hurriedly spoons it into his mouth.

"There's some of mine left. Do you want it?" Sara asks when Peter's scraping his bowl.

"Sure. Hey! This isn't bad. Sorry, I'd share mine, but..." he shrugs, "it's gone. I only packed for one."

Washing dishes at the river, the air, heavy with moisture, smells soft like freshly laundered towels. The sky is inflamed with shades of orange, salmon pinks, cardinal reds, interspersed with bands of eggshell blue. The surface above the first ledge, smooth as glass, reflects the sunset; liquefied streaks and gyrations of gold, scars of crimson. In the shadow of the fall, the water is sullen, gravely ominous as it buries itself into the heart of a standing wave, a foaming luminescent white with a cap tinted sugar-candy pink.

The maelstrom is unremitting, kills conversation. Peter crouches at the water's edge, utensils beside him, while Sara stands, tea towel ready, staring up at the blaze of colours. She taps him urgently on the shoulder, points to shadows fleeting back and forth above the rapids, changing directions so fast that one imagines they've vanished.

He rises, leans close behind her shoulder, and speaks directly into her ear. "They're nighthawks. Watch for the white bars on their wings. They're nocturnal, feeding on mosquitoes all night - millions of them." Peter reels, the perfume in her hair wings into his head. He closes his eyes, hunts for words to prolong the moment, but his mind fills with his own nighthawks, whirling, like running a rapid but more. He drops, breathes again, and rinses her plate as if it's her hand.

Following Sara back to camp, the fear that she will have an accident is gnawing at him. Arguments, like moths beating against a lit cabin window, urge him to change his plans. They coax, cajole, and almost wheedle surrender. It's no good, I must go on, he repeats to himself, almost aloud. I have to, for Danika.

"We'll go by your old fireplace. I saw some firewood there."

They swing left, trace a path to the cliff overlooking the rapids. They stand side by side, their thoughts afloat on the water, surfing memory. Peter leans a hand on the gnarled trunk of the twisted jack pine he's grown to love like an old pal.

"I took a photograph from here a few years back. It's on my study wall, my icon to click on when I need a break."

"It's exquisite," Sara says. "I wish I was a poet or a painter."

"You could be."

"No, it's too late to learn."

"It's too late when you're dead."

"I should have bought one of those instant cameras. At least I could show them back home how beautiful it is."

Peter snags his breath. Danika used to say the same thing. At the same spot. They'd sit on an evening and toss their wishful coins into the fountain. Peter's desire to reach out, hold her hand, Danika's hand, is so strong he has to swallow and grip the jack pine harder. The bark cuts, just retribution for his longing.

Without a word, he turns, fills his arm with firewood, and almost runs up the slope.

When Sara arrives with the dishes minutes later, the fire is a crackling blaze. Peter, gazing into its core, cannot understand why he's crawling in a cave, unable to find the way out. Shadows crowd him: Shorty Sara Paull Rocktrout. A red sweater hangs over the exit sign.

"Aren't you cold?" Sara asks, wrapping her arms in a fabricated shiver.

"Uh-uh."

"You haven't told me where *you* are heading."

"Upstream," he replies automatically, as if he has no choice, his fate already cast.

"Where to? Are there towns?"

He chuckles at her ignorance, looks up at her. "Sure. Fort McMurray, Yellowknife, and Tuktoyaktuk."

"I've heard of Yellowknife. Where's, what did you say, Tukyuk something?"

"Tuktoyaktuk." He pronounces each syllable slowly, emphasising each k and t. "It's on the Beaufort Sea. It's as far as the explorer Alexander Mackenzie got to when he was looking for the Pacific."

"All by canoe? How far is that? How long will it take? Do you have enough food? Can you get there before winter?" Her questions tumble out before Peter can answer.

"That's my dream," he cuts in, his gaze back at the fire. He wants to feel the tug of the Mackenzie River flowing north, to ache from sore muscles as did the voyageurs when they portaged their pelts around Skull Canyon on the Clearwater River, to hear the whisper of Alexander Mackenzie's Silent Rapids, and finally stand where he did, looking out onto the Arctic Ocean at the mouth of his Disappointment River. He wants to smell the caribou, the flowers of the Barrens, walk the Methy Portage in the footsteps of Peter Pond, the first white man to do so.

"And you're going all the way by yourself?" Sara asks, her eyes widening.

"Well, not entirely. I met you, didn't I?" Peter says with a laugh. "It's surprising how many people one meets on a trip."

"When will you finish?"

"Depends on the weather. October maybe, or next year perhaps, maybe never…" Peter leaves failure unannounced, resolves in his mind to succeed. "If I get bored with my own company I'll pack it in at Île-à-la-Crosse. That's where I pick up my next load of supplies."

"Oh, I'm sure you'll make it," she says confidently, as if her reassurance is pivotal to his success.

For an hour they chat, like strangers on a Greyhound bus, a litany of their lives for contemplation, comparison, but more personal thoughts and feelings remain neatly tucked away. Like a river, their conversation meanders, flowing deep into history, over sandbars of politics and geography. Borough Polytechnic, shorthand, typing; four years at the University of Saskatchewan – mathematics, then education; worked in the City, commuting every day, stockbroker; teaching, various places – Kinistino, Kamsack, Kerrobert, KKK he laughs, lastly a high school in Saskatoon; Saskatchewan names fascinate me – I'd love to visit Moose Jaw, Swift Current, I love walking in the Lake District every year; sailor in the Canadian Navy, destroyers, docked in Portsmouth for a week, I arrived nine months later.

"After the war, Mom and I emigrated to Canada. Never found my father. Mom died ten years ago, her life drained."

"Mine are in Dorset; Dad's retired. Pension lets him garden - he loves growing flowers and veggies."

The fire's a bed of coals when Sara stretches her arms above her head, grudgingly stands, rubs the log's hard impression from her buttock, and announces she's ready for sleep.

"Thank you so much for a most enjoyable and fascinating evening," she says politely, "I will never forget Rocktrout Rapids. G'dnight."

Before Peter can respond, taken aback by her move, she's gone, and his "Sleep well" falls upon a shadow by the fire. Her quick departure, maybe, is a signal – had she sensed he may want to share more than conversation that night? Had she perceived and misconstrued his thoughts by the river?

He suddenly feels terribly lonely, deserted. The silence engulfs him; crackling fire dead, roaring rapids muted by trees. His desire for this girl's presence has taken him off guard, inflicted him with pangs of guilt. He's used to being alone. For months after Danika's death, friends had programmed his life, showering him with meals, diversions, had tried to fill his void. They were well meaning but trying. He had become irascible. People soon lost their patience and eventually left him to himself. Now, he's quite content to travel alone.

Maybe I'm just afraid. Maybe this girl is the welcome diversion from what lies ahead, from the inevitable. His fate may well be that that had befallen many a voyageur, finding death on some remote body of water, his remains to feed the wolves. Again he contemplates turning around, backtracking, delaying the unavoidable parting and following this girl instead of his dream. To douse the fantasy, he extinguishes the fire impatiently, and heads for his tent.

In his sleeping bag, he stares at the ceiling. His mind flits across the clearing. He can almost hear her breathing, like a spring breeze sighing in the trees. Tomorrow their paths would go – must go – their separate ways, upstream, downstream, miles apart.

The rush of the river from inside his sanctuary is soporific. His eyelids fall, he rolls onto his side, and sleeps. The river fills his dreams, its challenges, its beauty, and recaps the events of the last three days. His dream touches Sara and Sarah. The one next door, and the other in Ottawa. Sorrow weighs on his heart; his lips mutter a groan. Her departure from home had been unexpected, had left him and his wife distraught. They had not talked in years, and now he wishes he had picked up the phone, even on the pretext of saying a veiled goodbye. Her mourning, when he dies, will be insignificant, he thinks bitterly.

Danika's image floats into focus, ethereal. She is the fabric of Rocktrout, not like that afternoon's demonic encounter. Her lips brush his frown, her nose caresses his, traces its profile until their mouths meet in a kiss. For thirty years, they had said goodnight this way. Often it led to love, whispered words of endearment, or just gentle play beneath the bedclothes. Idiosyncrasies, insignificant at the time, live on in his memory and keep his love for her as intense, an invaluable legacy.

Peter doesn't notice the sounds of the night, the whir of male nighthawks' wing feathers as they dive for mosquitoes, the occasional hoot from an owl as it glides through the trees, the scratching of insects, the incessant buzz of mosquitoes probing for access, for blood. Sara, on the other hand, hears them all, wonders what creatures are making the strange sounds. But it's not the noises alone that keep her awake. An idea struck her as she undressed, and now it's buzzing in her head. Peter has unwittingly planted a seed in the soil of her imagination. Is it possible, could she do it? She'd have to pick her words for him to agree. She's still exploring the ramifications when, finally, she drifts off.

Above the sleepers a half-moon rises to its zenith, hiding the stars, illuminating the rapids in an eerie light. A mist lifts from the river as a chill spreads its icy fingers up the gorge. Leaves rustle, awakening, restless in a breath from the north-east. Roosting birds fluff their feathers, entrapping warm air. The forest awaits the dawn.

A four-pound pickerel resting on a rock-sheltered bed of gravel perceives the breaking day, unaware that a wind, hard as granite, is storming at its harbour. A flick of its tail drives it into the current where it stems the rush of water pouring over the bottom ledge of Rocktrout Rapids. Eyes rove independently, vigilant. It slips from side to side like molten lead waiting for river-born prey, muscles primed, lethal as a torpedo. A black leech, body undulating gracefully, drifts downstream thirsting for an unwary host, angling for a lifeblood attachment. Both are alerted to the other when their paths converge. A shadow. Mouth agape, the fish waits. Suddenly, a vice grip stabs. Near the dorsal fin. A hook pierces an eye. Vision oozes darkly. The pickerel flies from the water, airborne in the talons of a bald eagle. Scales flash gold. Spasms shiver through its body, once, twice. It accepts fate. The glint in the other eye dies; the eagle's gleam, vitalised by the life forfeited.

The leech continues its journey, unattached.

The bird's approach in the grey dawn light, sailing up the valley, was effortless. Now it has to beat against the gale to return to its roost on Mountney Lake. The bird swoops to the water's surface and takes advantage of island wind shadows. Soaring over a ridge, it drops onto its eyrie, legs and fish thrust forward, wings beating the air. The babble from a hungry chick, shabby in a fluffy brown and white coat, has no effect on the urgency with which the adult plucks a morsel of translucent flesh. It will take all day to pick the fish clean. Will sustain the whole family.

It's Thursday. Peter stirs at six that morning, unaware of the drama that has taken place just a few yards away. Moaning treetops and tent-fly drumming; he knows the weather has changed. He peers through the mosquito netting. The gunmetal sky is no surprise; low clouds, heavy with rain, are scudding just above the trees from the north-east. That breath, that warning whisper that had touched him on Nipew, had indeed been the herald of foul weather. Peter is somewhat grateful that the energy-sapping heat wave has snapped, but he doesn't want rain – rain always dampens his spirit, bites into his resolve. This wind, though, pleases him. On Trout Lake, it will be at his back, will carry him the twenty-kilometre length of the lake.

Out of his sleeping bag, Peter shivers, pulls on extra clothes – shorts covered by green wind-pants, a polypropylene undershirt, his usual red shirt, red fleece sweater and a royal blue rain-jacket. His Tilley, wedged onto its habitual perch, hides his mussed hair. Danika forever teased him about his colour sense. Called him a toucan. His retort, in an exaggerated English accent, was always the same: "I'm not dressing for Henley, your *lady*ship."

Night gear packed, Peter ducks out the door and spends a few minutes stretching. Sara's tent is silent; she'll stay put with this wind, he reckons, as he strides down to the river.

In short time, a pot of water is boiling over a fire. Peter huddles near the heat gripping his mug, feels the coffee uncloud his head. His second cup is half-gone before there's rustling in Sara's tent. Her exclamation, when she pokes her head out, is as close to a curse as Peter thinks she's likely to utter.

"Oh, darn! Your red sky at night was wrong."

"Can't be right every time. Bundle up," Peter advises, "temp's down at least fifteen degrees. I'm cooking oatmeal which you're welcome to, and fresh coffee's perking."

The aroma of coffee invites, hastens Sara's dressing. She dons yesterday's wear, an extra sweater, windpants and an anorak. Peter grins as she squeezes like toothpaste from her tent. He has the notion it's the Michelin Man sitting on the log beside him.

Peter spoons out oatmeal and adds raisins and brown sugar to each portion. They eat in silence hunkered down next to the fire, wary of the enraged forest besieging them, duck instinctively when loud cracks from snapping limbs reverberate from its midst. Sara warms white hands by embracing her cup, shivers nonetheless. They finish off the bannock.

"Listen," he says, refilling her cup with the last of the coffee. "Because of your inexperience, stay put for the day. You'll never cross Nipew in this wind, the waves will be whitecaps. Even hugging the lee shore is unsafe. Rest up for the day. Write some poetry you talked about last night. This system will blow over in twenty-four hours and tomorrow will be fine again. Mind you, I've known of canoeists storm-stayed on Nipew for three days, so… weather up here can be fickle."

"You're going? In this gale? You're crazy! Must you go? Do you *really* have to?" Her voice rises, fear crystallises in her eyes.

"I have to. It's a tail wind. I can easily cover fifty kilometres today. You'll be okay. Here, give me your plate. I'll wash the dishes."

Peter strides away, oblivious to Sara's alarm. The last four days had gone without a glitch, every mile bringing exhilarating vistas, untouched panoramas of forested islands and endless cobalt sky. Her solitude had been Byronic, poetic in the stillness of golden dawns and reflective evenings. Her fear of being alone had dissolved, supplanted by a rare self-confidence. The weather's change has soured the adventure and Peter's ire last night has sown a seed of doubt in her mind: her confidence wilts like peonies in a dry vase. He's leaving, taking the safety net from under her. Sara bolts to her tent. Inside, she's safe, surrounded by the familiar – spilled clothes and homely aromas, paraphernalia of the night.

The squish of Peter's nylon-coated legs approaches, passes. Back on her heels, she watches him at the fireplace through the fly-screen. He neatly packs his wannigan, collapses his tent, and stuffs everything into the Duluth bag. A couple of times he peers into the forest. Once he looks towards her tent, takes a pace or two, but stops short, a frown creasing his forehead. She hadn't realised until then that she's invisible to him.

What's on his mind every time he stops? Hopelessness had engulfed her heart, but now it's anger. Anger with herself for not knowing what to do, anger with him for deserting her. How can I keep him here? She bites her lip, watches his back depart.

Sara's eyes cloud, saline fills her lower lids, spills. She blinks rapidly, sniffs thickly, wipes wet cheeks with her fingers. There's a reason she's met this man. Her face pales, her hands visibly shake. This is no accident. Something, someone, has ordained the encounter. Premonitions like this frighten her. This one somehow predicts she will go with him. There's nothing in England to stop her; never again will such an opportunity come her way. But how? How do I convince him that I can do it, that I won't be a hindrance? He probably doesn't even like me. Straight out and prepare to argue, or use feminine guile? Uh, uh, that's humiliating, and he's not likely to concede to such a tactic. She sifts a few ideas, elects on being upfront.

Peter is back, looks around, shrugs, hoists his canoe onto his shoulders, and is gone. Sara sits in a daze, knows her fate right now is packing his canoe, that procrastination has beaten her again.

On the first trip to the trailhead Peter notes Sara's green, overturned canoe, a sixteen-foot Old Town Scout, a craft that can be paddled tandem or solo. On the second, he's somewhat baffled, where's Sara? He remembers her Paull River story and his subsequent anger. So she drowns; so what? He immediately regrets his insensitivity. He feels her tapping his shoulder, the nighthawks whipping by. Maybe in her tent, but it's quiet; gone for a walk perhaps and got lost. Serves her right, shouldn't be out here. He jogs back for the canoe; shrugs. Too bad. In the shallows, the rapid ten yards distant, Peter loads and ties-in with a long cord. Zipping into his bright red life preserver, he turns, wanting to see Sara coming through the trees. He shakes his head and walks back once more.

He stops by the tent. "Sara, are you in there?" he asks quietly, unsure of himself, reluctant to intrude.

"Yes. Just a minute."

Sara crawls out and stands directly in front of him, long fingers entwined.

"I didn't know where you…"

"Peter, I've been thinking about your journey," she interrupts, her voice shaking, her throat in a noose.

"Oh! Don't worry about me. I'll be fine. I've paddled in worse conditions than these. It'll clear by late afternoon…"

"You said twenty four hours!"

"…and then you can decide whether to stay here or paddle on a few miles. There's a great campsite just before the river runs into Nipew."

"Peter." She looks at him, meets his eyes. "May I…" Her head sinks. The ground blurs, she focuses furiously on green cranberries growing at her feet.

"What is it?"

"I don't know how to ask this…"

"What?" he says bluntly, certain that she's going to beg him to stay longer.

She looks up. "May I go with you?" she blurts.

"Excuse me?"

"May I canoe with you for a few days? To the Arctic even?"

"I had an inkling that's what you were driving at," he mutters. "Of course not, impossible," he says, shaking his head, and laughs cruelly.

"Please…" she pleads, and immediately bites her top lip.

"How could you? No! That's ridiculous. Impossible! Shorty's expecting you back in Missinipe on Saturday, Sunday at the latest with the weather the way it is, and if you don't show up, he will organise a search. You have food for four more days, five at the most. I have none to spare. You said you're not a good canoeist, you're lucky you've got this far," he says sternly. "You have no idea, not a clue, of the hazards. And… And… You have to fly back home."

"I have an open ticket," Sara interjects.

Responses ready, like cannonballs piled on a monkey on deck at Trafalgar, Sara launches her hastily prepared salvo. "Food's not a problem – you can catch fish. You said it's easy to catch fish. I love fish. You said you always meet people. We can give them a message for Shorty. My canoeing is improving, will get better still. I'll do my share: cooking, setting up tents, chop firewood, wash clothes. Please think about it. Meeting you has given me an opportunity that will never, ever come my way again. If I don't do this now, I never…"

"Hold it! I'm sorry, it's impossible. I have reasons. I don't want your company for a start, nor the responsibility of baby-coddling you."

"A few days?"

"No! Forget it! It won't work. Finish *your* trip. Go back to England. Where you belong…" Peter tails off, uncomfortable with his last rebuff, and is not surprised when Sara turns and dives into her tent. He catches the glint of a tear. He wavers.

"G'bye," he says after a minute, shaking his head, unhappy with the rift that's suddenly driven between them.

Peter shoves off into deep water and hops in. He paddles against the current, moving slowly, as if the river wants him to stay. His daughter must have felt exactly as he does now when she had left home. With unresolved differences, she had left in anger and they had not seen each other since, not even at Danika's funeral. He shoves the shadows aside and concentrates on the river. Doesn't look back. Paddles hard. Hard!

Face down on her sleeping bag, Sara fights back the tears, infuriated with herself. She hears Peter go and crawls from the tent in time to see him disappear down the trail. She hesitates, then follows on a whim. From the bushes, she watches like a child playing capture-the-flag, ready to rush in and grab the trophy when the guard is looking elsewhere. When Peter departs, she runs forward and stands at the lip of the water. She waits. A hand hovers. In books, films too, the hero always turns, waves, and the instant lovers run into each other's arms. Always. Peter *will* turn... He will...

Head down, her mouth a thin line, Sara walks back to camp, tosses wood on the fire and sinks onto the ground. Cross-legged, chin in hand, she stares at the fire. Unkind. Mean. He could have taken me. Jumbled thoughts of anger and disappointment invade her. In an unusual show of temper, she kicks a log sticking out from the fire, loses her balance and tips onto her back. She's stuck, can't get up, giggles. Her clothing has made her into a pudding. The silliness makes her giggle hysterically, sees herself spread-eagled for the rest of the day, a whole week, newspaper headlines reading: 'Canoeist Starves Flat on Back'.

Sara suddenly falls silent, goes rigid, head to one side. Was that a bird whistle, or what? There it is again, definite. A shout. Someone coming up the portage?

Again. A call for help.

Sara rolls to her knees, heaves herself up and, heart pounding, races to the cliff above the rapids. Nothing. Nothing upstream, nothing downstream.

A scream sends her awkwardly to the trail and to the river. Peter's canoe, on its side half submerged, is drifting towards her, approaching the rapids. Peter's in the water struggling with the painter, tangled with something attached to the bow. She plunges in, slips and would have completely submerged if her hand hadn't jarred bottom, giving her balance. The water's up to her knees when she figures Peter is beyond reach.

"I'm here," she yells.

Peter gives the rope a vicious yank. The shock chord pulls from the bowplate and the painter flies free. Turning onto his back, he kicks and paddles like a turtle away from the canoe. He hits the riverbed and staggers upright but falls backwards. Sara wades further. Waist deep she reaches Peter and together they grasp the rope and back out. The bow swings towards them, the stern still clutched by the current. Gradually they gain the shallows. The canoe wallows into the bay.

Peter slumps onto the shore, his head between his knees, his breathing laboured.

"What happened?" Sara asks indifferently, still smarting from Peter's heated departure.

"I dunno. Happened too quick. One minute I was paddling okay, next moment, phttt, I'm in the water. I don't believe this."

"Hit a rock maybe?"

"Uh, uh. I made a draw stroke. The paddle must've gone under the side and made me lean over. Too far, I guess. Thank goodness I had tied everything in," he says, eyeing his gear swimming in water. "Ah crap, my long paddle's missing."

Peter wades to the canoe and levels it. He shakes his head, splashes to shore and follows the rocks beside the rapids. It's fifteen minutes before his return.

"Damn, damn, damn! I have to find it. I can't continue with one paddle, without my whitewater paddle."

Sara has managed to beach the canoe. He unties the cord and together they lift the dripping bags onto land.

"Thank goodness I waterproof my stuff, otherwise I'd be wasting a day drying out. It's only my wannigan that I'm worried about. There's a week's food and it's not completely watertight." Opening the lid, Peter finds the inside is damp but the food unspoiled.

"I have to find that paddle. I'll take the packs to the fire. Change your clothes. You'll freeze to death," he says. "Make some coffee."

It's an hour before Peter returns, walking up the portage brandishing the lost paddle like a war trophy.

"It had gone down the canyon, round the corner and down some fast water. I found it in the reeds on Mountney Lake. I can't believe how far it went."

Behind the tent, Peter peels off his wet clothes and changes into dry ones.

"I made coffee."

"Great, I need some." Sara pours, adds milk powder and sugar and hands Peter his cup.

"Thanks. You must be laughing inside seeing that I'm supposed to be the expert, the guy heading to the Arctic. Maybe I should quit now and head back to Missinipe with you."

"Surely you expect some things to go wrong, don't you? How can you take on a thousand-miles thinking that you're invincible?"

"But not twice in the first four days."

"Twice?"

"I nearly swamped yesterday lining a rapid. Easy one, too. Even *you* could run it."

"Not if I come with you."

"Don't start that again," he snaps. "Besides, with my record I'm more of a hazard than a help. Look. We don't know each other to just up and go off together. It's too much of an undertaking, for both of us."

"Stay for the day, while the weather is bad, get dried out and perhaps you'll change your mind."

"Doubt it. A dunking isn't going to stop me."

The sky darkens. The wind shrieks and rain falls. The fire hisses in protest, smolders as rank upon rank of raindrops bullet into the earth.

"Shelter in my tent," Sara shouts, picking up her scattered clothes, closing the wannigan and leading the way. Peter hesitates momentarily, then follows, diving into the tent behind Sara.

"Reminds me of another time. Three of us. We'd just dished out supper and it teemed. Three like sardines in a two-man tent for half an hour."

Sara sits cross-legged on her sleeping bag in the subdued green light, gathering clothes to her side, like a bird plucking at her nest. Peter stretches across the width on his back, fingers locked over his stomach. His eyes close. The rain pounds. Sara prays that it won't stop until nightfall.

But it does. A half-hour deluge, then drizzle. Large drops falling from the trees drum like grape-shot on the tent's nylon walls.

"I left my canoe at the bottom of the portage," Peter announces, and crawls from the tent.

The boat on top of the bank is partly filled with rainwater. Peter tips it over; the water gushes out and down the slope. He slings the canoe onto his shoulders and squelches along the trail. The roar of the rapids, sporadically muffled by the wind, sounds like breaking waves of the Arctic Ocean and the smell of fresh rain mixed with a parched forest floor has the salt-laden tang of sea air. His shin hits a tree stump. The pain stings like a sliver piercing his heart. He drops the canoe onto a tangle of Labrador tea and limps through underbrush and slumps onto a patch of low-bush cranberries overlooking the gorge. He rubs his leg, diluting the pain, spreading it like butter on toast. Like a drifting canoe, he keeps hitting against the same rocks: his daughter storming from home, the doctor's tapping pen, his mother's final breath from her withered breast, Danika's staring yellow eyes. He must stop recalling the dead. Remember something pleasant. Sunrise on a mist-shrouded lake nighthawks against a red sky tea hot and sweet racing down a tumble of water Sara crouching over a stubborn fire and then her face looking up at him, bloated and white and still. No! No more death.

Go with her, you need her, she needs you. Peter's head drops to his knees. She'll slow me down with her backpacks, her silliness, her female chatter.

You didn't think that way last night; you wanted to hold her as if it was me. You were ready to... No, not true. Never.

Two years have gone by, quit mourning. He rolls over and lays flat on the ground, sharp cranberry stalks and cold wet leaves press his cheek. He groans. Although lying there alone, he feels crowded, all these people directing him, not with words, but by their faces pulling and pushing in a tug-of-war. Danika's face is beside him, lined and yellow.

She will show you the way. Take her, care for her; she'll care for you.

He rolls over, his face as grey as the clouds flying overhead, lines pressed into one cheek wet as from weeping. Sara's pale face with its dull eyes looms and he knows that he will have to talk to her.

"I've made some lunch. Noodle soup and crackers and cheese." Sara, sitting on the wannigan, is swinging wet socks over the fire. Between two trees, a line carries her windpants, jeans, shorts and white frilly panties.

"Sara, listen to me. No more brash decisions. This isn't going to be easy. For a start, there are countless rapids to navigate, some are miles long. The Methy Portage that crosses to the Clearwater is twelve miles. Twelve! Can you imagine lugging your three packs and canoe twelve miles? By the time you're done, that's three there and two back, you'll have hiked sixty miles. You won't make it, you're just not strong enough."

"I'll throw half my stuff away," she counters. "Peter, I laid awake most of last night caught up in your dream, longing to take on the same challenge. My life has been some forty aimless years, years buttressed by storybooks. I have no ties; I can go where and when I please. I want to learn from you – how to run rapids, how to light a fire. I want to know how to live in the wilderness. I know I'm asking a lot and I know I'm weak, but I promise I'll pull my weight."

Impulsively, he crouches down and grabs her hands, grips them hard. The socks fall to the ground. She counters by holding almost as tightly, gritting her teeth as pain travels up her arms. He looks into her eyes, inches away. "Sara, we met yesterday and chatted for a couple of hours. Now you want to take off with me, a stranger, to sleep under the stars with a person you don't know from Adam. For all you know I'm a convicted criminal. A rapist."

"Rot! Such drivel," she cuts in. "Give me credit for at least being able to judge character. I see a gentle man who loves nature and being in the wild and loses his temper when he meets foolhardiness. It's simple – be my mentor, make me your apprentice. Criminal! Huh! Imagine…" she laughs, eyes sparkling, "me, a 'Sorcerer's Apprentice'."

"Isn't there someone at home waiting for you? Someone special? A husband?"

"There was. Divorced. He's locked up – Brixton." Her bitterness shouts, unmasking the hurt. "I lost my job thanks to him, so came to Canada to forget. I told you, to visit my aunt and uncle."

"Kids?"

"No. I didn't let him…" Her body shudders, perhaps from the horror of her last thought.

"I'm sorry, I really am, but…" Peter says sincerely. "But you have no idea. This is not paddling on the Thames, or hiking in the Lake District. This is like… like swimming the English Channel without practice, without a support team," he adds earnestly. "There's no turning back."

She shrugs, continues to look determinedly into his eyes, her head slightly tilted.

Peter releases Sara's hands and stands. She massages her fingers, surreptitiously feeling for broken bones.

"Will you promise me something?"

"If I can."

"You are to tell me when you realise you've taken on more than you can handle."

Sara nods.

"Pinehouse is five days from here. There's enough in between to satisfy your thirst for adventure. If we have to, we can phone Shorty from there and arrange a pick-up."

"That won't happen."

"Don't be so sure, Sara! There's more. This is vitally important. I don't want you stranded on, say, the Clearwater or at Fort Chipewyan, but it may happen." He sucks in through tight lips, holds his breath momentarily. "I'm no spring chicken. Suppose I become ill? Two months ago, I was... I..." Peter's mind blanks. He's blocked the word 'cancer' from his vocabulary. He fumbles for words. "I'm not as healthy as ten years ago. I might fall... have a heart attack, a stroke. Then what would you do? How would you get home? That's why I travel alone?" he says quietly, "It's not that I dislike company, but I don't want to impose on someone else."

She shakes her head. "I'll take that chance. My mother was a nurse before she retired. She taught me enough that I could look after you."

For several tense moments their eyes lock, searching for the hidden strengths, scrutinising for any hesitation, or a hint of compliance.

"Okay. If the soup's good, we'll go tomorrow."

Sara bounces up, hugs him briefly and impulsively kisses his cheek. "Thank you! Thank you! You won't regret this, I promise."

I hope not, he thinks somberly, aware of the changes that he'll have to make, concerned that his pace will be slowed to the point of making the Arctic unattainable.

But her closeness has unexpectedly quickened his pulse.

TWO

Twice during the night, Peter awakens to the incessant sound of dripping inside the tent and irritably moves aside, sleeps on restlessly. At last, with dawn's blessed arrival, he dresses in clothes kept warm and dry inside his sleeping bag, and exits through the rear vestibule because a puddle sits across the doorway.

A blustery wind, out of the east, pushes heavy clouds close above the trees. The day before yesterday day's sunny park now resembles a miserable graveyard; olive, grey and black, with tree-trunks like pillars of a mausoleum. Peter bare-foots to a tree; the peaty soil squelches, water squeezes cold between his toes. His urine puddles where it splashes, acrid to his nose.

"Sara!" he calls. "Time to get up."

He squirms his feet into wet booties, his teeth screaming against the wretched cold. In the firepit, last night's remnants are a soggy grey mess and wipe out a possible quick fire and hot breakfast.

Sara appears from her tent, looking no better than the ashes, pale grey shadows under crusty eyes and hair a birch-broom. At least, he surmises, she's taken his advice, wearing shorts under rainpants, his polypropylene undershirt, her red sweater, and the green anorak. "Jeans are lethal on a canoe trip," he'd cautioned her the night before. "Once wet, they take months to dry. Cotton's as bad." With toiletries in hand and arms hugging her violently shivering torso, she heads to the river, returning ten minutes later, hair brushed, suntan peeking through, and looking a tad better.

They labour over bowls of water-soaked granola, munching monotonously, swallowing reluctantly. Striking camp is difficult as they pack one wet item after another: red tarp into its stuff sack, tents into theirs, clothes waterproofed in plastic bags, and then into packs that double in weight because of the added water.

Sara trudges along the portage trail panting like an ill-prepared athlete on her first marathon. The backpack bends her like a willow under a clutch of spring snow. She pauses to catch her breath. Hands braced on two trembling knees, she shifts the weight over her hips. White bunchberry bracts litter the green carpet. Yesterday, Sara had likened them to confetti at a wedding. Today, in sombre light, they remind her more of snowdrops in a churchyard.

A small ball of brown fur, partly hidden by leafy undergrowth, scurries not two feet in front of her. It freezes. Sitting back on miniature haunches, the intrepid animal scrutinises Sara with black eyes. Its pointed nose and thread-like whiskers tremble, aggravated by unfamiliar floral scents. It scratches an ear vigorously with a wee paw, adding to the comical picture of a puzzled rodent.

"Hello, Mr. Mouse. Or are you Vole? Or Mole? Is Badger visiting you for tea and cucumber sandwiches?" she whispers. As though reminded of the pending tea party, the vole drops its front legs, turns and bolts. Sara, amused by the rodent, smiles, straightens, breathes in deeply, and resumes her trek.

At the river, she wriggles the pack off her shoulders. It thuds beside Peter's canoe that's already loaded and halfway into the shallows.

No longer sheltered by the forest, Sara's face is lashed by a gust of wind that reminds her of school holidays at Brighton on England's south coast. Rather than brave the gales that roared off the English Channel, she'd hide herself in the worlds of Enid Blyton, Agatha Christie and Jane Austen while curled cat-like into a lounge chair beside the hotel fire.

"What say we take a brisk walk to the Pavilion for a fish-and-chips tea," her father sometimes suggested, tempting her to stir from her fantasy.

"No thanks, Daddy. You caught me at a good part." A jaunt along the sea front, brisk or otherwise, dodging screaming seagulls, failed to excite her.

Now I have my own adventure. How well has her reading, stories of spies and love and fantasy and murder and action, prepared her for what she's possibly about to face?

Peter arrives with her remaining two packs and drops them into the canoe Sara is dragging towards the water. "Have you brought the kitchen sink?" he demands. "You have enough stuff to equip an army."

"No!" she replies indignantly. "Only a platoon. Better too much and safe than too little and sorry."

"You'll be wishing you had half of it when we hit the first mile-long portage. Load up and let's go."

The Old Town canoe, with a seat at each end, bow and stern, differs from Peter's. Sara has to stow her packs toward the front to counterbalance her weight in the rear, a difficult position from which to manoeuvre, especially in windy conditions, a situation not yet encountered.

"I think we should tie in your gear," Peter states, crossing to his canoe and pulling a length of cord from a side-pocket on his daypack, "just in case."

A capsize! Not this soon, surely? She stares over her shoulder. The waves swell before her eyes, the whitecaps climbing higher than a house. A lump catches in her throat, her heart stampedes.

"Can you front-ferry?" Peter's question snaps her trance.

She turns. "I'm sorry. Do what...?" Sara asks, gawking at Peter threading the cord through straps and tying it to a thwart.

"Front-ferry."

Sara frowns and offers an apologetic "I don't think so."

"I guess not, not with only two days of Shorty Hayes' instruction," he growls. "We have to cross to the other side and it's easier if you use the river's current."

"Can't we paddle fast straight across?"

"We could, but you'd soon run out of gas, so we use the river's dynamics to help. It's the best way to move upstream against a current."

Sara shrugs, but guesses he's talking physics, a subject she never grasped despite old Mr. Lockyer's dogged perseverance from the day she entered Form One. Nonetheless, she nods. "It will be smoother paddling over there?"

"Yeah. The rapids are close, so be careful. Can't afford a mistake like yesterday's. Here, I'll show you."

Peter kneels and with a piece of driftwood, scratches wavy lines in a patch of sand. "Water," he says. "The river." Methodically he explains, as he has for dozens of students, how to set the canoe's angle in the current, and by tilting downstream, how to vector sideways, at right angles to the bank.

"You make it look simple," Sara says, with a nervous laugh as he stands up. "I'll give it a shot," and moves to her boat and eagerly tugs at the bow. Peter helps slide her canoe into ankle deep water and then his a few feet upstream of hers. She licks dry lips, tastes panic. A glance at Peter tells her he's unaware of her fear.

"Stay close," he shouts as they push off.

Sara watches Peter glide away and follows in his path, concentrating furiously on his every action as they cross the river in line. At mid-stream, thinking this is easy, she glances over her right shoulder. She stares, fascinated by the way the river slides and swirls, its surface smooth like black satin, somehow sensuous. Behind the water-horizon, prancing up and down, points of white foam are all she can see, and a rock cliff beyond. White horses, she recalls, like the manes of the Lippizaner stallions. The roar, muted, is catapulted into the air by a carefree wind. Sara slows. The canoe loses way as if the river has sprouted fingers that are taking hold, that are luring her away from Peter. She smiles, feeling seduced. A tingle runs from her fingertips to the pit of her stomach. The spell is wonderful...

Whack! Terror smacks. Eyes fill her face. What *am* I doing? She swivels her head. Peter's beyond reach. Her throat tightens. Her mouth aches for saliva. Muscles lock. Can't breathe. A sudden wind rocks the canoe, steals the last of its momentum. She doesn't realise that she's drifting downstream – backward. A couple of strokes would have saved her, but, unwittingly, she flings the paddle aside and grabs the gunwales. Sara screams, but only a croak leaves her lips.

Often she has speculated on what one feels when facing inevitable disaster – a truck approaching in the wrong lane; a crippled aircraft gliding for an emergency landing, its passengers' foreheads tight to their knees. Now she knows. It's a blank, voided by naked fear.

Sara's knuckles blanch; closer, the roar is deafening, like an avalanche about to engulf her.

"Peter! PETER! Oh God. HELP!"

Peter's head turns, offhandedly, reluctant to stop. In a flash his canoe spins and he's racing towards her. Too late!

"Paddle! Paddle!" she hears. "Paddle for Christ's sake! Head to shore!"

Somehow – she never did figure it out later – she grabs the paddle and splashes it frantically through the water. Hardly breathing, her heart thumping, she gradually stems the current, drenches her face with a crab stroke, then creeps forward, angling towards the left bank. Peter comes crashing into her bow, rocks her violently, almost tipping her overboard. She recovers her balance and can't believe that she's facing the shore. He back-paddles out of the way. Sara drives harder, faster, and is virtually safe when the bow strikes a submerged rock. She pitches forward. The stern, still in the current, sweeps through a half-circle like a gate and jars into more rocks.

"Jump out! Quick! Grab the gunwale."

Using both hands, Sara jumps, swinging sideways like a gymnast on a pummel-horse and lands in the shallows. She slips on the slimy bed, twists awkwardly, and sits heavily in four inches of water. A stab of pain shoots into her tailbone and up her spine. She cries out, looks up just as Peter bucks over the white horses and disappears.

With the last of her strength, Sara heaves her canoe ashore. Water trickles icily down her legs. She squishes across the rocks between the two sets of rapids, trips on an edge and falls on her face. Her first instinct is to surrender and bawl, but fearful for Peter, she drags her head up in time to see him shoot the second rapid, missing a breaking curler by inches.

Sara stumbles back to her boat, sinks to the ground shaking uncontrollably, horrified by an image of her body floating away downstream. Wet, battered and bruised, her body refuses to respond. Breathing comes in weak gasps. Tears spring from her lids and the river splinters behind a salty veil. Why did I ever want to do this? I must be out of my mind. I'm useless. Not for two years has she felt so broken, not since that Friday night when her husband had walked out. A failure then, again now. In seconds, the river has shown its contempt for her experience, has stripped off her outer layers of who she is and proven her insignificant, no stronger than the vole she'd met on the pathway.

The sky, as though commiserating with *Missinippi*, suddenly opens. Rain falls in torrents, stinging her head and hands. The river hums as each raindrop spawns a bubble on the surface, a glassy dome that lives and dies within a second, leaving a circle that ripples into others like chain-link fencing.

Sara senses Peter's arrival, shrinks further inside her shell. He slips, crouches behind her, and places a hand on her shoulder.

"Everything was wonderful, now... ruined," she blubbers.

"Hey, snap out of it," he says, sharply. "There's no harm done. No one capsized *this* time. The only thing damaged is your silly pride. Where's your hat?"

Her hair is matted to her scalp, rivulets course down her neck. "Top pocket of my blue pack." She swipes her nose with the back of a hand, sniffs.

Peter extracts a yellow sou'wester and plonks it on her head, a sudden splash of sunshine. Grabbing her elbows he pulls her up.

"I'm soaked. Again." Sara shivers.

"Any more tears and the river will overflow its banks."

She smiles weakly. "It seems that you're destined to be stuck here. If you want to change your mind, about taking me that is, I quite understand." They are standing close, facing each other. Water drips from their hat brims, falling in unison, sometimes merging.

Peter unties the blue bandanna from his neck, wipes first her eyes, then her face. Her heart flutters from his closeness. She follows his pupils as they examine her. Sara senses his hand slowing, warmth spreading in her cheeks. Their eyes meet... All Sara can think is how blue his are, as blue as a Mediterranean sky.

"My fault," he apologises, his voice husky. "I shouldn't have expected you to do a ferry under these conditions. Something in me wanted to teach you a lesson. Stupid of me. It takes practice. A lifetime of practice. I should have stayed beside you, between you and the rapids... Look, I said I would take you to Pinehouse, on probation as it were, and I will. We just have to find a different way past here. It's kinda jinxed," he adds with a short guffaw. Peter turns and points. "The river flows through that gap. We have to get there, make a hanger right, and then we'll be cruising. Guaranteed!"

All Sara can see is a confusion of rocks and trees, but she vaguely remembers from two days ago a narrow channel, a sharp bend, and fast flowing water.

"Are you sure?"

"Hundred percent," he states reassuringly, wringing out his bandanna and retying it. "Wait here while I get my boat... and keep moving, or you'll freeze to death."

Sara hunkers down beside her canoe, her back to the rain, eyes stuck unfocused on the ground, remembers Peter's eyes. Never has she been so cold and wet, yet inside she's glowing. She chuckles at his speech, using words she's heard at the cinema – *hanger right, cruising.* Only in Hollywood films. Water drips off her lifejacket, flows down rainpants that cling coldly to her legs. It drips from fingertips that are wrinkled like prunes. The world around her drips: off leaves of willow and aspen and bearberry; the rocks ooze.

Peter returns, lining his canoe up the rapids.

"Are you absolutely sure you want me with you?"

He takes a hand and leads her to the water's edge. "We're going to line along the shore until we're beyond this fast water. *Then* we'll cross to the other side. I don't accept failure. Never have, never will." Sara smiles bleakly and nods.

Often she slips and occasionally stumbles into the water, but they forge upstream. Where the current slackens, they rest. Peter instructs her, twice.

"Do you think you can do it?"

"I think so."

"Okay. Go for it."

Sara pushes hard against a rock, strokes four times on her left, switches, and repeats on her right. Sooner than expected, she glides into still water on the other side. Her spirits rise. She laughs to herself. A few moments later Peter slides in beside her.

"Feel better?" Sara nods, gives Peter a grin. "Now follow right behind me as we tackle the next stretch."

They edge upstream against a medium current and reach the eddy below the turn. A high cliff obstructs the view around the corner.

"Notice how fast the current is on the outside but slower on the inside?"

Sara nods.

"You have to paddle hard out of the eddy. As your bow hits the moving water, called an eddy-line – do you see? – paddle even harder on your left and you'll turn the corner. Then straighten up close to the side and... go for it," Peter says, slamming his hand on the gunwale. "I'll be right behind you, just in case..."

On her first attempt, she's too slow; on the next, the angle is too wide. The river swings her left and she has to circle back into the counter-clockwise eddy. On the third try she yells, "Rule Britannia!" to the river, to the rain, to the rocks. An echo replies, seems to cheer her on. Gathering speed, she hits the eddy-line and disappears from Peter's view. Holding her breath, she grapples with the river, slicing into it with short rapid strokes. Almost scraping the cliff, every detail seems magnified. Long strands of green algae on the riverbed wave somnolently. Rainwater trickles down cracks and into crannies, washes around black lichen that looks dead. A solitary six-inch spruce sapling is eking out an existence from a fissure. Tiny pearls hang from every needle. Sara senses an odd kinship with it: soaked, desolate, rebirth. A speck of life in a remorseless world. Strangely encouraged, Sara forges ahead, pulls away from the current's clutches and, at last, glides onto Stack Lake, into the shelter of a high bluff.

Sara flops backward. Shoulders wedged between the gunwales, her head sags onto the stern plate. She grabs the sou'wester and drops it into the canoe. Eyes close. The rain, reduced to a drizzle, mists her face, settles like dew. The whisper of a paddle and the gentle rocking of her boat heralds Peter's arrival. For fifteen minutes they rest, absorbing the peacefulness of a lee shore; serenity returns.

Sara's eyes open. The grey ceiling is so close that it seems solid. She wants to reach up and touch it. Strength is creeping back. Sara turns her head, inwardly smiles. Beside her she sees a character from *Punch* magazine; arms and black-booted feet drooped over the gunwales, a battered hat hiding its face. A hand is clutching her gunwale, keeping them together. She remembers its strength when it crushed her fingers, a grip toughened from handling a paddle and wielding authority. She notices how a gold ring digs into the tanned skin and wonders why he hasn't mentioned a wife. Is she the person bringing his supplies, or has she gone from his life? He'll tell me when ready. His trimmed nails are grimy from their daily scraping in camp dirt. Without rocking her canoe, Sara sits up so that she can see more of him, her turn to stare.

What has made this man? What is it that evokes the sudden outbursts that had frightened her? What, just as suddenly, turns him gentle, sensitive and caring? Like nature itself: a storm is followed by a tranquil sunset; vicious as a wolf's kill yet tender when caring for a wayward pup; as biting as winter's gales before March's soft rains. She hopes that in the days to come, as they journey deeper into the Canadian north, she will understand some of his mystery.

"Peter." Her whisper strokes the silence. She wants to tell him how fired up she feels, but suddenly it's not so important, that it would mean little to him. All she mutters is, "Thank you...so much."

The mallard, stock-still on a clutch of nine blue-green eggs, is virtually invisible. Its nest, an intricate weave of twigs and grass lined with white-and-brown-flecked down, is tucked beneath a red osier dogwood. Scabs of bark and tangled reed-grass camouflage the expectant mother. Only her eyes, onyx in a dun head, disclose her island habitat at the far end of the lake. Wind sporadically penetrates the sanctuary, rustles leaves, fluffing crown feathers. The return of her pretentious mate, emerald head, white neck-ring and chestnut breast, is expected. Patiently she waits, unaware that he's a mile away eyeing two motionless canoes.

A whim, possibly from tedium, prompts the female to rise and waddle the four-foot beaten path. Once clear of overhanging branches she springs into the air, wings beating. Head down, she skims the water, calling boisterously for her mate.

A raven, inert in the only white spruce on the island, stirs, ruffles its shaggy crop. Watchfulness rewarded, it falls, like a tomahawk, on jet-black wings. It struts to the nest and chortles, a grating laugh like a rusty garden-shed door. Voraciously it attacks, hacking the eggs with its Roman-nosed beak. Some are split and the yolks sucked out. Others are lifted, tossed, and swallowed whole down its gullet. Within minutes the nest is empty save a few shards of shell.

Issuing a raucous cackle the bird lifts off, pushing branches aside with a brutish disdain, and flies to the north shore. An unholy commotion erupts from the top of a giant jack pine. A brace of ravenous chicks, half as big as their parent, is fed in turn a yellow-white discharge laced with shell fragments.

Meanwhile, the mallard returns, peers forlornly into its barren enclave, turns and takes off to rejoin the ever-vigilant drake. Instinct brings her back three times, but in late afternoon she departs forever. Later in the season there may be further attempts to breed, but survival is doubtful. Winter would arrive before the brood's southern migration and only the parents would have the stamina to fly the two thousand miles to Texas.

Mist rinses the landscape of colour; distant pewter-shores fuse the leaden sky into leaden water. A whorl in the middle of the lake – blue, yellow, red and green – brings to mind the initial smear on a painter's canvas. Sara, knuckle-white, is petrified by the swell as soon as they leave the lee. She's like a kite flying free as they race across the lake, striving to maintain a straight course as the canoe pitches and yaws. She's in Peter's wake, about twenty feet back, rapidly approaching a landfall alongside a slim incision in the bedrock through which white water plummets. Peter arrives, vaults from his canoe a fraction before it smashes onto the steep slope, and heaves it ashore. With legs apart, he braces like a combat-ready wrestler. Sara surfs in on a breaker. Peter catches the bow, staggers to almost sit, recovers, then tugs fiercely. Sara topples backward, arms and paddle akimbo. "Sorry," he says, laughing, and proffers his hand as she clambers over her packs. "A wave was right behind you."

His grip, gentle and warm, surprises her. She had expected it to be like hers, stiff and cold. Oddly, it reminds Sara of her father. As a child she had wandered with her hand buried in his warm paw through Kew Gardens. On Saturdays, he'd travel by train and Underground to Craven Cottage to cheer-on Fulham's football team, but Sunday afternoons were devoted to gardening and Sara. Lingering at flowerbeds, she had listened to his quiet, passionate narrative, had learned to differentiate between annuals and perennials, shrubs and trees, native and exotic. Now she longs to prolong her tie to *this* mentor, gripping his hand to somehow absorb its strengths.

"This is Stack Rapids," Peter announces, outwardly unaware of Sarah's lingering grip. "A short portage, only seventy yards."

She surveys the climb across bare rock and mats of flattened grass leading to a break between willows and the conifers behind. A gust snatches her sou'wester and it sails to tango like a sunflower in the dancing bushes. Scrambling up the slope on hands and feet, Sara rescues her hat then looks back over the white-flecked lake. The canoes pitch with each incoming breaker, buffeting noisily against the rocks.

"It looked much nicer the day before yesterday," she remarks. "Actually had a swim here I was so hot." She recollects the shock and subsequent goosebumps when she had slid naked into the water. Her face unexpectedly warms, imagining herself franticly stumbling from the lake, gathering clothes, a towel, anything, to cover her nakedness as he rounds the nearby point. How fortunate she had met Peter at Rock Trout and not here, she thinks.

The rain falls again, angry sheets of water hissing into the lake. The sky blackens.

"No point stopping for a break," Peter says. "I have jerky we can snack on once we're on Trout Lake."

Sara nods, puzzled by his word 'jerky'. She has strange notions of what they might be eating, unable to connect food with her first attempts at driving a car. She skids down to her canoe and grabs the heaviest pack.

"Let me..." says Peter, a hand on her arm. He lifts the pack and Sara slips her arms through the straps. Her back buckles despite straining to remain upright. She begins to doubt her strength, inadequate unless she reduces her load. She climbs the bank, one foot placed solidly after the other. A rough path wends between thickly cloistered jack pine and aspen. Under the tree-canopy, it's like nightfall, dark and silent. The trees, tall and straight, make the wind seem far away, muted to a whisper. Rainwater trickles down leaves and needles, pools and falls, bouncing off her hat and the underbrush. Hollow plops, like pebbles falling down a well, echo around her. She squelches through the gloom, her sneakers imprinting dimples in the mud. Her chest aches and her shoulders rub raw from the searing straps. The trail slopes gently downward. Sara thrills to catch sight of smooth water through the shoreline willows and inwardly cheers when she delivers her pack. She presses a fist in the small of her back and stretches muscles. Half way along the return hike, she steps aside for Peter to pass, Duluth bag on his back, canoe riding on his shoulders. She hears a muffled "Okay?" as he goes by.

"Yes, thank you. Nice and short."

Back at the landing, she finds her packs and paddles at the top of the bank. She grabs the smallest and a black-bladed paddle for each hand. They pass each other again and smile grimly – forced cheerfulness in a cheerless tunnel. "Plop Portage," she says to the air, to a nearby tree, to herself. Sara's heart and every aching muscle bleeds gratitude when she sees her inverted canoe approaching through the trees. She thanks Peter.

"No problem," echoes the gruff response from inside the green shell. Peter is also packing the wannigan.

Only her third pack and Peter's paddles remain. By the time she's loaded, Peter's striding toward her.

"I can take those. I'll carry your backpack if you want?"

"I can manage, thanks," she says handing over the paddles, determined to carry her own. "Why is this one bent?" she asks, noticing for the first time the bend between the shaft and blade.

"From beating lazy paddlers," Peter replies, chuckles. "It's supposed to be more efficient. Good on flat water only. The straight one – thank God I didn't lose it – I use in rapids."

"That wasn't so bad," Sara comments when they reach the end of the trail. "Thanks for carrying my canoe. I've been dragging it on the ground, but that's hard work."

"At least this portage and the next are short. In fact, only Birch Rapids portage is of any consequence in the next four days. We'll soon have a system down pat. You'll get stronger. But it will be easier when you dump some of your stuff," he harps, "you don't need it all."

They reload, push off, and cross a small lake to a minor rapid, a wide chute running aslant from right to left.

"We'll skirt round the haystacks and line up the left side," Peter suggests. "It's quite easy. Then there's a short but difficult portage around Trout Falls."

"I actually floated down this one," replies Sara, her voice firm with pride, but Peter doesn't seem to hear, seemingly ignoring her boasting intentionally.

Trout Falls portage, like Stack's, begins on steep-sloping granite, plunges into a dense dark forest of black spruce, and is ruptured by moss-coated boulders that jut up like petrified carbuncles. A slip on one could easily twist an ankle at best, or break one at worst. At the end a gravel path drops precipitously to a bay that is like a millpond. Resting in the shelter of the land behind them, Sara and Peter look out onto Trout Lake, fascinated by the gradual transition from black velvet to whitecap, one with rising trepidation, the other... exhilaration.

The rain stops, the clouds thin and lift. A white-throated sparrow immediately sings jubilantly from the willows. A pair of yellow warblers darting amongst the dripping leaves heralds the increasing light. Every time they perch on thin red branches, song bursts forth, bright and cheerful, a proclamation for better weather. The air tastes clean.

Peter suggests they walk over to the falls. From a cliffhanging rock they gaze at the boiling water twenty feet below. Sara feels dizzy. Standing with their shoulders touching like helium balloons on strings, Peter points out a possible route around the boulders piercing black through the foam. "The secret to running rapids is to find the greenest water," he shouts. "There's a line right-of-centre that is somewhat greenish. Follow that and cross your fingers. I've run this one once. See that wave at the bottom – the curling one – it almost flipped us. But we made shore without a swim."

Why's he telling me this? We won't be going down rapids; we're going upstream. Ah, he wants a pat on the back. Well, he ignored my boasting. She pouts her lips, squints an eye. Give me a chance, I'll show him.

"I've always wondered if the voyageurs ran Trout in their hurry," he adds as they retrace their path.

Peter cuts the glass surface of Trout Lake elatedly. The stop-start-stop-start that portages bring is over for the morning. He glances behind in time to see Sara hop into her canoe. He powers his paddle, expecting the push of the wind any moment. The muffled voice of the falls strokes his ears sporadically, reminiscent of the outcry of grief and hope from loved ones bidding farewell to a warship going to sea as his mother had done decades ago. Imperceptibly the force of the wind strengthens and whitecaps rise and foam along the gunwales. The surfride is exhilarating; Peter's excitement sparkles in his eyes.

A knot of fear suddenly tightens his stomach. He has forgotten Sara. Glancing over his left shoulder, then his right, he's relieved to glimpse a smudge of green a hundred feet behind. He stops. Paddle square to the water to prevent broadsiding. Sara races by, her face stark, whiter than the breaker she's riding.

"Is this safe?" she yells. Peter misses her next cry, its words carried on spindrift, gossiping with the wind.

Peter bends to his paddle, catches up and grabs a gunwale.

"Hang on to my boat. There, just behind me!"

Both canoes immediately stabilise, held together like the pontoons of a catamaran. Peter hooks his right leg over and into Sara's boat. He rummages in his daypack and pulls out two lengths of cord from his seemingly endless supply. The first and longest piece he ties between the two amidships. Then, stretched precariously across his Duluth pack and Sara's canoe, he reaches over and snugs both bows with the other.

"Right!" he says, easing back onto his seat, "You can let go."

Adjusting the rear cord, Peter cautiously allows the sterns to spread apart so that each canoe becomes the arm of a vee.

"That's better. Sailing without a sail." A broad smile creases Peter's face. "You'll have to steer because your canoe is the longest. I can put my feet up and let you do all the work."

The effect is remarkable. Attached at the nose like Siamese twins, the wind catches in the vee and carries them along at the same speed yet perfectly stable. All the same, Peter watches Sara until she has the hang of steering with her paddle.

Peter relaxes. "Now... some jerky?" he says, reaching for his daypack.

Sara gawks at what plainly resembles a strip of ragged leather. Peter tugs at his with his back teeth. His head and hand suddenly fly apart. Sara laughs.

"Is *that* why it's called jerky?"

"No idea. Maybe. Here, have a piece."

Sara rips off a chunk between clamped teeth, chews for several minutes.

"It's tougher than old boots," she protests.

"Keep chewing. It gets better." He sniggers at her grimaces, but gradually her frown melts.

"Hey! This is better than its looks. *Really*. I like the salty-spice taste. What is it?"

"Dried deermeat, but I'm not a hunter. It was given to me," he adds hastily.

They careen past a scattering of small islands that partly steal the wind. Ahead the lake stretches wide and unbroken to a thin line of trees on the horizon. The western sky, visibly brighter, adds hope.

The crossing is fast. They approach what looks like the end of the lake but is in fact a narrows that branches into a maze of channels that encircle many islands. The waves gradually build to four-foot rollers marching over the shallows. Rocks scattered in the gap take shape, appear like shadows in the flying spume.

"Be careful," Peter warns. He struggles to keep the canoes riding perpendicular to the crests, his paddle in a low brace like an outrigger. They bear to their left, aiming for a low promontory with its thatch of trees bowed, the leaves showing their silvery-grey undersides. He glances sideways. The point flies by. Breakers wreak pandemonium with the shoreline vegetation. Spray drenches their faces.

They duck into a pocket of a bay out of the wind. Peter and Sara stare at each other and chorus a "Wow!"

"What a rush! I've never done anything quite so thrilling yet frightening at the same time," Sara says, wiping her flushed face.

Peter agrees. "That was riskier than what I expected. We don't need these cords anymore," he says and slips the knots.

Trout Lake ends where the Churchill River spills out of Black Bear Island Lake down Birch Rapids. An hour later Peter says: "There are two parts to the rapids. We can line the first but must portage the second. We've done okay and the weather's improving so I say we camp after the portage. It's better to do your portages than to leave them to the next day even if you're wiped."

Relief floods Sara's face. "Those are such sweet words. I don't think I could go another mile… but I will if I have to," she adds quickly.

"You're going to get your feet wet again."

"They haven't dried yet, so no matter."

"Did Shorty teach you how we name each side of a river or lake?"

"No. Left and right I suppose."

"Not quite. Imagine you're facing downstream."

"Uh huh."

"Then we say the left side is *river-left* and the other side is *river-right*. Obvious as long as you remember to think downstream. So, here's a test."

"Here cometh the teacher," Sara says with a grin.

Peter laughs. "I guess. We're going to line-up on our left. Which side is that?"

"Err. River-right?" she says after turning her head.

"Right on," he says. "Above this section the river splits in two. On river-right, the same side we're on now, there are two waterfalls. On river-left there's a kilometre-long series of ledges, impassable except for a twisting route that native guides go up and down in their fishing boats, and expert canoeists follow when heading downstream."

"Are you an expert?" Sara asks.

Peter shrugs, "I s'pose."

"Excellent," Sara says. "I feel that I'm in good hands. An expert canoeist as well as an expert teacher. What more can a novice girl want?"

"A lot less clothing," Peter replies, his mind thinking ahead to Birch Portage.

"The portage is somewhere along here," Peter says after crossing the current below the lower waterfall. It takes four passes before Peter spots the break in the river alders that hide the path.

Ten yards into the forest, the canoe on his shoulders, Peter's premonition is verified. The trail, brown, slimy, and sweetly pungent, is awash. Water trickles between green curbs of club moss, Labrador tea and bearberry; dripping green ash and hazel shoulder in. Where the ground dips, water pools black, bowls of mud-soup and last year's rotting leaves. Tree limbs stripped of bark lie half-submerged, slimy bridges engineered by canoeists in their attempt to keep dry feet.

It is bug heaven. Hordes of blood-sucking mosquitoes swarm, zoom in like Stukas. With uncanny know-how, they find the softest flesh, a smorgasbord of ears, neck, backs of hands, ankles. The females land, probe and feed undetected until an itch alerts the invaded host. Slaps miss and the mosquitoes launch to a different dish. Black flies, furry hump-backed diptera, wage war commando-style. Their *modus operandi* is to steal down shirt collars, nestle into hair, or sneak up sleeves and pant-legs where they nip off chunks of skin before injecting a brew of poisons into the raw flesh. Sara's insect repellent is quickly gone. Even Peter, who usually scoffs at bug-spray, is driven to using some.

"I'm baptising this 'Pesky Portage'," Sara says at the end of the second leg.

"The *Guardians of the North*," Peter responds. "Black flies can kill a deer, even a moose, in three to four hours. I've heard of trappers driven to suicide by them."

"I'm not that low, but I'm getting close," Sara discloses.

The portage takes over an hour. An hour of torture. An hour of wishing that they were elsewhere. An hour of cussing. An hour of tears and mounting anger.

"Fucking tree!" after a collision that sends Peter reeling, his head inside Sara's canoe. "I've a mind to cut you into toothpicks!"

"By God, you're going to dump your bloody gear!" Peter again, this time up to his knees in mud. Sara, following behind, didn't dare argue.

At long last they shove off, exhausted, filthy, and itching all over. One blessing is that the edge of the storm has reached them. Above, ruler-straight, a cloud-edge stretches from north to south. The western sky is egg-blue; the land ahead is bathed in sunlight.

"We'll make for that one," Peter says, pointing to an island rising from the water like a Scottish castle, dark green trees like a crenellated parapet. Sara sighs and smiles.

"I love your war-paint," he says, indicating a streak of mud down her cheek and across her chin. Sara spears the air with her paddle, pokes out her tongue then laughs. Peter laughs with her.

On weekdays the alarm clock stirred Sara from her bed at six. She washed in a poky bathroom freshly perfumed with shaving soap, brushed her hair and applied a light smear of lipstick and eye shadow, breakfasted on cornflakes, toast, marmalade and tea, and, still sitting at the kitchen table, had proffered her cheek for a kiss.

"Bye, Daddy."

"God bless you, luv. Brolly weather t'day. Will mess with the cricket. Make a mint."

Ten minutes after her father had pedalled away on his bicycle to the bus depot, she too left the house, closing the front door quietly to not waken her mother and walked briskly to Woking Central station, indifferent to driving rain, dank fog, keen frost or thin sunshine; in summer daylight or winter darkness.

A five-minute wait at the north-east end of the platform, surrounded by grey nondescript passengers, lonely. Brakes whisper as the electric train glides to a halt. Doors slide open. She would look for a window seat on the left side, facing forward, and for the next forty-five minutes observed suburban London shaking off the night. Going toward the City, semi-detached dwellings with tree-hidden fenced gardens imperceptibly mutated into row upon row of drab terraced houses with squalid, brick-walled backyards. Well-kept warehouses with yards piled high with crates, pipes, drums of wire, gave way to chaotic factories, grimy gantries, haphazard heaps of coal, broken windows and paint-faded signs.

Anonymous individuals permeated her journey, actors in her own tragedy appearing on cue. She watched for them expectantly, gave them names; the milkman, Winston, at Surbiton; the paper boy, Harold, at Wimbledon; the white-smocked Indian, Ghandi, leaving his home at Clapham by the back gate; Maggie T, hard-faced with netted hair, invariably pegging laundry on a clothes-line near Battersea Park. Individuals seen fleetingly through the carriage window, individuals that developed character with each glimpse as she followed them with her imagination.

On dark winter mornings, the window became a mirror backed with lights streaking by like comets. On such days Sara loved to secretly scrutinise her fellow commuters, their profiles ghostlike in the window, faces supposedly hidden by morning newspapers. She speculated on their jobs or transformed them into characters in her current novel: horn-rimmed glasses behind *The Times*, LeCarré's Smiley; thin legs, small feet, definitely a ballet dancer; over there, college scarf round his neck, a student teacher; wary eyes, nicotined fingers, beige unbelted Macintosh, a plain-clothes detective. For one electrifying week, 007 occupied the seat opposite; her smear of lipstick and eye shadow had increased noticeably, applied with fastidious care. *She* was Miss Moneypenny, but on *her* 'Black Monday', he vanished, never to reappear. She hoped that he hadn't met a ghastly end.

Her journey terminated at Waterloo. Sara often wondered how the Duke of Wellington would have felt about the naming of the city's busiest railway terminus for his bloody victory, his moment in history trivialised to a train station. Sara's own victory each day was to thread her way through the crowd of commuters scurrying like ants, goaded by a booming female voice echoing within the smoke-encrusted glass canopy; "The train arriving at platform twelve... The 8:20 express for..." Alluring faraway destinations – Bournemouth, Winchester, Salisbury, Exeter St. David's, places she had read about but never visited. From the concourse she plunged underground, conveyed on endless downward escalators, scanned advertisements for Wonderbra, Beefeater Gin and Shakespeare's *Henry V* at the Globe.

Sara hated the Underground. IRA activity in the City frightened her and the 1987 fire at King's Cross Station still haunted her. She expected water to flood in at any moment as they wormed their way under the River Thames. Nothing would have made her shelter in the tunnels as Londoners had done during the war. Awed by photographs of white smiling faces back-dropped by the black circle of the tunnel, she would rather have faced the rain of incendiary bombs than spend five minutes cowering underground. She didn't relax until Bank – the station beneath the Bank of England, the City's heart – where she re-emerged into daylight. Gasping for breath, she'd arrive at her place of employment: Babcock, Williams & Evans, Stockbrokers, on Lombard Street. Interminable days spent in front of a keyboard and monitor, she had pounded out dockets, orders to sell or buy, processing the business of making clients wealthy or destitute.

Around her, anchored to shabby desks, ten women similarly attired in white blouses and black or navy skirts, spreadsheets or text reflecting green in their eyes, their long fingers darting over worn keys. The office hummed; the murmur of keyboards punctuated by beeps from concealed computers, a whisper of shuffling papers until twice a day by silent clock-watching agreement – no bells rang – everything stopped and the room stilled – noon; or five o'clock.

The lunchtime exodus dispersed the women, vagaries of the weather, to nearby pubs or to Woolworth's or to a bench besieged by pigeons in the churchyard of St. Mary-le-Bow. A habit-loving woman, Sara favoured a cosy sandwich-bar on Holas Street for a bowl of soup and a cup of strong tea. Propped open in front of her at her window seat, the current paperback provided an escape, or romance, or flight into fantasyland. At precisely ten minutes to one, she would fold in the top corner of the right hand page, slip the book into her handbag, place a half new p under her plate and return to the office.

At the end of the day she had followed the morning's commute in reverse, but once aboard the train, she re-embraced her world of fiction; journeyed to Africa on the words of Wilbur Smith, solved a mystery, clue by clue, with Mary Stuart, or went horse-racing in a Dick Francis saddle. Subdued passengers shared the carriage, weary from their labours, their day of mindless activity. Either they conversed in low voices or rustled through the evening tabloids waiting for the expected soundless lurch that began the homeward journey. Only the headlines would raise her head, otherwise she ignored the microcosm racing over the rails, tracking the spokes that radiated from the great metropolis. If no labour disputes, signal delays, or a mis-function at Clapham Junction slowed them, Sara would key open the house door at ten to seven to be greeted by the familiar West-country accents of *The Archers* coming from her mother's portable radio.

"Dinner's ready, dear. Got yer some noice pork chops. Kettle's on the boil. Go an' change," a maternal greeting that immediately brought tranquillity, reinstated the familiar surroundings of home and dispelled the drudgery of work.

Sara leaned into the sitting room.

"Hello, Daddy," she greeted her pipe-smoking father sitting over a glowing coal fire, his eyes glued to the tele. Faces of mostly austere uniformed men in front of old aircraft or open-topped sports cars looked out from frames hanging on three walls of the simply furnished yet cosy room. A pall of blue smoke hung in the air like a shroud of gossamer, a smokescreen protection from wartime ghosts.

"'Ello, Sara, luv. 'Ave a good day, did ya? Saw one of your teachers on Number 15 today. Geography. The one you liked. Asked afta ya."

"Mr. Swithins."

She ran the steep flight of stairs to her tiny room at the back of the house, drew curtains, braced for the damp chill and gooseflesh and changed quickly into a pair of slacks and a yellow wool jersey. She ran a brush through her coal-black hair, tweaked life into her pale cheeks. Along one wall, opposite a single bed, a library of books sat wedged into a cheap bookcase primed to explode, to scatter a rainbow of colour over the polished wooden floor, a jigsaw puzzle of humanity, a world of words.

"How many shirts do you have?"

"Huh…"

Peter's question punctures her daydream, ferries her mind seven thousand miles; across an ocean, a continent, a lifetime, to the fire blazing before her.

"Shirts! How many?" She focuses, through the smoke, on Peter sitting on the wannigan, his face rosy in the firelight.

"Ten. I think."

"I have two. Dump seven."

"But they'll get dirty…"

"Have you heard of washing?" Peter cuts in tersely. "I've been wearing this one," he says, tugging its front, "for a week."

"But the smell!" she grimaces.

"Who's worried about smell except yourself? You'll soon get used to it. And no deodorants – they attract bears. What else?"

"I have three wool jumpers and…"

"Take two. We call them sweaters, but I know what you mean – my mother used the same word. A jumper in Canada is a deer. And no jeans. I've told you that."

Against Sara's protests her clothing is decimated to what can be carried in two packs. She finally stops arguing when Peter demands "You want to carry it, fine, then pack it. But I'm not Sherpa Tensing. You have to carry your own load."

"Shall I leave my cook-set now we're using yours?"

"Yup. Leave a note with your name care-of Missinippi Outfitters and if an honest person finds it you'll get everything back. Otherwise it'll sit here and rot. Mice will love your stuff for their nests."

The wind, its work done in bringing them to their haven, has calmed. The cathedral ceiling sky is the darkest of blue in the east, azure at its zenith, and a golden radiance in the west. The lake, peaceful after its day of torment, mirrors the sky. The distant shore, a black saw-toothed line against the horizon, is the only indication to Sara that she's not in fact floating in space, not an atom suspended in the cosmos.

Subsequent to the miserable portage past Birch Rapids, the dying breeze had helped Peter and Sara reach their camp, perched on the eastern tip of the island, thirty precipitous feet above the water. Looking out from their vantage point, there is a sense of remoteness, as though aboard a ship at sea. The tiny pinnacle of resistant rock has survived the

85

scouring glaciers of the last ice age, has survived thousands of years of white winter following blue summer. Little has changed since its birth. The dense stand of black spruce and lush bed of moss shows that the island has escaped fire, that nothing has changed for centuries, and is as well dressed now as when Alexander Mackenzie passed by.

The tents, pitched side by side, no longer separated by mistrust, are a few feet back from the cliff, protected by a spacious stockade of tree trunks. Their beds are softer than a feather mattress, impressionable for tired limbs. Wet clothes hang limply on a line. The fire burns in a fireplace that's a relic from past voyageurs.

Following the habitual cup of tea, Sara disappeared into her tent for over an hour. Peter had peeked in and found her sprawled on her sleeping bag, fast asleep. Considering the day's events, culminating with 'Pesky Portage' (he had adopted Sara's label), he realised that she must be exhausted, physically and mentally, her energy drained. While Sara slept, Peter sat by the fire, reflecting on the day. Despite the uncertain start, Sara had performed better than he expected and had not impeded his plans. In the coming days she would adapt to his habits, and may even become an asset. He looked forward to sharing places that he loved: mystical Silent Rapids, Needle Falls, Drum Rapids and Snake Rapids.

Later, when Sara reappeared, refreshed and sporting dry, clean clothes, Peter had suggested fish for supper. Astride a flat rock, he made a half dozen casts. A red and white spoon flicking through the water had lured a pickerel from a reef twenty feet off shore.

"Got one!" Peter cried, feeling the line jig in his hand. It took ten minutes to land the fish, alternating between reeling-in and releasing. Peter's apprehension rose whenever the pickerel raced away, seeking freedom, the rod zinging like a factory siren. He marvelled at the golden flash each time the fish leapt from the water, its scales gold in the western sun, but was raked by guilt when eventually the limp body lay on shore.

Peter had broiled the four-pounder over red-hot coals, Indian-style on a grill fashioned from a willow branch. They picked the smoke-flavoured meat off the skin until not even a morsel remained to reward the trio of grey jays, camp thieves, that had hopped and glided around them while they ate. Sara laughed at their clowning, amused by the coquettish tilt of their heads and whimsical whistles when they called each other.

"I'll go and sort my things before it gets too dark," Sara says, surrendering to Peter's dogged advice. "Then I'm going to hit the sack." Peter soon catches sounds of unpacking and imagines Sara besieged by sleeves, trouser legs, shirts and sweaters – vivid colours over-painted tent-green. Much later, Peter replies to a muffled "Goodnight."

The ensuing silence brings emptiness, a loneliness that he cannot fathom. He has spent many solitary vigils beside dying embers. Why should he feel any different now, he ponders? Before, memories had returned and kept him company until sleep beckoned. Memories of happier times with Danika, of trips they had taken, of nights they had loved each other beneath a heaven of stars, their fingers caressing, lips tracing curves with adoring gentleness. Tonight, however, the memories refuse to focus. They are distant, beyond reach, pieces of a jigsaw that won't fit. Peter is conscious of his mind reaching out to Sara, entering her tent, eyeing her like a covert visitor. Only the top of her head shows, her body cocooned in the sleeping bag. Gently he eases back the cover until he sees dark eyelashes, trembling slightly, hears her breath whisper on nylon. Sara's face is pushing Danika's image aside, arousing self-reproach to cut like a filleting knife. He remembers his earlier guilt when he took the pickerel's life.

A sudden mournful falsetto cry breaks the silence. Peter flinches, believing that his lascivious mind has sub-consciously caused him to groan out loud. But when the cry is repeated from the lake, a tremulous *ha-oo-oo,* he realises a loon is calling. A weird, maniacal laughter bursts from his right, immediately below. A second bird, re-surfacing, has verified the absence of danger, that it is safe to dive. Peter searches for it from the cliff edge, straining his eyes for a glimmer of light. He thinks he detects a loon's neck-ring on a wedge-shaped shadow, but it's probably his over-active imagination.

Unbelievably, birch bark canoes emerge from the darkness, five of them in V formation. A brigade of voyageurs, bow waves surging, eager to reach their destination. In unison, long thin paddles are plunging into the water forty times every minute. A short figure standing in the high bow of the lead canoe, in a rich baritone, is leading them in a rollicking song:

> *"En roulant ma boule roulant,*
>
> *En roulant ma boule,*
>
> *En roulant ma boule roulant,*
>
> *En roulant ma boule..."*

Proud steersmen, leaning on their long oars, look down on crews of six, middlemen, dressed in worn buckskins or wool jackets, caribou breeches, gaily coloured *ceinture fléchée* around their waists, heads covered by misshapened bowlers or toques sporting an eagle feather. Feeling a slackening in the pace, one of them calls out "'ey, Henri, old man, are you dreaming of that little woman you left behind in Lachine?"

Peter's imagination blossoms. He discerns the agents and the bourgeois sitting behind the middle seats, tall beaver hats firmly pressed on their heads. As they head west, bow waves spreading, the water corrugates behind them. Peter catches the occasional jingle of song, drifting like smoke across the lake, or is it the loon again penetrating his brain, its yodelling warped by humidity?

Before entering his tent, Peter checks the campsite once more. The lake's black surface is peppered with starlight. No sign of the voyageurs remains. Every ripple has evaporated like the vapour trails of high-flying jets, their passage unmarked.

To the east, an aura hints at the silent approach of the moon, elevator of oceans, flashlight for a myriad nocturnal creatures, the passive recipient of one step for mankind.

*   *   *

Sara twists and turns in her sleep, groaning as she dreams. She's
drifting in a canoe on a gentle stream, absorbing sunshine. A voice is
calling. Imperceptibly the current increases, eddies boil up. Lofty overhanging trees reach out from the bank. The river turns sharply, makes a
whirlpool. Revolves lethargically. A cosmic black hole. Getting closer.
She stands, balancing like an acrobat. Debris floating round and round
merges to make a face, burnt branches form eyes, the vortex makes a
mouth. Twisted into a grotesque shape. She steps out and stands on the
water. The surface dimples under her feet, like a pond-skater's. She peers
into the mouth, into the orifice. Robert! She cries in horror, jerks back.
Why are you here? What do you want?

A wailing rises in the distance. A wolf's howl. It's Robert who's
calling. Suddenly she's afraid. Her feet are cold and wet, frigid water
slides up and between her legs, encircles her waist, covers her breasts,
her neck. She's helpless against the icy pull. Her head submerges;
breathing stops.

Sara wakes, shivering in a sticky sweat, elbowing the sleeping bag
that's wrapped tightly across her face. She lies still, breathing with
shallow gulps, staring up at a green sky.

Several seconds pass before the nightmare evaporates, before Sara
grasps where she is. Her heartbeat has just slowed when a howl invades
the tent, embraces her with tingling skin. Wolves! Involuntarily, she
visualises bared fangs ripping her bloodied flesh. Cowering into the
sleeping bag, she tells herself, unconvincingly, that she's on an island,
safe from the blood-lusting predator.

Diffused moonlight illuminates the tent. Her watch tells her that it is
shortly past three, that she should go back to sleep. Abused muscles are
begging for rest.

Sara rolls onto her stomach, wedges one arm under her head. She
pushes her dreams to home. Seated in their cosy kitchen, Mum and Dad
are breakfasting at a white-clothed table. Everything shines white,

sparkling in morning sunlight; Daddy's shirt, Mum's hair, distempered walls, micklemas daisies in a vase. Are they talking about her, do they have any inkling what's happening to their daughter? Daddy, his large white mug of tea at his lips, washes down bacon, eggs, and fried bread coated with marmalade. Mum, the top of her boiled egg sliced off, dips a finger of toast. Suddenly, Sara feels dreadfully homesick. She aches for their simple humility, for their love of her and each other. She wishes that she could phone, just to hear their voices, to chat about innocuous things; the weather, the garden, the Test Match, the neighbours. I'd tell them about Peter. Daddy would like him.

For thirty minutes Sara dreams, craving for sleep, but to no avail. In the end she gives up, dresses and crawls out of the tent, hands and knees sinking into the bed of moss at the door.

At the fireplace, she feels faint warmth on her hand. A bunch of kindling and a few strong puffs springs life into the fire. Orange tongues push back the dark and warm her legs.

Sara wraps her arms around herself. Above, the Milky Way hangs, a scintillating veil stretching between horizons. She traces familiar constellations: *Ursa Major*, the Pointers direct her eyes to Polaris at the tail of *Ursa Minor*; to her right, Cassiopeia; Orion is in the south. A meteor flares briefly, shooting across the north-east, tempting Sara to wish as she used to as a child. She closes her eyes and places her palms together. A wish...

Sara is following a satellite when she hears Peter's tent-zipper.

Peter has also woken suddenly, wrenched from sleep by a stab of pain. Drawing his legs up, he massages his side gently to ease the frost of fear as much as the ache. A sweat breaks on his forehead. Tears mist his eyes. A forced belch fills his mouth with bile that burns his throat. He feels like an animal caught in a leg-hold trap and wants to vomit.

Unquestionably indigestion, he reasons. Ate too much fish by itself; should have eaten bannock as well. Cucumbers are the same – hard to digest. Need roughage – a slice of bread would do.

Cancer darkens his mind but is kept out, refused access. It drones in his ear like a tenacious mosquito thirsting for blood.

Peter peers through the netting. The sky to the north is duck-egg blue. The moon silvers the lake, casting inky shadows. A sigh from *Missinippi*; the murmur of Birch Rapids comes to him, carried through the night on a rising mist.

To his surprise, Sara is silhouetted against a flickering fire. He pulls on moccasins, shorts, and a fleece jacket. Brows knot. Why is Sara not asleep? Leaving his shelter, he's relieved to feel the indigestion easing.

Sara turns.

"I didn't wake you, did I?" Sara asks quietly, as if loathe to break the morning's serenity.

"Uh, uh. My bladder did," Peter replies from behind the tent. "Can't sleep?" he rasps, emerging from the trees. He inhales the crisp air to cool his burning throat. Licking his lips, Peter swallows, trying to lubricate his words.

"No," Sara replies, moving to the opposite side of the fire. Peter rummages in his wannigan.

"I was having a bad dream. Wolves woke me. I wasn't sure where they were – in my dreams or on the island. Their howls seemed to be inside my tent. Then I couldn't get back to sleep."

Smiling, amused by her naivety, Peter moves to her side and offers a bag of jelly beans.

"Thanks," she says, selecting a red and a green. Sara's face is stark in the moonlight, bleakly white, but with each flare-up, her cheeks blaze a dusky gold. Her eyes, in shadow, contrast balefully, like cavities in a skull. Her hair smoulders like obsidian.

"There's nothing to fear," he says confidently, then, holding up a candy, "I prefer black ones. There are no wolves on this island. And, despite the stories, wolves don't attack humans unless they are dead or dying. Red Riding Hood gave wolves an undeserved bad reputation."

"I was only scared at first," she admits, "but I soon realised that they were across the lake."

Dropping the ziploc candy-bag into the wannigan, Peter drags it closer to the fire and sits, tossing a couple of logs onto the blaze. Sparks spiral, crackle cheerfully. With out-stretched arms, he shields his face and warms his hands at the same time.

"Come and sit here. There's room," invites Peter, edging over, leaving enough space for a leprechaun.

In a sphere of golden firelight they perch, chewing candy, divining heat through fingers that almost touch. Each is acutely aware of the other, their first intimate contact.

"We should have a better day…" Peter starts at the same time as Sara says "Tell me a canoeing story…"

"Sorry. Good timing! What did you say?" Peter says, chuckling.

"You first."

"Uh, uh. You're *my* guest."

"You must have a canoeing story or two, or something…" she urges, her voice somewhat hesitant.

Peter stares into the coals and visualises faces, two in particular; one distinctly, his mother's, the other, remarkably like his own yet never seen – his father's.

"During WW2, in England," Peter begins quietly, "thousands of women married hastily because of the war – war brides they're called. Many became widows by 1945 or their husbands had returned home to countries of the Commonwealth. Hundreds were wives of Canadian servicemen.

"One nineteen-year old girl went to a dance at the local social club. She was waltzing with a young sailor in blue, RCNR flashes on his shoulders, when the air-raid siren sent them dashing to the air-raid shelter. They laughed as they ran hand in hand, unafraid of the scream of falling bombs. They giggled at the silliest things, intoxicated by too much beer. During the following week, the romance flourished, mostly in the air-raid shelter after the pubs had closed.

"Two transatlantic convoys took our jaunty sailor away for two months, but on his return, he found his girl frantic with worry and in the family way. To avoid the scandal of being an unwed expectant mother – people at that time were quite narrow-minded – they married three days later at the registry office.

"Constance, the new Canadian bride, enjoyed a one-day honeymoon, and then went back to work at the dockyard, packing food supplies for warships. The sailor in the meantime returned to his destroyer..." Peter's voice falters. Bending forward, he rubs his side.

"What is it?"

"Nothing. Indigestion. Supper is still swimming in my gut." He laughs at his joke. "Must have eaten too quickly."

Gradually the spasm fades. Peter inhales deeply and continues, "...he went back to his destroyer and was immediately transferred to Scapa Flow for escort duty on the Russian convoys, to Murmansk, and he never returned to Portsmouth.

"He survived though, including a sinking, and at war's end, arrangements followed for the brides to emigrate to Canada, fares paid, once their husbands were found. The rules of conduct, however, were intolerable but thought necessary. The women weren't allowed to fraternise with the ship's crew or servicemen returning on the same ship. If caught, they weren't permitted to disembark and had to immediately return to England, and subsequently their families had to pay for the passage.

"Constance received notification when her husband was located, and within a month she and her son boarded a boat train to Southampton and embarked on the *Aquitania*. The goodbyes to her parents broke her heart, not knowing if they would ever see each other again. Constance didn't even know her destination except that it was somewhere in the middle of Canada – they had no atlas or maps.

"Imagine; a voyage of sixteen days on a ship with a thousand homesick servicemen restricted to the lower levels and, on the top two decks, hundreds of war brides, with and without children. Socialising was forbidden. Conversations banned, even when exercising on the promenade decks. Some did chat, however; the brides were punished, not the men.

"Constance slept with seven other women and nine children in a cabin designed for four.

"Three days out, a violent storm hit them and nearly everyone became seasick, yet the women could not remain in their bunks. They had to sit on deck, in or on their life jackets as cushions – there were no chairs. The only salvation was the food, if one could keep it down. Especially memorable were white bread, beef, real coffee, and sugar, unattainable items in England during the war. For years afterwards, Constance would talk about the white bread they had had on the ship. She even saved a few crumbs and sent them home to her parents in her first letter.

"They docked at Halifax, at Pier 21. Immigration admitted them, the Red Cross clothed and fed everyone and herded them onto trains. Five days on a train. Five days to cross Canada. Miles and miles of woods, lakes, prairie, with the occasional small wooden houses appearing to break the monotony. At whistle stops, one or two women would disembark to be greeted by joyful husbands and in-laws. Departing hugs from those going on, and floods of tears to launch uncertain futures.

"At Saskatoon, early in the morning, in the middle of a winter storm, no one met them. Eventually, a Red Cross transport woman took them, with two others, to a collection depot.

"Three days later, two women turned up – my father's mother and sister."

"Constance is your mother?" Sara interrupts.

"Yes."

"They would be your grandmother and your aunt, then."

Peter nods. "Yeah."

"How old were you?"

"Three." Peter pauses, then continues before any more questions interrupt.

"Another train took us to a small town called Kindersley where we lived on a farm for a year and a half. We never saw my father – he had moved to British Columbia when he learnt of our pending arrival.

"My Mom was miserably homesick, but was determined not to quit and return to England. That would have been admitting failure. My Canadian so-called grandmother and aunt tried to make us a home, but too many differences proved insurmountable. We eventually moved to Saskatoon, and that's where I grew up."

"Did your mum ever go back?" Sara asks.

"No. Her parents died soon after, within two years of each other, still quite young – in their fifties. Mom passed away ten years ago. Worn out, I think, from staying alive."

"I'm sorry," Sara says softly. "I know how you feel – I remember loosing my grandparents. She never re-married?"

"Men-friends called from time to time, but I guess she never loved again. Maybe she didn't find the time. We lived from hand to mouth, never a nickel to spare. She worked as a store clerk. When she found a permanent job at Eaton's we found a bit of security, but not much."

Peter, leaning forward to grab another log, suddenly clutches his stomach. The pain is a dentist's drill striking a nerve. He lurches to the brink of the cliff, sits with his legs dangling over the edge. He stares bleakly into the void. He swallows violently, conscious of sweat running down his temples, down his spine. Something has snared his genitals.

Sara crouches beside him, holding his arm. "Can I get you anything?" she asks.

"No!" Peter gasps.

"Is it *only* indigestion? It seems worse. I have Rolaids."

"Yeah. I'll be okay. Just leave me alone for a bit."

"It's not appendicitis, is it? Or an ulcer? Or a…"

"No! Leave me alone!" Peter cries impatiently. "If I want your suggestions, I'll ask," he adds brutally.

Sara stalks to the fire. She toes the burning embers, eyeing Peter resentfully.

Peter's head droops. Saliva dribbles from his mouth, a silver thread that falls into his lap. He inhales through flabby lips, licks them. His doctor's voice echoes in his head "…it could be next week, or next month, or next year. We don't know…"

Slowly his body relaxes, tension eases, and the pain subsides as quickly as it had arrived.

Not till next year. Never! I know I can beat this. His mind races down his roster. Exercise. Canoe harder. Healthy food – not as much fish. I *have* to win. Many cancer victims survive, he's heard, by holistic means. He's been fine until now – it must be food poisoning. That damn fish! Have to… 'Upchuck' his students would have said. Peter detests the coarse word.

He jams a finger down his throat, gags, and vomits onto the rocks below. The stench makes him gag again, painfully, but only mucous dribbles down his chin. He swipes his mouth with the back of his hand. His open palm comes away dripping from his face. Remarkably, the tightness has gone; the pressure has subsided.

Sara's suddenly kneeling behind him, rubbing a hand along his spine, massaging his ribs.

"Get some water," Peter croaks through a scorched throat, as raw as if he had eaten a jalapeno. "Please," he adds politely, regretting his outburst.

He hears her go, pots clanking, reviving his image of her at Rock Trout, an image that assuages his mind and body, a tonic.

When she returns he drinks thirstily, dashes what's left onto the mess below. The second billy he pours more carefully, washing away all residues.

"Thank you," he says, returning the pots to Sara.

"Any more?"

"No, thank you. That should be okay."

Sara kneels and rubs his back through the layer of fleece. "Feeling better?"

Peter nods.

She slips her hands under his jacket. Peter's flesh prickles, his skin responding to cool moist fingers. The gentle rubbing generates warmth and relaxes his nerves, but also excites them. He opens the zipper, and his expectation is rewarded as Sara caresses his ribs, sliding her hands over his torso.

"Look at that moon," he mutters, distracted by unfamiliar sensations, emotions he had forsaken the day he scattered Danika's ashes into Otter Rapids. "It's like a giant Ritz cracker." Sara stops momentarily. Peter senses her eyes over his shoulder and feels her breath brush his ear.

"The sun will be up in half an hour. The voyageurs used to start their day at this time. '*Lèvi! Lèvi! Lèvi nos gens*'," Peter calls out, imagining a scatter of bodies huddled beneath their blankets. "If any supper left-overs remained in the cooking pot, that would be their breakfast, otherwise they'd get up, paddle until eightish and then stop for a smoke."

"What did they eat?" Sara asks. Her fingers had slid to the side of his neck, squeezing his trapezoidal muscles, pressing knots, seeming completely at ease.

"Peas and pork grease between Montreal and Grand Rapids. Pemmican and dried fish here in the West."

"Ugh!" Sara's face wrinkles in distaste.

"They were nick-named 'porkeaters' – *les mangeurs du lard*. They had no time to hunt or fish. They'd paddle from dawn to dusk, resting only to smoke their clay pipes. Just back there..." Peter points, " ...there was a trading post, a rendezvous for the Cree Indians from Lac LaRonge."

Sara sits beside Peter. He closes his jacket.

"Thanks," he says awkwardly. "I haven't had that done to me for a long time, not since... well, a long time ago." Peter can't understand why he avoids Danika's name.

"I think you wish you had been a voyageur," Sara suggests, quickly looking away.

"Without a doubt they were exciting times," he replies, nodding, "but brutally rigorous compared to today's comforts. There was pride in being an *hivernant* or 'winterer'. Many died; drowned, or injured from a fall. They didn't know at the time, as with any discovery, but those men established Canada as it is today. Yeah, I guess I admire them – for their tenacity and courage and honour."

To the north-east, a wash of gold brightens the sky, sharpening the horizon. Above it, a delicate pale blue pushes back the darkness, stars flicker, vanish.

"Breakfast?" Peter asks, surprising himself that food should already be on his mind.

"What's on the menu, garçon?"

"Pork and peas!"

"I'll pass, thanks."

Sara stands. Peter grasps her hand and pulls himself up. Their hands remain together.

They stay close, each waiting for the other, to speak, to move.

"Thank you for your concern. I'm sorry I yelled at you. It's a bad habit of late. You didn't deserve that."

Sara shrugs, smiles imperceptibly.

"Now – breakfast. I'm actually hungry. Oatmeal or the last of my pancakes – what would you like?"

"Pancakes, please." Sara leans forward and gives him a brief hug, and before Peter can reciprocate, she runs to her tent. Puzzled, Peter thought he saw the gleam of a tear. With strange feelings tugging at his heart, he busies himself at his foodbox, preparing breakfast as the sun's red rim climbs above the tree line.

THREE

"There they are," Peter announces, pointing his paddle mid-way up the hundred-foot cliff. Half-hidden behind ground juniper, a mosaic of yellow, russet, and ash lichens camouflage the blood-red paintings. Peat-stained rainwater, seeping from fissures, has streaked the bedrock reddish-brown, crafting an image of a wounded giant, bloodied and torn. Higher, on a ledge beneath a cusp-shaped overhang, a jumble of sticks lays evidence that ospreys have nested here.

"May we stop for a closer look?" Sara asks.

The canoes turn toward a jumble of massive rocks.

After their early breakfast, Peter and Sara left the island before the sun dispelled the morning chill. They had paddled leisurely for over four hours. The cloudless sky promised the return of the heat wave, but a sporadic north-west breeze kept the air fresh. Weaving through a maze of islands, they followed narrow channels, crept across expansive bays, absorbing a collage of magnificent scenery. Rock-lined shores and steep cliffs framed a landscape cloaked with dark green trees – spruce, pine and tamarack. Sculptured into the terrain were ravines filled with pale coloured birch and aspen. Only the sun warming her left shoulder told Sara that they were heading west.

Sara felt the tension from yesterday's turbulent ride melt away. The backpack of fears she had carried when alone gradually shrivelled: gone were thoughts of fierce animals, of capsizing into freezing water, of becoming lost.

Her mind touched a mid-morning conversation. Her cheeks warm again as she recalls Peter's praise: "You're okay, you know. You handle a canoe reasonably well. Better than I thought possible. It's not easy to solo a straight line, but you are."

With bows lodged on buff-coloured rock, they stand side by side, necks craning. The red lines, circles, and squiggles, an incomprehensible message that only scholars would dare to interpret, are virtually invisible behind the leaves of a trembling aspen.

"Come on," Sara encourages. "There's a ledge. We can climb right up to them. It looks easy." With youthful enthusiasm and the agility of a mountain goat, she scrambles over rocks, her bare legs straddling gaping cavities. At the base of the narrow shelf angling up the cliff, she has to squeeze by the straight white trunk of the aspen. The tree had taken root a foot from the cliff, had grown erect and tall as if aware of its guardian position. Pushing off her knees, Sara scales the steep climb.

Peter's ascent is more sedate. He arrives several minutes later. Sara is still panting.

"You should slow down," Peter rebukes Sara. "A fall could break a leg. We're a long way from a hospital."

"Right. Sorry. Point taken."

In silence they examine the crude design. Sara turns to Peter. "Do you feel anything?" she whispers. "In the air?"

Peter nods his head abstractedly.

"It's eerie, mystical almost. It's as if spirits are hovering around us. Do you *really* feel it?" Again, Peter nods. His eyes have a far-away look, glassy.

"Thank goodness. I thought it might be only me. Mmm. It's wonderful. Can you figure it out?" she asks. "It's a camp, isn't it?" Sara's eyes trace two vertical lines, shoulder width apart, that have five or six small triangles, like pennants, daubed on their insides. "And this might be the shoreline," she continues, indicating an arc that connects the lines at waist height. She squints at a square cross inside a circle under a serrated arch-shaped line. She drifts into the past, imagines red-stained hands of a half-naked native inking in the motif, trembling a little from fear.

"He's drawn a sacrificial stone inside a meeting lodge. This is a witch doctor maybe."

"The Woodland Cree used medicine men or women, not witch doctors," Peter corrects gently. "They made sacrifices, but not human ones like the Mayans or the Zapoteks of Mexico. I'm not sure, but I think the cross may have something to do with the Jesuits. They were here at the beginning of the 1800s."

"Only two hundred years ago? But I thought petrographs were anywhere from two to four thousand years old."

Peter shrugs. "Possibly that's so in Europe, but I don't think archaeologists can age them. Not like fossils. There's no carbon. The red colour is iron oxide. One theory I've heard is that the drawing represents a medicine man's visit to the spirit world. Suppose he happened to be here on a fast and went into a trance; when he returned from the dream world, he would immediately paint what he could remember, usually the last thing he saw. Subsequently, this became a sacred place, like a religious shrine, and Indians journeyed here for the sole purpose of a vision-quest, to commune with the spirits."

Sara crouches in front of Peter. Two figures, their arms raised, are facing a long squiggly line with a horned head. Her forehead creases. She puzzles over the riddle. "This is a man and this a woman, but why three fingers. What do you think?" She looks up at him. "This is a snake or a serpent, isn't it? Do you have legends in Canada like our Loch Ness Monster?"

Peter chuckles. "There's O-go-Pogo in the Okanagan. That's out west, in the Rockies. They say that the medicine men assume the form of an animal when they enter the spirit world. You'll always find animals in rockart. And this... with wings. It's a thunderbird." Peter snaps his fingers. "Of course! It hadn't occurred to me until now. We're not far from Pinehouse, and the Cree name for Pinehouse Lake translates into Snake Lake. And I recall reading that the voyageurs found a unique species of garter snake in this vicinity. Maybe the Indian came from there. A bit of a stretch, but anyone's guess is as good as mine."

"Oh, Peter, this *is* fascinating." Sara rubs her arms. "I get goose pimples thinking about the Indian standing here hundreds of years ago painting his story. Do you think he knew that later generations would puzzle over his message?

"My favourite place back home," she continues, excitement bubbling, "is Stonehenge. I love to stand in the circle of stones, beneath the high arches, and let my imagination loose. I've read piles about the druids. I actually went a couple of times for the summer solstice to watch their sunrise rituals, but the hippies spoilt it by rioting. I never went again."

For thirty minutes they squat on the ledge discussing the artwork, making sense of primitive artists; short, dark-skinned, dressed in tanned leather – moose or beaver – long black hair, nomadic, sustained by fish, their faith bestowed on men who held power with tales of life-threatening spirits.

Before they leave, Peter extracts a small leather pouch from his pocket. It contains tobacco. He pinches a wad, briefly holds it to his nose, smells its sweet aroma, then reaches high above the painting and squeezes it into a crack.

He turns to Sara and smiles. "For the spirits," he says quietly, reverently.

Sara leads the way down. At the bottom, she swings round the tree then leaps from rock to rock until she is back at the canoes. She turns and watches Peter's steady descent. He's easing himself down the smooth rock on flat feet. Suddenly his legs shoot from under him. Pebbles scatter, roll. He falls heavily on his back. Is sliding. The tree breaks his fall. He's wedged between it and the rock face, hidden from Sara's view by a colossal rock.

Stunned, she moves forward and sideways a couple of steps. "Are you okay?" She spots the top of his head.

"Yeah," a muffled reply. "I think so. Just stuck – ha, stuck between a rock and a hard place. Nothing broken, I hope. And I was telling *you* to be careful…"

Sara is climbing back over the rocks. Suddenly, a scream splits the air. Amplified by the amphitheatre of rocks, it's a cry of pure agony, the like of which Sara has never heard and never wants to hear again. The clatter of wings follows as birds in nearby trees take flight. Sara's heart stops. Hairs at the nape of her neck prickle. She runs the remaining distance, oblivious of the pain when she slips, unaware of the blood that seeps from her grazed shin, aware only of the sobs that echo pitiably.

Peter is on his right hand side, crumpled into a foetal heap, wrapped around the tree, which he's gripping with both hands. His back's to the wall, legs dangling over the edge, four feet above a hollow that's partly filled by the wrinkled trunk of an old aspen. A graze on his left leg stretches from ankle to kneecap. Blood oozes, pushing away dust, conceals embedded grit and folds of white skin. His Tilley hat has fallen over the side and lies between two rocks, dirty and desolate.

"Where do you hurt?" she shouts above his cries.

"My stomach!"

"Again? Not your leg?" Sara says, confused. She hovers by his body, indecisive.

"Don't just stand there!"

Peter's shout shakes her. "Tell me what to do. Can you move?"

"It feels like I've been stabbed. Get me out of here."

Sara scrambles onto the slope above Peter, grabs him under his arms and pulls. He moves an inch. Gradually, with much sucking of breath and many cries, Peter is unwedged. Once his buttocks are through the gap, Sara drags him clear of the tree. She drops below him, swings his legs over and supports his weight as he slips off the ledge. They stumble a few steps and collapse. Peter stretches out on a grassy patch and leans back against the old tree.

"Thank... you." Peter's face is ashen, eyes half closed. "My God, he was right! This is agony. Please! In my day pack... I have... a... a," Peter sobs, forcing his words through tight lips, "bottle... pills, white plastic. Please – quickly. And water."

Sara hoists herself from the hollow and hurries down the rocks, unmindful of danger, and wades into the water beside Peter's canoe. She finds the bottle as soon as she opens the flap. Her hands tremble. Was he expecting this? Reading the label brings a lump to her throat. 'Morphine'. Panic electrifies her. Nobody carries morphine without reason. What's wrong? She fills the bailer and climbs back, slopping water.

Sara kneels beside him.

"How many?" she asks, prying off the safety cap.

"One."

She places a single green tablet between his lips and then the bailer, spilling water onto his shirt. Peter tilts his head back, swallows. Sweat is trickling off his forehead, down his temples and into his eyes. The thought of shock presses her mind and she tries to remember the correct treatment. Keep him warm; raise the legs higher than the head. Panic jolts again.

His eyes squeeze shut. His breathing shortens, becomes shallow.

"I need your bandanna," she says, and fumbles with the knot against his neck. Using the leftover water, she soaks the blue cloth and wipes his face, carefully washing off sweat, crusted salt and dirt. Turning to his leg, she cleans the wound, coaxing grit out of raw flesh. She fetches a small red bag, a St. John First Aid kit, from her pack and applies a dressing, tenderly winding a bandage around his shin.

For half an hour he barely moves, not even when Sara sponges his forehead. His waxy face gradually regains some colour, the lines soften. The moaning stops.

"This isn't indigestion this time, Peter. What's wrong?" Sara demands, unsure if he's heard her.

Peter lifts his eyelids, searches for her face and focuses. "I have colon cancer... It's terminal. Flared up sooner than expected... maybe ruptured from the fall... screws-up the trip. Sorry."

"Peter, oh God, no," she mutters. Sara blinks rapidly, fighting back the tears. "Are you sure?" Horrified, she remembers the pill bottle, its potent contents readied. She nods to withdraw the question.

"Now I understand what all yesterday's talk of illness and injury was about. This is why you tried so hard to discourage me from going with you."

Peter smiles grimly, nods his head once.

"You said terminal. How long do you have?"

"Three to four days, I think."

"Days!" she cries, pulling back, staring aghast. "Don't you mean months? Years? You can't die in three days! That's ridiculous."

Peter shakes his head. "The doc warned me this might happen."

"We have to get help!" Sara says quickly, feeling her heart racing, her stomach in a knot. "How far to Missinipe? Or is Pinehouse closer?"

"Sara," he says, reaching out, clutching her hand. "Please don't. It's no use. There's no time. Find us a campsite overlooking the lake, and let me… rest." His hand falls to his side. His head drops against his chest. He moans quietly.

"No, no, no! Peter. Listen to me," she cries urgently, shaking his shoulder, shaking off the despair that has suddenly, like an autumn fog, fallen upon him. "Help me. You know where we are. I don't. Which way? Missinipe, or further west?"

A frown wrinkles his forehead. Sara holds her breath, imagines his mind calculating, adding distances.

"Missinipe. One… two… three. Four days."

Peter shakes his head. "It's too many," he groans, slumping sideways, as if he has capitulated. His head rests on the grass.

"Too many? Cancer can't spread that quickly. Peter." She shakes him gently, then more urgently. "Peter!"

The drug has deadened all his senses, Sara realises, making him drowsy.

"We're going to make it," she says. What was the word he used yesterday. Yes. "Guaranteed!"

Peter's eyes close.

Sara sits back on her haunches. Different ideas race through her mind. The rustling leaves of the tree canopy are comforting. She drinks the remaining water from the bailer, frowning at its saltiness, but it cools her hot, dry throat. I mustn't lose it, she tells herself. Check the alternatives. Decide upon a plan. Wilderness is a state of mind. That was what Peter had told her, not something to frighten you. You'll not get lost if you stay positive and keep tabs on where you are. Was that another hint to her that Peter was not as he appeared, that he may need her help? My God! He's been dropping well-disguised messages all the time; she hadn't picked up on their significance.

At the canoes, she's suddenly aware of the incredible burden she has assumed, cognisant that Peter's life rests in her hands. Has she unsuspectingly been following *her* road to Damascus? Which path do I choose? Where's the signpost?

"Obviously he can't paddle alone," she decides. "We'll have to leave his canoe and go in mine."

Dismayed, she weighs up Peter's packs. She drags the boat further out of the water, feeling his angst when it grates on the rock. She wrestles with his Duluth bag until it rolls over the gunwale. It thuds to the ground. And he said my packs are heavy, fuming, half-carrying, half dragging it to her canoe and tips it into the middle. The foodbox and daypack follow, placed behind the Duluth. Not until her packs, spare paddles and Peter's fishing pole are all re-stowed amidships and tied in does she rest. She mops her dripping face with Peter's bandanna that she has absent-mindedly tied around her neck. Sara cannot remember ever having to physically work as hard in all her life. She takes another drink and chews on a piece of jerky, a reward from Peter's daypack. Finally, she sets Peter's map, as he had done, between the back thwart and the foodbox.

To her right the view is obscured by a headland, but to the left, about fifty yards away, willows are growing at the lake's edge. This seems to be the one possible location to conceal Peter's canoe until their return. She slides it into the water and unsteadily climbs in. She's scared of tipping while sculling to a break in the bushes. Her foot slips on the rocks as she disembarks and she splashes into the water up to her thighs. She grabs the canoe just before it floats away.

"A good start, Sara!" she admonishes herself. "Can't even land. How in the Lord's name am I going to paddle all the way to Missinipe?" She shakes her downcast head, resigned to defeat.

It takes thirty minutes to hide the canoe with a cover of willow branches. A sombre thought cuffs her, chills her to the bone in fact. I'll not see it again; it's unlikely Peter will either.

She starts back along the shore over a jumble of rocks. She needs to pee. After, she sits, her eyes on the old aspen. At its foot, a grizzled face, blue eyes pinched by pain. There are doubts. Her mind, now that she's had the time to sit and think, is a huge question mark. Sara shuts her eyes and whispers a prayer, requesting the spirits to protect them, to safeguard their journey, and to guarantee their return. Why *their* return? I mean nothing to this man. I've known him just forty-eight hours. Yet without a second thought, she has committed herself to his rescue. There's an inkling that she's falling for him. Is this commitment hastily made due to love? Love? Hold on. Sara shakes her head. She mistrusts the word – that mental state she has yearned for, seemingly found, then brutally lost. All she wants at the moment is to see Peter safe, and possibly to come back for his canoe later. Love doesn't fit into that equation, not yet.

Back in the hollow she takes Peter's hand, is a little flustered. He doesn't move, his fingers limp. For a ghastly moment she thinks he's dead. His chest rises; relief swells in hers. She whispers "Peter, please stay with me," acutely aware of the double meaning of her words.

Sarah shakes his shoulder, gently at first, then firmly. "Peter. Peter, wake up," her voice rising, "We have to leave. Wakey, wakey."

Slowly, Peter sits up, nursing his head. "Where are my books?" he demands.

Sara is puzzled. "I'm sorry, what did you say?"

"Where are my books, damn it?" Peter says crossly. "Where's my mark-book?"

Sara giggles. "Peter, you've been dreaming. You're on the Churchill River. Not in school. We have to paddle to Missinipe."

Peter peers at Sara, his eyes mere slits, eyebrows closely knitted. "Who're you? Missinipe? No, I'm going to Fort Chip."

"Peter," Sara says patiently, grasping his wrists, "you've had a fall. We have to go back." She urges him up.

Peter sways, brushes her away and vigorously rubs his face. He stares at the lake and then the rock painting and slowly his frown fades.

Turning to Sara, he prods his stomach and says, "Boy, that pill sure did the trick. I feel that I'm floating on air."

"It did the trick alright," Sara mutters, quietly so Peter doesn't hear. "It's playing several tricks – a wonder drug," she says normally.

Climbing from the hollow, Sara turns to Peter. "Grab hold."

Peter shuffles forward and takes Sara's hands, allowing her to hoist him out of the hole. She leads him via a circuitous but safer route.

"Where's my canoe?"

"I've hidden it. It'll be safe until we come back. But we have to go now. We have to do four days paddling in less than three."

"In case there's a need," Peter states pragmatically, "I have morphine ampoules and needles. Some in the wannigan. More in my daypack. By then, though, I won't be much use. I'll be dead."

"I don't want you to talk like that. We'll be home before anything happens, you'll see," she says lightly, in an effort to boost both their confidences. Her self-belief, however, remains bleak and misgivings lick at her resolve.

"Do you want to take the front or the back?"

"Bow or stern!" Peter snarls.

"You know what I mean," she says, laughing, "I'm glad you still have your sense of humour."

"Bow."

They slip the canoe into deep water, and while Sara steadies the stern, Peter eases himself in. He tucks his good leg under the seat, and stretches the other into the vee of the bow. Sara kicks off. Being afloat again revives her optimism. A ghost of a smile crosses her mouth and a shine returns to her eyes. As they move from the shadow of the cliff, Sara looks back. She feels a caress from something in the air. Though she can't name it, she knows that it is good, and when she fills her lungs, she feels ready for whatever lies ahead.

After watching Peter for a few strokes, Sara picks up his rhythm. In no time, they are surging ahead, paddles in unison as though they've been partners for years. The bow rises and dips with each thrust, breasting wavelets that chuckle as they part.

The sun is below its zenith. The wind, still from the north-west, has freshened with the afternoon's heat. As long as it remains behind them hope lives, but, she knows, they are at its mercy. A storm like yesterday's but from the west would be a lifesaver. From the east, on the other hand... Sara suppresses the thought.

Sara's ears ache. For half-hour her eardrums have analysed every sound: a breeze scallops the water; belligerent ducks jabbering as they lift off; sighing reed-grasses resonating with shifting air. Everything bar her ears' desire – the murmur of moving water.

They had maintained a steady pace for the first hour, but as the afternoon wore on Peter's strength waned. He kept his rhythm, stroke following stroke, switching sides frequently. But with dismay, Sara watched his shoulders sag. She tried desperately to take up the slack, her face turning sheet-white, eyes glassy beneath quivering lids. Her arms and shoulders are crying out for rest.

Sara has followed the map closely, watching each landmark approach and slip by. The rapids *must* be around the next point, two kilometres away. Why don't I hear them by now? A wrong turn? We're lost? Self-doubt returns like a tsunami.

The breeze that has been gently pushing them peters out. Silence; no ripples, no birds, not a sound except from the monotonously dipping paddles. Then... a whisper. No! Aspen leaves trembling in a breath of air. Is imagination tricking her again? There. Once more, whimsical, perhaps a little firmer. Sara almost leaps from her seat, but her strength allows only a cry as conviction sweeps through her.

"Peter, it's Birch Rapids. Can you hear?"

He barely nods, raises his paddle half-heartedly.

"We have to take 'Pesky Portage', don't we?" she asks forlornly, wondering how they'll manage it in their weakened state.

Peter shakes his head, jabbing his left arm.

"What d'you mean?" She remembers the two waterfalls from the portage. Sara examines the map. "Down river-left?" she asks, hope sounding faintly in her voice.

"Yes," Peter croaks, nodding determinedly.

"There are lines drawn across the river. Doesn't that mean a waterfall?"

"No. A long rapid. Don't you remember? I told you."

The noise intensifies. Then, like a symphonic poem, the tumult climaxes, orchestrated for their rounding of the point.

Sara stares in utter disbelief. Pandemonium crowds her view. Water rages from bank to bank, as far as the eye can see. White horses sparkle, dance. Spume hangs in the air. False horizons, indicating ledges, span the hundred-metre width. In the distance, the river curves to the right and disappears. How on earth can we possibly survive?

Peter signals to pull ashore. Sara jumps out, steadies the canoe. Peter slowly disembarks.

"You can't see it from here," he shouts, "but there's a route on the left – easily runnable."

"You can't be serious," Sara utters in disbelief.

"You take the bow. I'll shout instructions – either draw or cross-draw, nothing else. Remember, the water's fast. You *must* react instantly. Don't hesitate."

"What if I make a mistake?"

"We end up in the river. Don't grab the gunwale on any account. Keep your paddle in the water to slow us down. And don't forget, if we tip, swim on your back away from the canoe, feet pointing downstream. That way you can avoid any rocks. Heads and granite don't get along. Normally this is a rush, a roller coaster ride. Unfortunately, I don't feel much like it today."

Sara hangs back, deliberating with her fears. Despairingly she tries to visualise their over-loaded canoe cresting the last wave. But another vision – bodies adrift, a sunken wreck, and rescue washed into oblivion – overwhelms her.

"Do we have to? Is there no other way? This isn't the best time to be running my first rapid. It's huge. Peter, is there really no other..."

"You can do it!" Peter yells impatiently, cutting in. "We have no choice – sink or swim."

Peter moves in front of Sara, zips-up her lifejacket and makes sure it's snug. He grips her shoulders and smiles. "You'll do okay. Don't worry so. It may even be fun."

Sara opens her mouth to object, but, lost for words, smiles with thin white lips. His eyes hold hers, steadying, breeding encouragement.

"I'm ready. Let's go." Sara tries to breathe normally. Staring at the water, she suddenly wants to pee. Her knees, hard against the sides, send jolts of pain into her thighs. She compels her heart to quit pounding in her ears so that she can hear Peter's commands. Sink or swim; *his* words, she recalls, and hates them, hates him. Her worst nightmare – her head weighed down by relentless forces and the sudden gulp when she can no longer hold her breath. What's it like to drown? Would her eyes stay open? Would the water go up her nose first or fill her throat? How long does it take to die? Would they die together?

The instant Sara's foot breaks with the land, *Missinipi* takes charge. Gripping with invisible fingers, it buffets the canoe from side to side.

Despite frantic back paddling, Sara and Peter race into a channel between a small willowed island and almost sideswipe the shore. They burst onto the main flow. They must U-turn to the left, around a rocky spit.

"Cross-draw-left," yells Peter. "Hard! Hard!"

Sara sees a foaming ledge across their path and, two feet from the shore, the slim green slick of a chute. They've turned too much! Sara braces for the capsize.

"Right draw, Sara! Once! Now, power ahead!"

Sara obeys. The canoe hits the chute like a torpedo slicing a target. Sara catches a glimpse of foaming white on both sides.

They plunge into the melee, following the main run between the left bank and ledges that stretch to their right.

An audience of rioting willows, like sports fans against a crush barrier, spills into the river, trailing their green fingers in the current. The canoe meets one challenge after another. Walls of water, white and sea-green. Malignant boulders nose the surface like crocodiles, or expose rounded backs like hippopotamuses on the Zambezi.

Paddles flash, parrying the thrusts of the river. Braces and draws and cross-draws and backstrokes and pries fend off rocks, keep waves at bay and allow the canoe to side step each adversary. Shouts spin into the air and are drowned by spume, drowned out by stampeding white horses.

On several occasions, the battle is nearly lost by little more than a hair's width. The first skirmish is with a red giant, a granite mass camouflaged by jade-green algae warts. Waiting in ambush, it occasionally surfaces, baring a shoulder that silvers in the evening light. Sara doesn't see it beside her. The canoe strikes and lurches sideways. Sara grabs the gunwale, rule number one broken. All her weight shifts right. The canoe keels over, hangs momentarily on the brink. Water floods in. Peter counters, leans outside the canoe on a high brace, compensating until it slips off the rock.

They suck in wet air, steady the canoe. Immediately two standing waves, in line, tower over them – a brace of white-headed monsters. For a fleeting moment, Sara considers a sidestroke, but the confrontation is unavoidable. They must muscle through by frontal assault.

The first wave hurls the bow to a breathtaking height. They catch air. For a split second, Sara is looking down the whole length of the rapid. They plunge. She stares into the black-green heart of the second wave. Sara's eyes burst from their sockets. She discovers how a mosquito must feel when it's about to be swatted.

The bow submerges. The canoe shudders. A mountain of water strikes Sara in the chest, takes her wind. It slaps her face with a stinging blow. She screams, then gags and chokes, nearly drowns on the river that has filled her mouth. She's flattened against the packs, saved from being washed overboard by legs wedged under the seat. Stomach muscles stretch. Sara fears damage.

The canoe is swamping, unstable. Peter holds his paddle in a brace and yells to pull to shore. They edge across the current, barely missing a series of towering haystacks, volatile waves that play at the bottom of every rapid. Frisky for the most part, they can strike the final *coup de grâce* to the unwary, or swallow a flooded canoe.

The craft slows, drifts into an eddy. The combatants collapse. Sara, on her knees, limply holding the gunwales, drops her head. Peter flops back onto the stern cover, one hand on his stomach, the other covers his face.

Sara cannot believe they are still afloat. She is wringing wet. Despite the chill air, warmth floods her body. A radiance is coursing to every capillary. A congregation is applauding in her head. She has triumphed over her greatest ever challenge – her first rapids. She wants to run an Olympian's lap of honour with a Union Jack drooped across her shoulders.

Speed, flirtations with danger, physical exertion, and a test of skills. What a tonic!

Sara lifts an arm, but something has nailed it to the gunwale; a blender in her stomach is mixing nausea and hunger. Her head settles, comprehends Peter's love of whitewater. The passion that drives mountaineers against impossible heights is suddenly clear. Canoeists and climbers enjoy similar emotions, thrilled by surfing the highest wave or conquering the ultimate summit; passion for adventure, a desire to challenge oneself, and an infinite love for life. The result: excitement that exceeds the high of an alkaloid drug, that surpasses the tension of an action movie – a Hollywood fabrication, or outstrips the thrill of a roller coaster, a contraption for synthetic delirium.

Peter? She sits up with a jerk and twists in her seat. Anxiety cuffs her. She reaches for her paddle and pulls to shore. Jumping out onto wet rocks, she grips the gunwale and stumbles to him.

"Are you okay?" she asks, a hand on his brow, the other gently wiping his face. "Do you want a pain-killer?"

An imperceptible nod sends her to his pack. She hopes that this time it won't induce sleep. She gives him water, then bails out the canoe.

Slipping off her lifejacket and wet tee shirt, Sara's white skin protests with a shiver of goose bumps, inciting tiny hairs to stand like soldiers on her torso. She drapes the shirt over the packs, and from her own, extracts a towel and dry clothing. She glances towards Peter. His eyes are closed. She removes her sports-bra and stands naked except for yellow nylon shorts. She towels herself vigorously, stimulating a pink blush like a prickly wild rose to effuse her skin and the nipples on her small breasts to harden. Her hair stands in a tangle of black spikes.

A feeling of eyes prompts a second glance. Peter's watery-blue irises meet hers. She moves to cover herself but stops. She's not embarrassed, surprising herself that she's no longer apprehensive with her nakedness. In fact, she cherishes his scrutiny and warms to his stare.

"I like…" Peter says, pausing suggestively, "your farmers' tan." A smile obscures the crease of pain that now perpetually features on his face.

"What do you mean?" she replies, aware that he's not referring to her naked body as she had first thought, as he wanted her to think, but to something quite different.

"Your arms are brown and the rest of your body is white. That's a 'farmers' tan'; what farmers get by wearing a T-shirt while working the land in summer."

"Would you prefer a full tan? I can work on it."

"I think you are beautiful as you are."

"Now you're teasing," Sara replies, surprised by her pleasure at his words, words she has read in romances, meant for fictional women, never for her. "Stop your joking. We can go when I'm dressed."

Peter eases himself upright and climbs out.

"How much further can you paddle?" Sara asks, threading herself into a dry bra and a clean shirt. She brushes some order into her hair.

Peter doesn't reply but moves to her and holds her hands.

"You were great, Sara. I really thought we were history when we hit those waves. They were keepers for sure, but you hung on and kept us out of trouble."

"Thanks, but you had more to do with our success than me. But I admit, I feel good. Sensations I've never felt before. I was both afraid and excited. I wanted to cry, laugh and cheer, all at the same time, if that's possible."

"It is. Good job. The next rapids are class one. Remember we waded up them yesterday? We can run them, but you take the stern this time. You might as well practice in case you have to later."

"How're you feeling?"

"Tired, and in pain. We'll make for an island three klicks from here. There's a wilderness camp where we can stop for a while."

"Good idea, as long as you can manage."

"I'll make it."

Slow, wide and shallow with few obstacles, and a deep channel corkscrewing down the centre, Peter pilots a passage. All Sara has to do is steer, keeping the canoe straight in the current. As they pass pillow-rocks, Sara learns their effect on the water. Those just below the surface make waves behind the rock, breaking upstream. Those that break the surface produce waves in front, on the upstream side, as well as downstream eddies. Peter has told her that it is possible to tuck into eddies such as these and be out of the current, just as one can hide in the shade of a power pole.

Four pelicans eye them as they reach the bottom of the rapid, acknowledging them by nonchalantly gliding in single file across the agitated surface.

The wind dies, exhausted for the day. A ceiling of vermilion and saffron stretches between horizons. The sun is flaring the backs of the canoeists as they edge towards the island. Halfway, on the last lap, they are dallying in their own dream worlds, barely moving.

A discordant racket suddenly shatters the silence, wakes them from their stupor. The din grows to a high pitch, then, as suddenly as it had started, cuts to a rhythmic beat.

"It's a plane," shouts Peter. "It must be at the camp. Paddle, Sara! Paddle for your life! We must catch it."

Paddles splash, fatigue forgotten and hope renewed. The canoe surges, like a racehorse leaping from the starting gate.

"There he is!" shouts Peter.

Sara scours the distant shore, her heart pounding, yearning to see their rescuer, their deliverance. A prick of green light attracts her eye. There – a pink silhouette, a floatplane nosing out from a bay on the west side of the island. It pauses, turns towards them.

"Can they see us?" Sara shouts.

"I doubt it. The sun will be in their eyes even if they look our way."

A roar fills the air again. The plane slowly moves forward, then accelerates. A bow-wave swells in front of the floats. The aircraft is approaching at a widening angle.

"Wave," yells Peter, swinging his paddle. Sara whips off her life jacket and waves it frantically.

"Over here!" she shouts. "Help! Here. Please look."

She stands up, rocking the boat violently. The lifejacket sails into the water. She rips off her shirt, sending a shower of buttons over the side. Surely they will see this, it's almost white. How can they miss it?

"Help, help. Heeeeyyy... Please God, make them look!"

The white bow-wave disappears. The plane lifts into the air. The pitch of the engine changes, softens. It heads towards them. Banks... left, away from them...

"No, no, nnooo..." Sara cannot believe they haven't been seen.

...away from the blinding sun. Only a lucky glance in their direction would pick them out. From above, the canoe would be a mere smudge scuffed on a maroon sea.

"LaRonge, that's where it's heading," Peter says as he watches it turn south, but as it continues its circle, he adds "No. It's going to Missinipe. If it keeps on turning, they've seen us."

Their hearts stop, their fists tighten, eyes mesmerised, hoping, praying...

Five seconds and Peter says flatly, "Missinipe. They'll be there in ten minutes. Oh well, that's that."

Sara watches the plane diminish and disappear into the mauve sky. She feels her blood run cold. Her fingers go numb and desperation encroaches on her sanity. Tears run uncontrollably down her cheeks. She weeps quietly, stifling the sobs in her throat. Selfish with her grief, she hides it from Peter. She buries her face in her shirt as distress washes away hope of rescue.

"Another half-kilometre," Peter says, speaking listlessly over his shoulder. "Let's get this son of a bitch to shore," he adds vehemently.

Sara's arm and shoulder muscles rebel. Her fingers refuse to bend when she hooks her lifejacket from the lake with her paddle, throws it with the shirt at her feet. She paddles aimlessly, totally spent. She hasn't the energy to even think.

Waves well up as if a leviathan is moving beneath the surface. They pass underneath, roll the boat, and continue toward the sun. The wake taunts with a nauseating lullaby, haunts Sara with a closing wave… so long, farewell.

Peter staggers from the canoe the moment it grates onto the sandy beach. He collapses to his hands and knees at the water's edge. His stomach locks in a cramp. Back arched, wolf-like, he retches. A claw grabs his testicles and twists viciously. A repugnant green slime slides from his mouth, hangs momentarily on a silver thread, then falls. Through half-closed, watery, bloodshot eyes, Peter's appalled by the sight of the partially dissolved pill. The mess is like a giant amoeba with a green nucleus. The doctor's prediction is verified. No longer will he be able to hold down food or water, let alone painkillers. An angry red tumour grows in his mind, like a napkin ring encircling his colon. I might as well put a noose round my neck, he contemplates darkly. End it now. Quicker. And painless…

Feeling Sara's hand on his back as she kneels beside him, Peter quickly covers his vomit with a scoop of sand.

"Let me help you up to the cabin," Sara offers, taking his arm.

Peter raises his head and through glazed eyes focuses on three overturned aluminum fishing boats six feet away, and beyond, two identical log cabins tucked into a dense forest of pines. Each has a small deck facing the lake, a picture window that fills almost half the front, a brown painted wood and glass door and matching screen doors. The green asphalt roofs are littered with russet pine needles, and blackened metal chimneys project from the rear. Peter catches a breath of hope – an antenna is strung between two steel rods attached to each cabin.

"The door should be open," Peter wheezes. "See if there's a radio."

Peter watches as Sara scrambles up the beach, jumps the three wooden steps to the deck and disappears into the first cabin.

Her crestfallen face when she re-appears within seconds tells him all he needs to know.

"There's only a microphone. The shelf is empty. What about the other cabin?" she asks forlornly, leaning against the waist-high railing.

"I doubt it," he answers weakly, "I expect they took it with them in the plane. Either it needed repairing or they're not returning for several days. When the cabin is in continual use, the radio's left here for contacting home base in LaRonge."

Peter struggles to stand. Immediately Sara leaps to the sand and takes his elbow. He wavers like a drunk.

"Let's get you into the cabin," she says, slipping her arm around his waist. "There are some beds. The mattresses look awful, but at least you can rest."

Peter remembers the room; a wooden box lined with cheap mahogany panelling, a well-scuffed plywood floor, and a ceiling of yellowing tiles. Nothing has changed since his last visit, a wind-stayed sojourn with Danika, a day of idleness waiting for a north-easterly storm to blow through. He recognises the bleak furnishings; the stained wooden table at the window surrounded by four mis-matched chairs, an old propane stove and refrigerator, and, in each back corner, black iron-framed bunk beds covered by rust-stained mattresses. The windowsill is littered with the dried-out shells of flies. Even the 1994 calendar with a gaudy picture of a heavy-breasted female in a black negligée still hangs above the potbelly stove against the back wall between the beds. The bare necessities for a huddle of fishermen willing to rough it in a wilderness camp, there for the fishing, the beer drinking and lewd stories.

Between the door and window is the empty shelf. A black wire dangles from the ceiling beside a hand-worn microphone – an umbilical cord to the outside.

Springs protest as Peter slumps onto the bed. He falls backward. Sara lifts his legs onto the mattress.

"In my day pack," he mutters. "There's a clear plastic, waterproof bag. Get it for me."

Peter's eyes close. His mind follows Sara floating towards the canoe, hovering over it, and returning with the small bag, its contents clearly medicinal. He hears doors open and close, then senses Sara at his side.

"I've never done this before," she announces nervously, "but I've seen it done on the tele. How do you…"

"All in the bag… ampoules, needles, instructions."

Silence. An interminable age. What's taking her so long, he wonders impatiently.

"You have to turn onto your side," she says at last, her hand resting on his hip. "The needle has to go into your hip. I'm sorry if I hurt you," she warns.

"It can't be any worse than now," Peter replies, rolling away from Sara. He feels her hand reaching to undo his shorts, tentative at first, then more purposeful. A touch on his skin as she tugs to expose his buttock is, for an instant, exciting.

"Here goes. Darts practice."

He winces as the needle stabs, penetrating his muscle, and he feels the pressure of the liquid enter his body.

"Aiea! I hope you improve with practice," Peter jokes, adjusting his clothing. He rolls back to find Sara kneeling close to the bed, still holding the syringe, her face aged by worry. Impulsively, he reaches out, cradles her head, and caresses her cheek. Taken by surprise, she grabs his hand, but his smile changes her mind, and rather than removing it, she gently strokes his knuckles.

A faint spark is returning to humour Peter's eyes. Before he can stop himself, he blurts "I wish you were undressing me to make love, not to bayonet me."

He notes the quick flush rise in her cheeks, like a red rose catching the early morning sun. Quickly dropping his hand, he laughs shortly, realising the inappropriateness of his remark.

After an uncomfortable pause, with Sara staring distantly at the wallboard behind his head, their eyes meet. What each one sees in the other has shifted through a subtle change, has raised hope, has bridged a gap.

"I wish… I wish things were different too," Sara says, her voice barely more than a whisper.

"I'm sorry we missed the plane," Peter says, matching her thoughts, "but we tried. Five minutes sooner and they'd have seen us."

"Peter, we *are* going to make it," Sara says earnestly, dropping the needle on the floor and grasping his hands in hers. "I know we can do it. Maybe we'll meet someone – fishermen or canoeists – who will help. I'll paddle you all the way to Missinipe if I have to."

He turns his head to the wall and bites down on his lower lip. They've missed the one chance he'd thought possible, and holds no hope that they'll now be rescued.

She pats his hand, like his mother used to when he was sick. "Go to sleep now. I'll wake you at dawn."

He wipes his eyes with the back of his hand. "Thank you… Sara."

Closing his eyes, he drifts into the air, floating like a cloud, settling as gently as a snowflake. Then, whispered words: "I'm leaving for two ticks. I need my sleeping bag."

Sara's move to the door triggers Peter's eyes to open. The room spins as though he's riding a merry-go-round. Despairingly, he concentrates on the bedsprings above but imagines a cage closing in like a coffin lid. The effort provokes such an ache behind his eyes that he snaps his lids shut, like cell-doors slamming, the echo reverberating in his brain.

As if by magic, his stomach vanishes; he sees his legs running off with a suitcase labelled 'Pain'. Has his lower torso evaporated? He wiggles his toes, but has no idea if they moved or not. His mother's smoke-cracked voice is ringing in his head. He recognises a childhood favourite:

How sweet to be a cloud

Floating in the blue!

It makes him very proud

To be a little cloud.

Vaguely he hears other noises; a door catch, hinges squeal. Strange aromas excite his nose. A smell of blossoms and warmth fills his head when Sara covers him with her sleeping bag.

He dreams… a small airplane, silvery pink with floats awash… floats morph into wheels, a single engine is racing, bouncing across a grass strip flecked white with snow… Grey clouds lash the windows, shadows caress the bundled stretcher… Him? No! A uniformed woman beside the door, dark blue with a perky white hat.

The picture spins, turning… into rows, desks in twos, young faces, eager, shoulder length hair… chalk dust misting the air… two people at the door… sorry to interrupt, Mr. Jordan, this is the new Grade One teacher, Miss Danika Medinski… Hi…!

Fiddles playing, also an accordion, a band. Polkas, old fashioned waltzes, the butterfly dance for trios – plucking wallflowers... bodies whirling... Two men, bushy eyebrows, lined faces, skin leathered by bitter winters. One pouring pale amber liquor into a glass from a square bottle, a five-point star on the side, the other – red wine... Head back, gulp, cough... They circle all night – stop, move, stop, move.

"Die bochu! To the bride and groom."

Again, around and around... later the liquid looks like water but kicks like a mule. Faces fade, shimmering as in a heat haze.

Men and women on opposite sides of the room... Music starts, bodies converge, partners meet by unspoken agreement... the room gyrates, couples spin, the shouts grow louder.

Dance, Peter?

I've never... I'll crush your feet. Is this a polka? God, my head's spinning, too many soasts... I mean toasts.

Hey, Pete, Danika... A shout from across the room. Let's get out of here... go for a drink.

Four in a red car, laughter, Harold and... can't remember his current girlfriend... five-minute drive, stop between ghostly tree trunks – Bohs all around. Oh shit! Let me outa here... sharp pain – jab, jab – a knife blade below the belt.

Green mucous... My God! ...missed the car, thank God. On my shoes. Shit! Yuch!

A voice, gentle, unbelievably angelic... is this heaven? "I wish things were different too."

Sorry, Danika... Here, take these green pills. The plane drops through clouds... Into a hospital... Pacing, pacing, pacing.

A baby girl. Yeah!

That's it!

That's it?

Sorry, she can't have any more.

Oh… Why?

Oh…

Exactly like you. My eyes though. Can we call her Sarah? Sarah Jordan – no middle name, middle names belong to someone else, are insincere.

Danika, Danika… A hand gently strokes his face, then a soft coolness that reminds him of roses on a mid-summer's evening. Danika's nose traces his, connects momentarily and a warm breath caresses his mouth. Their lips meet, linger forever… forever… forever.

"Peter, Peter… Wake up. The sun's rising. It's time to leave."

Peter's eyes open a sliver.

"Wake up. Open those eyes."

Glassy-blue irises turn in Sara's direction, but show no sign of focusing. She gently dabs a damp face cloth into each socket, wipes crusty eyelashes.

"You'll have to wake up enough to help me get you into the canoe." Sara orders. "Then you can sleep some more. I've arranged the packs so that you can lie flat."

"I can paddle," Peter murmurs. "Just give me a second."

Sara pulls back her sleeping bag, helps Peter swing his legs, and takes his elbow.

"Mind your head," she warns, as Peter pushes himself erect. He holds onto the bed frame until he clears the top bunk, and, through the window, he sees the soft light of the new day. He walks unsteadily onto the deck and sucks in cool damp air.

Leaning against the railing, he slowly wakens to his surroundings.

The bay, still in the shadow of the island, spawns tendrils of mist that hang like gossamer, awaiting dispersal by the merest of breezes, or evaporation in the first of the sun's rays. A chorus of birdsong – boreal chickadees, pine siskins and warblers – fill the air, bright, cheerful, greeting the day with joy. He looks up. A bald eagle is soaring, a black flake on the blue ceiling, its shadow traversing the landscape. Peter visualises the eagle's outlook: the wide expanse of unruffled water studded by pink rocks encrusted white by roosting pelicans; behind him to the north-east, a collection of long narrow islands separated by intense blue arteries. Every concentric circle from a rising fish is observed, its location stored into memory.

Sara opens the door and crosses the deck to stand beside Peter. Her packed sleeping bag is under her arm.

"Isn't this beautiful," he says, with a sweep of his hand, "So quiet. Nature at peace, delicately balanced. This is how the land was before man ripped off its skin and replaced it with concrete and asphalt," Peter muses. "Here in the North you can quench your thirst with lake water. You can breathe pure, clean air.

"*Death exists nowhere in nature,*" Peter quotes, "*...only in our forebodings, our formulae.* Death happens to sustain life. Like the fish we ate the other night, or the deer taken by a wolf pack. When a tree falls, a thousand insects benefit. The raven robbing a nest seems cruel. Yet life's diversity depends upon the survival of every single species. It's only man who's doing his damnedest to destroy anything that interferes with his idea of progress. Did anyone mourn the death of the last passenger pigeon? The woodland caribou has almost gone from Saskatchewan; you'll not see the Giant Blue butterfly in England again."

He turns, faces Sara.

"When I die, Sara, I want to be cremated." Speaking in a strange voice, as if reading his own obituary in a massive cathedral, Peter continues. "To change into carbon dioxide." He chuckles, takes Sara's hands in his.

"I'll become food, food for the trees. The little bit of water I'll generate will fall with the next rain bringing sustenance to any number of creatures. My ashes may catch in the crop of whiskey jack, will grind into atoms – calcium, phosphorus, gallium – and migrate into its cells. I'll be living and thriving somewhere else. For ever."

"I like your concept, but Mother Nature will have to wait because I'm not going to let you die, not yet," Sara responds with alacrity, unsure whether or not to take Peter seriously. "I'd rather talk *with you*; I don't fancy conversing with the rain. People will stare."

"I talk to my canoe," Peter replies seriously. "But not any more," his voice lower, remembering where it is.

"Come on! Let's go. We've no time for that kind of talk," Sara says, her forehead wrinkled. She jumps off the deck, landing squarely on her feet.

Turning, she says, "Ready? You'd better shut the door."

Standing in knee deep water beside the canoe, Sara packs her sleeping bag and re-arranges the gear in the middle of the boat. She deftly strings the rope through each item, tying them all to the canoe, while Peter sits on the nearest upturned fishing boat watching.

"I'm truly impressed," Peter remarks.

"I learnt from a master," Sara says, her eyes shining. "Still have a long way to go to match your skills though." She pulls the canoe off the beach.

"Get in." Peter eases himself into his seat. He notices that he's still wearing his neoprene booties, and pictures anaemic, atrophied appendages within them. Sara swings the craft until it's facing the lake and hops in.

"Let's take it easy at first," Sara says as she dips her paddle. "How're you feeling?"

"On a morning like this, how can I feel anything but hopeful. My stomach aches a little. A bit hungry, but that's okay. I'll only bring it up. I'll need another shot in a couple of hours. When we get to Trout Falls. Did you eat anything?"

"I snacked on some energy bars. I'm fine," Sara answers.

Paddles dip. The water ripples, chattering against the bottom of the boat. Birds are singing. The volume diminishes as the rift from shore increases. Rounding the headland that encloses the bay, Peter and Sara stop and look back at the camp; a crescent-shaped beach, a hint of habitation, a backdrop of greenery, and light intensifying, edging the saw-toothed skyline in gold; a mirror image, crystal clear, is inverted on the water.

"Gorgeous," whispers Sara, and with a sigh, resumes paddling. Peter falls into step, matching her rhythm.

Keeping close to the right shore, they head north-east, facing the climbing sun, into the collection of islands.

Sara feels the gnawing in the pit of her stomach, a combination of hunger, anxiety and fear. Despite what she had told Peter, she hadn't eaten. In fact, she had no energy bars.

Sara's thoughts turn to the events of the night, remembering the first spoken advance from Peter, unexpectedly coarse, flirtatious; her hour-long watch over him until fatigue, stiffened bones, and a quieter heart allowed her to drift into sleep on the other bed. Her dreams touched the question that had been following her since Peter's fall: is she falling in love? Was he playing last night, or did he actually feel something for her? Cold had eventually woken her, and the dawn-light through the window had alarmed her into action, had renewed her determination to get Peter to medical care.

Rounding a point, the widest expanse of Trout Lake opens in front of them. "Look at that pile of rocks like a little man," Sara points out as they paddle through the channel where they had wildly surfed. "I don't remember seeing it before."

"It's called an *Inuksuit*. Eskimos build them to lead travellers, like a signpost."

"There aren't Eskimos this far south, are there?"

Peter laughs. "No. I expect some canoeists built it."

As the sun climbs, its heat increases their discomfort. Peter shades his eyes with the brim of his Tilley; Sara puts on sunglasses and scolds herself for the umpteenth time for forgetting a hat.

Slowly, persistently, they edge across the water. Conversation lulls, an uneasy quiet settles over the pair as Peter shows increasing discomfort, missing strokes from time to time, letting out an occasional groan when reaching forward. His head sags.

A vee in the skyline appears like a long awaited friend. She remembers the cliff above the falls where she had stood. She recalls the trail and worries. At least it won't be slippery this time. With Peter's strength almost gone, the challenge of the portage seems insurmountable.

"There's Trout Falls," announces Sara, masking her growing dread.

"We'll run them," Peter responds.

Sara snickers. "You're not serious. We'll be smashed to smithereens."

"The portage will take for ever," Peter says. "I've been planning as we paddled. As I remember, enter from river left, aim right of centre, swing left, miss the big wave at the bottom on the right, and... *viola*."

Sara sits silently, terrified by a vision of them careening down the rapids, willing herself to trust Peter to steer them through. He said he had run Trout once. But had almost capsized.

"Peter, I'm too scared. I don't think I can do it."

"The worst that can happen is that we'll tip over. In that case, we unload, bail out, reload, and carry on."

"But, my God, we might..."

"I've made up my mind," Peter interrupts, "Do or die. Don't worry. Trust me, and... trust yourself. Keep the boat straight, that's all."

For the twenty minutes that it takes to reach Trout Falls, Sara frets. She fidgets, hands like a butterfly: she checks that the tie-down rope is secure, she unzips and re-zips her life jacket, makes sure that the stern painter is coiled and that the bailer is handy. Her sunglasses disappear into a pocket, and all are zippered shut. She licks dry lips until they are sore. For her parched throat she scoops water into her mouth. She forces herself to swallow scarce saliva, suppresses her nausea.

The whisper of the rapids grows louder. White horses spring into the gap, leaping above the horizon line where the lake overflows. They pass a river coming in from the left, the water gurgling over hidden rocks, flowing past trembling aspen that crowd the banks. Sara recalls paddling alone a few days back, before she had met Peter. She finds it difficult to reconcile what she did that day with what she is about to do. How is it possible that I'm here, taking on this test? In a moment of panic, she thinks... I must jump out, swim to shore and leave this crazy man to his fate, to his death if it be. Of course, she can't because of what he has done for her, because of her growing feelings that would make her follow him anywhere.

"Are you ready?" Peter shouts above the thunder. "On your knees, legs under your seat!"

The crescendo rises, drowning all thought. She mutters, "Oh my God" to herself a few times. "This is worse than Birch Rapids." Her knees are braced against the canoe. Her paddle, on her left, is in the water, back-paddling as if trying to stop the inevitable. Suddenly, the current grabs and she's looking down a mountain of seething white, down into the pool at the bottom. For a fleeting second, they hover on the brink, like the gladiator hesitating before entering the arena. Then the bow plummets, rises violently and jerks to the right. Escape is impossible, with no way to go but... into the mêlée.

* * *

"Hi, Shorty." The glass door of the village store closes with a jingle of bells behind a bear of a man. Close to seven feet, Shorty Hayes is the antithesis of his name. At eighteen he stopped growing. Friends had dropped 'Oliver' in preference for 'Shorty'. Basketball coaches had badgered him for years to join their team. But he lacked a competitive spirit and was soon left alone to pursue his own pleasures. The minute he sat in a canoe and propelled it quietly through the water, he sensed the promise of unlimited freedom and was hooked. The grace of the craft spoke to him, whereas the raucous echoes of the basketball court had left him on tenter-hooks.

A bushy coppery beard had sprouted on his first exploration into Northern Saskatchewan. Befitting his personality, it felt natural although it contrasted astonishingly with his blond hair and blue eyes.

"How you doing, Tom?" Shorty asks in a voice as lively as a mountain stream, unexpected – not gruff like a grizzly's. "Still baching, I see," he says nodding at the groceries being checked by the store clerk – sausages, hamburger patties, baked beans, soup, sliced bread, a carton of milk.

"'Fraid so. Not too many available women in this neck of the woods," Tom replies. "Now if Jody here wasn't hitched," he says, grinning at the young woman, her eyes large behind thick lenses, nail-painted fingers darting over the cash register, "I'd have a reason for staying put all year."

"What makes you think I would want you to," quips Jody, turning a bag of potatoes for the price tag.

Shorty, guffawing at Jody's wit, strides to the cooler at the back of the store. "Flying today?" he asks Tom, grabbing a Coke.

"Twice this morning. Contact Lake Mine and McIntosh Lodge. We've almost caught up what we lost on Friday and Saturday."

"That was quite a storm," agrees Shorty at the counter. "Did you see

132

anything of that English girl? She should be on Nipew or Hayman by now," Shorty asks, looking down on Tom's boyish face that now and then experiences the edge of a razor.

"You mean the one I took to Paull Lake last Sunday?"

"Who do you think I mean?" Shorty counters. "Maggie Thatcher? How many English girls are there in this part of the world? Besides, you couldn't take your eyes off her. I was surprised you managed to take off. I was waiting for you to hit the trees at the end of the lake."

Tom laughs. "Don't exaggerate. But she *was* a bit of all right. Sorry, I didn't see her. But then she could have been camping anywhere along the shore."

"Is that everything, Tom?" Jody asks, checking off the last item.

"Yes, thanks."

"That's $45.89."

Tom fishes out a fifty from a beaten wallet. "Here. I'll buy Shorty's drink."

"Thanks, Tom. I'm a bit concerned. I hope she stayed put on Friday and didn't try canoeing in that wind. Saturday wasn't much better."

"She seems sensible enough. Where did you figure she'd be by Friday?"

"Probably Mountney, but possibly as far as Nipew. She was due in yesterday, but now more likely today. Tomorrow at the latest. She can't get lost, but you never know."

"I'm scheduled for Nemeiben at four. I'll swing by the Churchill on the way," Tom suggests. "I was at Maguire's on Trout last night, right on sunset, but didn't see anyone, going or coming back."

"Thanks, Tom," Shorty answers. "I must say that I'll feel better when I know you've seen her. Come over for supper when you get back. I'll tell Sandy to put on an extra steak – we're barbecuing tonight."

"Great! I'll pick up a case of beer. A guy works up a thirst flying in this weather. See you, Jody."

Shorty pauses on the top step, sucking his Coke, and watches Tom cut through the trees towards the airplane base on the shore of Otter Lake. From his vantagepoint, he looks across the gravelled intersection, the focal point of the village, to the two-storey log building that is the hotel and restaurant of the resort. He contemplates strolling over to chat with the owner, but decides against it, realising that he has too much work to do. He drops down the steps and heads right, back to his office and the task of planning two coinciding trips with only one available guide.

Walking past the village park on his left, he recalls his son Matthew's birthday party that weekend. All twelve children from the community had been invited. They had spent an afternoon burning wieners and marshmallows on a fire. How time has flown: it hardly seems seven years since his wife had been flown by air-ambulance to LaRonge for an emergency Caesarean. Two years later, Lisa had arrived without complications.

On his right sits a partly built house sheathed in weather-blackened plywood, victim of under-financed speculation. In the driveway is Peter Jordan's battered Ford truck, covered with a film of dust. Shorty wonders where he is. He would have lined up Great Devil Rapids into Hayman Lake, crossed Nipew, and portaged into Trout Lake. It's just possible, he figures, that he'd met the English girl, that their paths had crossed depending on how fast he had travelled. Chances are, though, he missed her by only minutes, a common occurrence in the north. He envies his friend. He wanted to go with him, had even suggested it to Sandy, well aware what her response would be. So here he is, looking after Pete's old truck while he's off tripping. What stories he'll have when he returns in September.

He pushes open the office door, a small wood building standing in front of three log cabins that butt up to the forest at the rear. The walls are hidden behind a montage of maps and sketches and paintings and photographs, a history of journeys and a scrapbook of canoeing feats in formidable rapids and waterfalls. Behind the counter, Shorty sits in front of a monitor. Flags fly at him on the screen. He stares, as if hypnotised. He remembers the English girl, her actions hesitant as he instructed her in some basic manoeuvre. Suddenly, he regrets sending her to the Paull River. If only she had waited a day, he could have hired Pete as her guide, knowing that he wouldn't have refused despite his plans. With a sigh, he hits a key and transmits his nagging concerns to the back of his mind.

"Peter! Peter!" Sara screams, swimming frantically towards the overturned canoe, still clutching her paddle. She reaches the stern, clings to it, spins her head urgently. She looks back at the falls, already twenty feet away. He's not pinned to a rock nor swimming behind her. Nothing. She scans the shore, wishing desperately for a canoeing party to be at the portage. Nothing. Her body goes limp; her limbs lose all sensation. She feels like... nothing. Tears stream down her face, indistinguishable from the water running off her hair. She wants to scream, to bawl like the child who has just dropped her mother's Sunday tea service.

The plunge down the torrent had been a rush. Frightening yet exhilarating. Gathering speed at the brink, they had cut diagonally across the flow. Halfway, they had executed a tight turn around a massive boulder, its black back barely revealed through white foam. Then a jig to the right, a rip down the one green slick in midstream, and, just as cheers burst from wide open mouths, they'd hit the angled wave at the bottom. They were within a canvas of success. The canoe lurched sideways and Sara was catapulted into the water. Her life jacket brought her quickly to the surface. She grabbed the paddle that was within arm's reach. The canoe was drifting away, its bottom shining in the sunlight like a green monster.

Sara pulls herself to the middle of the canoe and heaves on the submerged gunwale. The canoe rocks slightly. Fresh tears run down her cheeks; I'll never turn the brute over without Peter. It's hopeless. I can't re-float it, bail out the water and reload the packs. I can hardly lift them when dry. I may as well leave it here. Swim to shore. Wait for someone to come by. Sara scans the shoreline again, the island of rocks that she and the canoe are drifting on to.

Her mouth drops; her blue pack suddenly pops up beside her. Then her second one next to it, the canoe rocking and higher in the water. What's happening, Sara wonders; how have the packs escaped? Then it's Peter's red Duluth that emerges.

Sara gasps with joy and amazement. Peter's head and shoulders explode from the water on the opposite side. His hat's hanging askew, pouring water, covering one side of his face, the cord cutting into his chin.

Wheezing for breath, he straightens his hat, looks around, and, seeing Sara, says, "Good, you're okay," as though nothing has happened. He snaps a serrated knife back into its sheath strapped to his life jacket.

"Where were you?" Sara blubbers, her relief giving way to frustration. "I couldn't find you. I thought you had drowned."

"Under the canoe. In an air pocket," Peter replies matter-of-factly. "I had to cut the packs loose. The wannigan is still tied in – it would sink otherwise. Boy, that was close; we almost made it. I needed one more stroke," he says excitedly. "Head for those rocks and we'll flip the canoe," he orders, then seeing Sara's face, says, "You're okay, aren't you?"

"I am now." Sensing a rush of anger mixed with foolishness and relief, Sara says "I didn't know where you were. I was sure you had drowned. You could have let me know," she adds irritably, her voice rising, surprising even herself by its loudness.

Peter stares at Sara, a perplexed look on his face. "I said you'd be alright. And you are. Besides, my feet were tangled in the painter someone forgot to coil," he states sarcastically.

"I tied my end. I know I did. You were the one that forgot."

They stare at each other, across a rift that has opened.

"Once I freed my legs, I had to cut the packs loose. We'd never turn the canoe otherwise."

"I was scared that I had lost you," Sara bawls, "I couldn't see you anywhere. Everything was lost, kaput. If we had taken the portage and…"

"We would still be taking it!" Peter barks, slamming the water with a fist. "By about now we'd have the packs on shore."

"We wouldn't be *in* the water," Sara sobs, dropping her forehead against the canoe.

Peter swims round the stern and slips an arm around her waist. He lifts her chin, turns her face and apologises. "It's not as bad as you think. I've capsized more times than you've had hot Sunday dinners. So we're a little bit wet. So what. We'll soon dry."

The canoe wallows, has drifted into quiet water, close to a mishmash of low-lying boulders.

"Let's get to those rocks," Peter suggests amiably, "and we'll pull the canoe in by the painter. Push the packs ahead as you go."

A few strokes and Sara touches bottom. She scrambles out, dripping, darkening the coffee coat of dirt and dead algae left by the spring flood. The packs nestle pathetically in the shallows like the carcasses of drowned beasts. Peter struggles on hands and knees, the painter clutched in blanched fingers, his face warped. They lean on the rope together. The canoe resists like a waterlogged deadhead, until it too, floats beside the packs.

"We'll both have to lift from this side," Peter says as he stumbles back into the water, grimacing with every slip and twist of his body. "We'll never right her until we break the water seal." With backbreaking strength, they rock and heave until the vacuum suddenly relents with a 'glug' and the canoe turns over. Sara is thankful that Peter's wannigan, lopsided, is lying in the bottom. His daypack is still lashed to a thwart, and his bent paddle is floating in water up to the gunwales.

"Where's your other paddle?"

"Oh, shit!" Peter exclaims. "Where did it go?" His eyes skim the surface and the encircling shoreline. "Not to worry. If it isn't in the bay here, then it'll be down the next rapid. It can't go any further." Peter removes the pack and foodbox.

"Take the other end, Sara, and we'll empty out the water."

Confused with his meaning, she moves to the bow, then follows Peter's actions. Together they rock it back and forth. Water swishes over the sides; as the load lightens, their efforts become more effective. Eventually, they lift and tip the craft clear, hold it high until empty, then let it flop back onto the water.

Between them, they hoist the drenched packs aboard, retie the cords and finally sponge out the dregs.

Exhausted, they squat uncomfortably on the round boulders. Sara senses relief coursing through her veins. What had nearly been a disaster has proven to be just another obstacle to be overcome. She speculates how many they can survive, predicts pessimistically that by day's end they will most likely be raven-fodder.

"Sara, could you… I really need another shot."

Sara clambers to the canoe and opens Peter's daypack with shaking fingers, worried by what she might find. The contents of the plastic bag are dry and undamaged. She prepares a new syringe. Turning, she finds Peter standing, back towards her, his dripping shorts already down to his knees. She can't help but laugh, finding the situation ludicrous.

"Don't even consider dart practice from there," Peter threatens jokingly.

"Say, what a good idea. Revenge for your excessive concern for my safety – making me run impossible rapids."

He bends over, tense, his white buttocks shining like the moon. She leans into his ear and says in a loud whisper, "Revenge is *sweet*," and gives a cheek a stinging slap.

Peter yelps. "What was that for?"

"You know!" Laughing, Sara shoves the needle into the handprint that's reddened Peter's butt. He grunts, pulls up his shorts, and rubs his backside.

"Vixen. I'll get you." A smile brightens his face, lifts Sara's hopes. He squints at the sun nearing its zenith. "We'll soon be dry, unless we…"

Sara darts a hand onto Peter's mouth. "Don't say it. I've just had a ghastly premonition. Please, let's be careful."

"We're doing fine; *you're* doing fine. There aren't any more class four rapids."

"What about at Rock Trout?"

"In comparison, a snap, as long as we get there before the morphine knocks me out."

They shove off, turn into the current, follow the left shore and immediately find the lost paddle.

"All intact," Peter remarks. "Just a little less wet behind the ears, you might say."

Shortly, Peter is aligning the canoe with the small rapid that empties the bay.

"Keep the canoe straight," he shouts over his shoulder. "This is easy. Remember wading up it the day before yesterday?"

"Yes, and I told you I ran it. You ignored me."

Before Peter can reply, they are into the fast water, bouncing over a couple of haystacks, and pulling out to the left.

"Don't we have to portage the next?" Sara asks. "We did going upstream."

"There's an alternate route," he replies, pointing left. "A simple rapid on the other side of that island."

They run a set of two and paddle onto Stack Lake, cross it and are gliding into a steep-sided passage with a familiar right angle bend. Sara shakes her head. From the upstream perspective, she finds it difficult to see how she'd had so much trouble rounding the turn.

"We'll rest at Rock Trout," Peter suggests. "You need to eat and drink."

The canoe scrapes onto the sand from which their journey had so recently begun. Like an automaton, Peter holds the canoe as Sara disembarks. Their movements are slow, dreamlike. Words, emotions, drum in their heads, but cannot escape. They drop their life jackets in the bow. Peter takes Sara's hand and leads her past the first ledge to where they had stood on the first night.

They stand close, looking into each other's eyes. Peter's gaunt face tells more than he's been saying, more than he knows. His lips are cracked and dry, his eyes receded into blue-grey cavities.

To Sara's astonishment, he pulls her close, encircles her with his arms, a hand holding her head tight to his chest.

"We're back again. Seems I'm never going to leave this place," he says, his voice faltering. "I'm really sorry things have gone terribly wrong for you, for us."

She's feels his heartbeat increasing, pulsing in her ear. She wraps her arms slowly around his waist. The relevance of Rock Trout dawns upon her. Peter has called it his haven, his personal sanctuary. Is this where he expects to die? Was this what he was hinting at that morning, she wonders? This is where he wants his ashes scattered, into this torrent, his ultimate heaven.

She clings tighter. Thus they remain for an eternity, their bodies at peace while their thoughts rush, like the river, towards an ocean.

*   *   *

Peter drags open his eyes and stares into the curling wave that rises, falls, forever breaking, swallowing the river sliding over the ledge. It's hard to remember his carefree arrival four days earlier. A terrible loneliness washes over him. It's all over; the dream is dead. He shivers involuntarily.

He thinks about slipping into the river, taking heed of the Cree brave, distraught with sickness, and sinking into oblivion. What would that be like? To drift away with the current? Phobia of water up his nose scuttles the idea; hypothermia is much more inviting. It captures by stealth, creeps up on you before you can resist.

Peter sees his mother's image materialise in the foam. Water crashes around her, like her life's struggle amidst bombs and the uncertainty of warfare. Alone and in poverty she had raised him, in a culture that was inhospitable, in a climate that was harsh and unforgiving. He fancies he hears her voice penetrating the thunder, fighting to be noticed, her brogue as strong as the day she had left Portsmouth – dropped aiches and tees, ars added where there should be none. "Come 'ere, son. Pu' yer 'air straight'. Can't 'ave yer lookin' loik a gu'ersnipe, can we. Be'ter pu' yer jumper on, keep ya warm."

Peter opens his mouth, about to reply. The wave changes shape and his mom disappears.

Peter gently moves Sara's head into the crux of his shoulder. His cheek rubs against her hair, fingers move to the nape of her neck. Unconsciously, fingers massage her skull. He smells the green of the water in her drying hair. He inhales her vitality. He relives standing at the same spot -- dishes, erratic nighthawks. Four nights ago. Only four!

A blow strikes him fully in the chest. Bile scalds his throat. Guilt swells, overwhelms him. His head is sinking beneath black-green water. Impossible to breathe. Never has he held another woman except Danika the way he's now clinging to Sara. Roughly, he shoves her away, then catches her as, taken by surprise, she almost slips into the river.

"I'm sorry," he mutters, his face desolate. "Forgive me, I had no right to grab you. I was dreaming that you were Danika. No, I... I believed that you *were* Danika. No! Oh God! I don't know anymore... The morphine... it's curdling my mind."

Peter turns and rushes up the bank, staggering dangerously close to the edge of the gorge. He stops, leans against the jack pine, his old guardian tree still keeping watch, patiently awaiting voyageurs. He has to escape the demons. The river's pull is overwhelming. He holds his head.

Sara, still at the water's edge, watches him, her hands together at her mouth, as if in prayer. He suddenly enters the door of narcotic delirium. Colour fills his head: blood red, death black, steel blue, stark white, cold white. His mind clears as sharp as January air.

His mother had raised him.

Danika had filled his days.

His daughter had catalysed a family.

Three women had impacted his life; one had brought him from seed, the second nurtured him, and the third carried his strain.

A fourth has now barged in. Why? Why was she here? Is there a reason, or was their meeting truly a matter of chance? Look at the coincidences. She's from his birthplace, is compassionate like his wife, and has the same name as his only child. When setting out from Missinipe, he had not envisioned, would not have believed the twists of fate that now besiege him.

I have loved three women; can there be another? Peter considers the possibility then dismisses the idea. He puts his earlier advances down to flirtation, a consequence of being alone with a young attractive woman.

His mood swings sharply again, and a rush of anger strikes like a hot wind. He curses life's untimely consequences. He's irritated with himself for giving in to Sara's persuasiveness, for adding complications. If only I had listened to common sense, she would now be home and I would still be travelling up the Churchill River. No rock paintings, no fall. No pain -

– maybe later, if at all. The cancer was in remission, damn it!

No more golden sunsets on a tranquil lake, he reflects bitterly. No more paddling at night beneath the stars, their echo like diamonds on a jeweller's cloth. No more living... No more...

"Sara!" Peter cries.

Sara runs, pushes through the willows, and scrambles up the bank. She stands near him, hovering awkwardly from foot to foot.

"There's no future for us, therefore it mustn't be," Peter says vehemently, to himself as much as to Sara.

"Peter, what *are* you talking about?"

"You and me. Us. It's pointless."

"Us? What?"

"I'm going to die," Peter says, his face wretched.

"No. Not if I can help it."

"Sara, I am. That's why we're here. That's why we came back."

"Rubbish. You're so melodramatic. It's not going to happen," Sara replies forcefully, grabbing Peter's hand.

"When I started out, it was different. I had accepted the possibility but still hoped. I suppressed all thoughts of death, of failure. I left home knowing that maybe I wouldn't be going back. I was happy away from people. I had my escape, but I didn't know I would meet you."

"I'm glad you did," Sara says, unconsciously rotating his gold ring.

"But don't you see... All the coincidences. Unbelievable. We left together; we returned together. Your name; my daughter's name. Where you come from; where I was born. Danika's dead, I'm nearly..."

"Peter, you're *not* going to die," Sara cuts in fervently. "Please don't give in. Fight. For me, for yourself... for us. I'm not giving up. You mustn't. I promise you, we'll come back, right here and we'll finish our

143

trip. We'll do it together."

"Yeah…? No, I don't think so." His voice is so quiet that Sara has to turn her head.

"Peter," Sara says, softly. "By *us*, what do you mean… are you feeling… something?"

"I don't know. It may be the circumstance."

"When you were under the water at Trout, I felt empty."

Sara takes Peter's other hand and holds both tight.

"Would you hold me again? Please."

Peter pulls Sara's arms around his waist, then slips his around the small of her back.

"Peter, let's keep going," Sara says, speaking urgently into his ear. "Let's not stop here to rest."

"Aren't you hungry? You have to keep your energy up."

"I may still have some chocolate I can eat while we're paddling." They break apart, but their fingers remain interlocked.

"Is it possible to carry everything across the rocks rather than portaging?"

"Better. We'll line down the first ledge and run the second."

"Let's do that. I don't want to stop here. There are too many ghosts."

"Too true," Peter reflects broodingly.

Peter is encouraged floating down the gorge with the current, the roar of the rapids quickly fading. They make a sharp right turn at the bottom, the current dies and peace returns.

A burst of song fills the air, a pensive whistle across the water, a farewell from a white-throated sparrow. A short stretch of fast water empties the bay, takes them onto Mountney Lake.

"There's a bald eagle," Sara calls excitedly, as they head between islands covered by towering trees. The bird silently circles, following them across the water. They round a point and head south. Peter raises his paddle, pointing to the eyrie. A chick sits in the nest. By its size, he guesses it wouldn't fly for another three to four weeks. In a way, he feels a certain envy. Soon, it will take a leap of pure faith and would experience the excitement of a maiden flight – flying free, soaring, majestic.

The shoreline squeezes into a narrowing channel. Down to thirty feet, crowded between a dense growth of overhanging willows spilling from unseen banks. A slow-moving current seethes. Boils of black water that rise from the deep spin the canoe like a newspaper in the wind. The sun's heat beats down into the confined space. The River of Styx, Peter believes miserably, carrying them to Nipew, to Dead Lake.

The left shore retreats, breaks away as the river spills over the boulder garden familiar to Peter. He guides the canoe to the deepest channel. Nonetheless, the heavily laden canoe frequently scrapes the riverbed. At the bottom, Sara has to jump out to lighten the load and push the canoe off an anchoring boulder.

They are at the last rapids, the torrent that had nearly robbed Peter of his canoe, that almost cut his journey before it had hardly begun.

"You'll enjoy this," Peter flings over his shoulder. "Go in from the right then down the centre. Stand up for a quick look," he adds. He feels the canoe rock.

"Looks fast and tricky," she remarks.

Peter draws the bow into the downstream vee. Despite his fatigue and mental lethargy, Peter's pulse quickens as they bounce over the waves. Sara screams as the bow cantilevers off the biggest haystack then plunges into the next, causing water to pour over the sides. Seconds later they are drifting onto quiet water.

Peter tells Sara, who's bailing water, that that's the last rapid until they cross Nipew. "Do you know the meaning of 'Nipew'?" Peter asks after a pause.

"No."

"Dead Lake."

"Oh," Sara replies, sounding nonchalant, as though she's saying "So what!"

Baggy cumulus clouds, tea-clippers with mainsails set, are cruising across the blue sky before a south-west wind when they reach Nipew. Peter thankfully ships his paddle and lies back on the packs. He tries desperately to remain conscious. In a minute, however, his resolve falters and his mind goes as black as a grave.

Although Sara is paddling steadily, she feels that she's making little progress. The lake stretches as far as her eye can see. The shoreline to the right is a hazy line; the shore on her left is falling away as she creeps towards the middle of the lake. She feels like a cockleshell floating on the ocean; a mote surrounded by sky and water.

If a wind should pick up, she muses, we'd be in deep trouble. Alone, she had invariably hugged the shore, hesitant to put more than a hundred yards between her and land. However, their present situation demands a risk; that she takes the most direct route across the widest part of Nipew Lake.

She notices a small island off the left bow and corrects her course so that she would pass within its shadow. Its profile from a distance resembles a battleship; low in the front rising to a central peak with the tree-line mimicking turrets and radio antennas and then dropping sharply at the back, towards the stern-rail. But as the island comes closer, it loses its warrior image; masts become trees, guns become a rocky shore. Its changing appearance tells Sara she is making progress. Strangely she finds herself drawn, ponders the possibility of a visit. But a shudder through Peter's body cuts sharply through her musings and reminds her of her mission. She passes by, regretfully, sensing a belonging, a mysterious kinship.

Faint sounds, like a mosquito, or blowfly, buzzing near an ear. An airplane? Sara searches the southern sky. Hopeful imagination, she realises, when all she hears is the breeze messing her hair and the waves lapping against the canoe.

She scans the map, finds the island, and agonises over the proximity of Missinipe. I did hear a plane, she says to herself, wishfully. If only it would come this way…

A strange, sweet aroma teases his senses, ferries his mind across water, fleeing from his body cradled on the floating bier, a weave of red willow boughs. He glides over a half dozen slight, brown bodies, jumping and splashing in the shallows, their shouts and laughter shielding their innocence, their lack of understanding. Living for the moment, they play together, as all children of the world do, no matter their circumstance.

He's surprised to see, gathered in a circle, a cluster of tepees perched on a grass-covered promontory. Racks of drying fish and a stretched woodland caribou hide are clouded in smoke, the haze hovering in the absence of wind. A covey of birch bark canoes is pulled up on a stony beach. He sees no one, but hears noises, chanting, coming from one of the tepees. Unbidden, he squeezes through a small opening and is assailed by fumes, his head reeling as he inhales incense of sweetgrass and ground sage, indistinguishable from the bouquet of marijuana. A circle of squatting men is gathered; brown skinned, black braided hair, wearing grimy leathers. Behind them, almost unseen in the gloom, the women sit, hidden under loose dingy clothing, their hair pinned back in a braid or a bun. Kneeling before them is an old man.

Two or three oil candles chase shadows across his wrinkled face. His eyes shine like obsidian beneath black, tangled eyebrows. Straight hair streaked with white, hangs down to his naked shoulders. Loose folds of skin cover his body, shiny with sweat, the lower half fitted into leather breeches.

As Peter stares, the elder grasps a leather gourd and shakes it gently towards the ground, producing a whisper, a rustle of seeds. It is then that Peter notices the prone body, a man, clothed in only a loincloth, lying at the exact centre of the circle. Eyes closed, he shows no sign of life, only the slightest movement of his chest. His torso, coated in bear grease, shines like polished mahogany. The medicine man rests the rattle, placing it precisely in its original position. His hand, moving gracefully to a woven platter, picks up a braid of smouldering sweetgrass that is generating a blue haze of smoke. He waves the entwine above the prostrate head, producing a cloud, then smudges the upper torso with cupped hands, drafting the smoke downward. At the same time, he begins to chant; a rhythm of words that rise and fall, guttural on occasion, then unexpectedly falsetto. As the prayer proceeds, the family circle joins in, not in unison, but independently, their voices rising and falling at different moments.

The incantation goes on for many breaths, the tempo unchanging, interspersed with further smudging by the medicine man, shakes from the rattle in his right hand, and genuflects with an eagle feather in his left. The congregation gradually tires, their starved bodies exhausted, but they continue, sensing their worth, their faith in summoning the spirits to heal a sick brother.

Peter in his ethereal guise senses others floating nearby, gaseous shadows, some pungent and offensive, unearthly; others fresh as spring leaves, pure as birch sap, sublime. He feels the conflict between the spirits; sprites against wraiths, good versus evil, an intangible contest for this man's soul.

Who? Peter wonders. What is his position in the tribe? A chief, or a brave warrior? A provider of food for his family, a skilled trapper of the beaver that the white man, the *moonias*, come for once a year. He moves closer, using the dark to hide, but finds it impossible to see the man's face. Closer, nearer, to within a breath. Red welts cover the forehead, a rash of boils fills the cheek hollows. He searches behind the eruptions for an identity.

Then, a shudder courses through his body. Commencing at his head, it races down his spine and shakes his legs violently. It branches to his arms; his fingers tingle as if he had brushed a nettle. He recognises the face. He is looking at the image of himself ten years ago. A snapshot of his first encounter with the souls of Nipew Lake.

He backs out, pushing against the flap covering the entrance, escaping from the tepee, into the circular encampment. Fear fills his soul. He thrashes around like an unbroken stallion in a corral. Breaking loose, he stumbles into the fish racks, sending them crashing into the smoking fire. He turns for the shore, running, stumbling down the slope, searching for an escape. Unable to stop, he almost falls over the first canoe. He's astounded. The thin birch shell has been caved in, probably by a rock. He rushes to the next one; the same thing, the stone still sitting on the keel. To the next, and the next. All destroyed.

Turning, he faces the camp, looking back to the tepees. They are emitting apparitions, swarming out like bees, hornets, shadows that roar. Behind him, the children are shrieking, shouting his name. His name? How in hell's name did they know it?

"Peter! Peter, look. Here! Over here! Peter, wake up. Please wake up. It's a plane." Oh, my God. He can't be dead. Not now, not at the last minute.

A roar fills Peter's head interjected with soprano cries. The bier rocks. His hat falls off. Something is hitting his head, stinging his cheeks.

Forcing eyelids against crusty hinges, he opens his eyes, exposing his pupils to painful light. The roar reaches a deafening pitch and a shadow crosses his face. For a fleeting moment, he glimpses wings, pontoons, a tail-fin. The image registers. He mutters "Thank God," closes his eyes, relaxes, and the sounds wash over him: swish as the floatplane hits water, the roar as the engine throttles back, and a rhythmic chug as it taxies towards them.

FOUR

"Am I glad to see you... I'm sorry, I've forgotten your name," Sara shouts as soon as the engine dies and the pilot opens the small door-window. She recognises him immediately, remembering his fresh young face and excessive attention. He had flown her to Paull Lake, her nerves taut with excitement and fear, eyes mesmerised by an emerald land and crystal-clear lakes. She had learnt something of his upbringing in a small prairie town, the name of which she's forgotten along with his. Wants to fly 747s. Working as a bush jockey will log the required flying time in no time.

"It's Tom. I see you've picked up a passenger."

"Do you know Peter uh...? He's very sick. We have to get him to hospital."

"I know Pete. Move closer. Saves shouting." Tom opens the door and climbs down onto the float.

"What's the problem?" Tom asks. He crouches down and catches the gunwale. Leaning over, Tom places the back of his hand against Peter's forehead, lifts an eye-lid, and checks his pulse.

"Heat stroke, I'd say. Clammy skin, weak pulse. I reckon he's dehydrated from the sun."

"Please, we have to hurry. He has stomach cancer. He needs an operation otherwise he'll die. He hasn't eaten or drunk for days. He's drugged with morphine."

"Morphine?" Tom exclaims. "You don't take morphine on a canoe trip, unless... He knew?"

"Yes, but not this soon I think. He fell and made things worse. You must fly us to Missinipe."

"He'll have to go to LaRonge. That's the closest hospital. Hang-on, I'll radio Medi-vac."

Tom returns quickly to his seat and slips on earphones. After what seems like fifteen minutes to Sara, but was actually five, Tom jumps to the pontoon.

"Okay. The air-ambulance is on its away. Here in twenty minutes. They'll take him to LaRonge and then Saskatoon."

Saskatoon! Sara feels the blood drain from her face. Suddenly Peter is about to be taken, transported a long distance, leaving her behind. Questions tumble into her head. What should she do? How will *she* get to Saskatoon? Money, accommodation?

Sensing her anxiety, but misreading its cause, Tom says, "Don't worry, I'll fly you to Missinipe so you can return home."

"I have to go to Saskatoon." Sara hesitates, suddenly aware of the commitment she's made. "I want to make sure that Peter is okay."

Tom's face begs an explanation. Sara briefly tells her story - their meeting, canoeing together for two days and the accident.

"Shorty will find a way to get you south. He knows people. He'll find someone who can help. Don't you worry. Pass up the gear. We'll load while we wait."

Tom says, "These packs are a little wet."

"We capsized at Trout Falls," Sara replies, trying to sound

151

nonchalant, curbing the images that continue to invade her mind.

"Stand on the pontoon to lift the packs, otherwise you'll capsize again. Here." Tom extends a hand.

Sara is relieved to let him take charge, thankful that the responsibility for Peter is being shared. They hoist each pack precariously into the small cabin except for the one Peter is lying on. Tom climbs in and secures everything into the cargo net.

"Here they come," Sara announces excitedly the moment she hears the drone of an aircraft.

"Wake up, Peter," she urges, gently shaking his shoulder. "The air-ambulance is here. Can you hear me?" Peter is unresponsive, but she sees a ghost of a smile pucker his lips. Instinctively she caresses his cheek. She stands as Tom alights beside her. Looking south, a speck above the horizon grows, resembles the dragonflies she's seen flitting over the water, their jade-green bodies on iridescent wings, bulbous emerald eyes seeking mosquitoes. The silhouette takes form and before Sara can say the proverbial 'Jack Robinson', a silver and red single Otter is circling above them. It completes one and a half circles before it drops, banking steeply. Sara sees the pilot's face peering down. For a moment, the plane looks like it's going to nose-dive into the lake, but it levels off and glides for a landing. White surf sprays, the engine bellows, and the plane sags like a dog flopping into shade on a sweltering day. It loses momentum rapidly, turns as they rock in it's wash, and approaches with a melodic chug. A small door flies open the instant the propeller stops. The silence is eerie to the point of being sinister. The Otter comes to rest thirty feet away, dwarfing the Cessna like a mother bird taking to wing her wayward offspring. A sweet noxious smell of aviation fuel permeates the air, making Sara more nauseous, accentuating her hunger and fatigue.

A slender, uniformed figure drops onto the pontoon. "Can you bring the patient over in the canoe?" the nurse shouts. "We can't approach closer without risking a collision."

Neither Tom nor Sara had considered that. Tom clambers back into the cabin and retrieves Sara's two paddles. He steadies the canoe as Sara drops in to the middle, behind Peter.

"Wait a minute," Tom says. "Hold on to the plane." He reaches into the cabin for a coil of yellow rope, ties one end to a cleat and the other to the stern.

"We'd look a bit stupid if the wind picks up and blows the plane to the other side of the lake," Tom says, stepping gingerly into the stern. "Be warned. I'm not comfortable in a canoe."

"G'd afternoon. I'm Catherine, and this is George Kubinski," the nurse says as a bear of a man, similarly dressed in a white shirt and navy slacks, appears at the door.

"Oh, hi, Tom. I thought it might be you," the pilot says. "Long time, no see. You have a canoeing casualty I see."

"This is Sara Sutcliffe," Tom says when the bow nudges the Otter's pontoon. "She's from England. It's Peter Jordan you'll be taking. Sara's wondering if she can come with you?"

"'Fraid not. Against regulations except for immediate family," Kubinski replies, grabbing the canoe.

"I guessed as much, but thought I'd ask."

"This isn't going to be easy, Tom, lifting the body out of the canoe and into the cabin," Kubinski says. "Canoes are too tippy."

"Don't tell me!"

"Catherine, take Tom's rope to the aft cleat. Tom, you come on the pontoon with me. Catherine, take the casualty from inside the cabin."

The pilot directs the awkward transfer of Peter's limp body through the doorway and onto a stretcher.

"Thanks, Tom. Miss. Be seeing you." With a cavalier salute and wave, the pilot closes the door. Within seconds, Kubinski's head appears at the cockpit window. Tom quickly releases and returns to the canoe. He reels in the rope to the Cessna. Once they're clear, George waves and instantly the propeller grinds over. The engine shatters the silence. The last thing Sara sees as the plane taxies is the nurse's hand holding a transparent pouch above Peter, its plastic tube delivering fluid to his parched body.

Before they arrive at their own plane, the air-ambulance has turned and is racing past them into the south-westerly breeze. Airborne in a few seconds, climbing rapidly, it heads south.

Sara watches the all-too-quickly diminishing Otter, its angry buzz in pursuit. The whole operation was so slick she can hardly believe it's happened and that Peter has gone. She raises an arm but stops halfway, realising the futility of her wave. The lump in her throat swells and chokes, brings tears, not of sadness, but of relief and doubt. Were we in time? Will I see him again? She makes a prayer to a God she isn't sure about, a God that she never considers merciful.

In anticlimactic silence, both pilot and canoeist, privy to their own thoughts, load Peter's pack and lift the canoe out of the water, onto its side against the struts. Sara, balancing on the tail end of the pontoon, notices the breeze is freshening. The air is whistling through the ailerons. Tom lashes the canoe to the plane. She silently thanks him for not breaking out into his customary chatter, preferring his whistling and his out-loud thoughts as he clinches knots.

"That should do it," he says with an assuring flat-handed slap on the side of the canoe. "You have to climb in first."

Hanging on grimly, her toes catching the edge of the pontoon, she side-steps to the door. With a knee on the canoe and hands clasping the doorjambs, she pulls herself up with an assisting shove from Tom. She swings into the pilot's seat and then squirms to the passenger side, taking care not to knock any of the levers in the cramped space. Tom jumps in, slams the door, settles, and buckles his seatbelt.

Tom faces Sara, smiles encouragement, and points to the set of earphones hanging before her. She slips them over her head.

"Don't you know all that," she almost remarks testily as Tom, following a dog-eared chart, checks various controls. The cabin is stiflingly hot, the air pungent with a potpourri of fuel, hydraulic fluid and oil, leather and rubber, plastic and metal. Tom fits his radiophone over his ears. His voice, oddly distant, echoes in her head, startles her.

"Here we go." Tom pushes a button and the propeller blades cross her view. With a bark, the motor fires, the propeller blurs, and the cabin shakes violently. The pandemonium swallows her, the earphones ineffective. Again his voice. About to reply, she realises Tom is talking to someone else – a female voice in her ear.

Sara concentrates on watching the water. The surface has become choppy in the time it took to effect the transfer.

"I told base to phone Shorty. He'll meet us at the dock," Tom says as they taxi into the wind.

"Thank you," Sara shouts. Tom's head recoils.

"Ouch! No need to yell – talk normal."

"Sorry. I forgot," she says, pointing to the small microphone in front of her mouth.

"That's okay. It happens every trip if the passenger hasn't flown before. Here goes," Tom adds.

Tom pushes the red and black levers forward. Spray bursts beneath the plane. Through the windshield Sara sees only white clouds and patches of blue sky. Beside her, Tom is sitting erect, peering over the instrument panel. Noise thunders. She senses the tail lift. Trees ahead are closing. Suddenly the shaking stops, the engine pitch fades to a hum. They soar. Sara is exhilarated, understands Tom's love of flying small aircraft.

Urgently Tom points to their right, his hand inches from her face. Sara's eyes jolt, her mouth drops. The sky is a livid jet-black, the trees starkly emerald. To the north-west, the direction from which she and Peter had recently travelled. The top of the cloud billows, creamy white and solid, Thor's anvil is developing. The sky ahead hasn't changed since their arrival on Nipew; if anything, it's brighter, the clouds more majestic as they sail away to the east. Racing from the storm, Sara imagines, like ships flying for a safe harbour.

"A typical summer afternoon storm brewing," Tom announces. "It's coming our way, but we'll be in Missinipe in two shakes. Thank goodness we managed to get Pete out in time. The waves on Nipew will soon be four-footers. Too rough for this little plane."

At his mention, Peter's image jumps into her head, this time with more joyous episodes; jerky as they sailed down Trout Lake, his amusing stories; an island campsite with fresh pickerel and early morning moonlight, birdsong; soup and bannock lunch; red scars on a rockface from before time, a canoe still there... Forever? The droning engine closes her eyes. The emptiness in her stomach lets out a yelp. It dawns on her that she hasn't eaten since Saturday morning. Sleep is upon her when the nose drops.

When the aircraft banks steeply, her eyes leap open, fingers tightening into a knot. She was dreaming; she was running Trout Falls when the plane tipped.

Missinipe is below, it's cluster of roofs nestled amongst the trees, the resort dominant like a throne. An untidy clutter of boats, vehicles, machinery and aircraft are parked at the airplane base. They drop steeply and land on the black surface, the splash of white like a skunk's tail.

Ten feet from the dock, Tom turns the aircraft and backs into its parking spot. He cuts the engine, slides out the door. His head disappears and Sara catches indistinguishable words from the shore. Wearily, she slips off the earphones, unsnaps her seatbelt and moves into Tom's seat.

"Wait 'til I unload the canoe," Tom suggests, his head ducking into the doorway. "It will be easier to get out. Shorty's here."

Sara sees bare hairy legs in scruffy sandals on the wooden dock, then Shorty's Viking face appears under the wing.

"Hi, Sara. Pleased you made it. I hear you've had quite a time. I phoned before I left the office, and Pete's already in LaRonge. They're taking him to the airport right now. They said he was stable, what ever that means."

Sara bites her bottom lip hard, sensing tears brimming. It's all she can do to nod. Everything is normal here, surreal, yet Peter, miles away, is fighting for his life.

The canoe beneath her disappears, and before she can climb down, Shorty's frame fills the opening. He almost picks her up as she leaves the plane. Unashamedly, she steps into Shorty's encompassing arms, fighting back emotion. She clings to him, her head against his chest, strangely comforted by the smell of his sweat. She closes her eyes, shutting out the world, seeking only comfort from this house of a man.

"Like a cuppa?"

She nods, his T-shirt rubbing her cheek. Just the thought of a mug of hot tea has a soothing effect.

"Come on, then, we'll go up to the house. Tom will look after all the gear. Won't you, Tom?"

"You bet."

"You need food and rest. Then we'll see about getting you to Saskatoon. Sandy has the barbecue fired-up."

Sara feels like the child who has been lost and now found. They walk up the gravel slope from the dock in step. His grip holds her close, her head pressed in the crux of his armpit. Her legs feel as though they might give way at any moment, unable to support her weight. Her fingertips tingle. Running on pure adrenaline for hours, she hasn't noticed how taut her muscles have become. The confidence that has taken days to germinate in her evaporates in thirty seconds, leaving her vulnerable, overwhelmed by emotion. She's totally empty.

It occurs to her that she was this way once before – the day that her husband had abandoned her.

* * *

Sara changes gear, into third, and gradually climbs the steep hill, away from Otter Lake and Missinipe, away from memories reflected in the rear-view mirror. She passes a green sign – *LARONGE 80*. Miles or kilometres, she wonders. She glances at the speedometer. The needle registers zero kilometers. One question answered. What else on the old truck doesn't work? Apprehensively Sara flips dusty switches; a wiper creeks across the windshield, the horn croaks and dirt flies from a vent into her face. Head shaking, she resigns herself to a hope and a prayer.

Edging left as she breasts the summit, Sara shifts up, and swings to the middle of the gravel road when she sees there's no oncoming traffic. She settles into the bench seat, prepared for the rough ride to LaRonge, optimistic that the traffic will be light this early in the morning. She has been warned about the heavy trucks en route to the uranium mines up north that invariably hog the middle of the road.

"They barely pull over, let alone slow down," Shorty had told her. She's uneasy with her limited driving experience. The half-ton Chevy feels enormous and everything's on the wrong side. And what with having to drive on the left...

"Left? Not left! Right! Oh my God," she exclaims. Colour drains from her face. The steering wheel is suddenly sticky. Her mistake raises an image of a northbound vehicle rearing over her as it tops a hill. "Keep right!" she shouts, then laughs at herself.

Bright sunlight floods the cab, highlighting the accumulation of grime on the frost-cracked dash. The truck elbows aside tendrils of steam sweating from the road – the night's saturating rain evaporating into the cool air.

Last night, on the brink before sleep, Sara was vaguely aware of a premature darkening, the abrupt silencing of a cheerful robin outside her window, a ghostly hush. The storm she'd seen on Nipew had reached Missinipe. Sheets of rain pounded the roof and overflowed the eavestrough. Never had she experienced such furore, and like a child, she cowered under the bedclothes, peeking at the frenzied trees outside the window, petrified a stark blue-green by lightning. Sara's positive that her heart missed several beats when one synchronous crack of thunder and flickering light assaulted the house, shaking it to its foundation. Sandy screamed, bringing a smile to Sara when the men laughed beyond the bedroom walls. Despite her exhaustion, sleep was impossible. She watched in awe, amazed by the intensity of Nature's anger. Curled up, she hugged herself, frightened by an imagination that thrusts her into a crushed tent, that sets her adrift in a tossing canoe on Nipew with dead people floating around her. She cannot recall Atlantic gales bringing such violence to England, yet Tom had said, "…typical summer storm…" She refused to envision an *extraordinary* one.

Once the tempest passed, Sara slept soundly – naked between the sheets, exhausted, motionless, dreamless.

The road snakes, curving past tranquil blue lakes, cutting through granite outcrops, curling around blind bends. At every summit of the rugged roller coaster, magnificent views unfold; oceans of green, vistas of rolling hills carpeted with pines. The broken road keeps her focused; skirting rain-filled potholes, fishtailing through coarse aggregate, slip sliding on wet clay. It's like the Monte Carlo Rally on television. Her confidence grows, the driving is exciting. She presses harder on the accelerator.

Sara shoulder checks that the packs and paddles are where Tom had placed them. It was Tom's idea, endorsed by Shorty and Sandy, that she use Peter's truck to drive to Saskatoon. Her heart warms remembering them, their forced cheerfulness and sincere good wishes, waving farewell until she turned a corner. She wants desperately to return; to share their lifestyle, so different from the urban rat race she has endured all her working life.

The walk to Shorty's house is a blur, and it wasn't until Sandy's hastily prepared tea was consumed did she begin to feel human again.

The long hot shower washed away the film of bush-dirt, purged her fears, and returned her partially to normality.

"Tom!" Shorty's sharp rebuke cuts short Tom's stare, a can of beer poised at his lips, when Sara emerges bare-legged from the bathroom in Sandy's white terry-towel house-coat, her damp hair slicked back, framing a fresh, younger-looking face.

Tom gulps his mouthful of beer. "I'll get your packs. They're in my truck," Tom says and hurries for the door.

Later, dressed in crinkled but clean clothes, she picked at a barbecued steak, her appetite appeased by just a salad and baked potato. A pre-supper phone call to the Saskatoon hospital had told them that Peter had arrived and was in surgery. The news knotted her stomach and cut her desire for food. That was when Tom had said, exposing a mouthful of blood-dripping meat, "Why don't you take Pete's old truck? You have the keys, don't you, Shorty?"

"That's the best suggestion you've ever made, Tom," Shorty remarks. "I'll bring it over in the morning, Sara, and we'll load your gear in the back. You may as well take Pete's stuff."

Plans were made and directions to University Hospital in Saskatoon scribbled down.

Sara passes a road-sign for Stanley Mission. A picture of a clean, white, steepled church springs to mind, recalled from travel brochures. The first church built in the West, its simple lines rising from a point overlooking the Churchill River, charms her thoughts.

Sara sighs with relief when the tires hit the asphalt and sing in accord. Immediately, a massive grey truck, hauling two bulk containers, passes in the opposite direction, rocking the half-ton in its wake. A diminutive brown-faced figure behind the wheel raises his hand, a nonchalant greeting. She now appreciates Shorty's warning, thankful that she hadn't met the truck earlier – on that first hill!

She crosses a narrow bridge with white railings where half-naked shiny brown children are waving and diving; then she's rolling into the outskirts of LaRonge. She stops to refuel and buys a chocolate bar and a Coke, indulgences she has forgotten while canoeing. In no time, she's back on the road, heading south.

Later, all Sara would remember about that trip is a wide lonely road, a winding river of black asphalt stretching to the horizon. A broad ditch on both sides, backed by trees, two impenetrable walls. Logging trucks rumble by, heading north, the vertical bunks on the empty trailers like four-poster beds. The road is endless, dulls her mind, numbing her foot on the accelerator. She rarely moves the steering wheel. Two hours of driving forward, dreaming backwards, recalling a lifetime, memories both recent and distant.

Peter appears every few minutes, hovering in the cab, squatting on his wannigan, driving his canoe over waves, or smiling beneath his battered hat, then drifts away.

"Having trouble?" his first words. A greeting that had caught her in that hideous mosquito net. Words from nowhere, from everywhere. She smiles, remembering her stumble into the fire that refused to be.

"You were fantastic..." She grins. Never has she heard such praise, genuine words of gratitude, other than from her over-protective parents.

The road climbs a range of hills, twisting around lazy bends. Sara's hand drops to the gearlever. At the summit, she pulls off and grinds to a halt in a lay-by overlooking miles of forested land, a sapphire lake in its midst.

She slips from the cab. The sun's heat strikes her. She walks to the back of the truck. Impulsively, she grasps Peter's long paddle. Heavier than expected, Sara holds it gently as she would a baby. She takes an imaginary stroke, sensing its power in Peter's hands. It can change a canoe's course, spin it around obstacles. How many rapids has he run? How many lay ahead? If the surgeon wields his scalpel like Peter can this paddle, she muses, there will be many. Every malignant cell, every miscreant molecule must be nipped, removed dispassionately, the bad sacrificed for the good.

Sara remembers why she stopped. Her bladder is screaming for relief. Moving to the front of the truck, away from the road, she drops her shorts, and leans her back to the fender. She contemplates the yellow stream flowing from beneath her, soaking into the dirt. Peter's strange words revisit. "I will fall as rain sustaining any number of creatures." Parts of her are to remain here – molecules of water and salt. *I wonder if I will be sustaining an ant or two, or will everything evaporate into the dry air all too quickly.* She shakes her head as she adjusts her clothing, still uncertain with some of Peter's ideas.

Robert entered the office for the first time one extra-busy Friday, raising ten pairs of eyes, blue, brown, green, and one pair that were hazel with green flecks. In seconds, Sara absorbed all salient features, had labelled him 'The Saint', and dismissed him. On the train home that night, she had thought about him again, allowing thirty seconds of her time, which was thirty seconds more than any other man.

En roulant ma boule roulant . . .

Sara grips the wheel as she had the handlebars of her father's bicycle, steering from her pony seat on the crossbar when he playfully lifts his arms. Turning her head, laughing, long black hair blowing in the wind, she searches his eyes for approval. "Keep yer eyes on the road – you'll 'av us in the ditch," he exclaims, grabbing the handles as they begin to wobble.

Father and daughter filled weekends exploring the lush-green countryside around Woking, following by-ways that meander throughout Surrey before they succumbed to the scour of developers' bulldozers. Horsell Common is a particular favourite. They cycle on roads and paths, a labyrinth of horse or walking trails through woods of oak, beech and chestnut, wandering across the sandy heath that is blanketed with broom and yellow-flowering gorse. Breathing perfumed air, they locate rare flowers in season; orchids, bog asphodel and sundew. Their path invariably leads to a pub – 'The Cricketers' or Dickens' 'Bleakhouse Inn' – where Daddy quaffs a pint of ale and smokes his pipe, and Sara enjoys a bag of crisps and fizzy lemonade, or a beer-shandy when she's older.

When Sara outgrew the crossbar, her parents scrimped and saved until they bought a bicycle for her seventh, or was it the eighth, birthday. Sara's face beams. It was an unforgettable day; she remembers her excitement. A blue two-wheeler hidden behind the settee. Daddy running, panting like a bulldog, holding onto the saddle for her maiden ride. Within twenty minutes, they were both cycling down the road, Mummy waving vigorously and shouting, "Be careful!" as they disappear round a corner.

En roulant ma boule . . .

Robert's second visit, followed shortly by a third, and each time, his covert perusal of her, with Mr. Evans, a company partner, at his side. Unusual – clients did not, as a rule, enter the computer pool, preferring to discuss over tea and digestive biscuits in the boardroom. Sara recalls, with an unpleasant tremor, her surprise when kindly Mr. Evans placed on her desk an invitation for lunch, neatly written on the back of a business card.

"Mr. Robert Fielding is a new client," he says in his Welsh accent. "Do you mind?"

Sara acquiesced, and instead of her familiar sandwich bar, she had been whisked away in a taxi. Feeling apprehensive, she responded to questions in monosyllables, agreeing, expressing no opinions. Their conversation never once touched on business – that came much later.

En roulant ma boule roulant . . .

Ranging further afield, they pursued the essence of their lives. They visited the gardens at Kew and Henry VIII's Hampton Court, traced history at Windsor Castle and Runnymede, had bet on winners and losers at the races – Ascot or Epsom. When Mummy was off-duty from Woking's Brookwood Hospital, she'd meet them at their destination, complete with picnic basket, travelling there by bus or train. For longer trips, they would benefit from Daddy's job as a bus conductor, taking free rides on the top floor of a double-decker bus.

En roulant ma boule . . .

The luncheon was followed by theatre dates, dinner dates, trips to racecourses in a Jaguar sports car – one social event after another, his pound notes flowing like confetti in a hurricane. From time to time, Sara remained in the City, sleeping alone, as she insisted, in Robert's Fulham flat. Now that Sara is able to think rationally about her courtship, she realises that love, real love, never entered the affair. She could not even recall the word being spoken. At the time, though, she had evoked school days and understood what girlish hysteria was all about – she *thought* she was in love; had come of age, had graduated at last. She had found her tall, dark stranger.

The whirlwind of activity picked her up and delivered her to a Chelsea Registry Office. A cold, informal marriage with three witnesses. The best-man – a school chum they were told; Mummy unable to hold back the tears; and Daddy, her closest friend, who was loath to give her away to a man he disliked from their first meeting. The wedding was their second.

* * *

She squirms involuntarily in her seat, as if settling more comfortably behind the wheel. But, in truth, she's remembering the pain of losing her virginity and the emptiness that followed. Their lovemaking, weekends of groping, revolting coalescence of sweat, soon became mechanical. Sara found no physical pleasure, but was content to give Robert the satisfaction of climax, and made, she thought, the requisite noises – groans and sighs.

A week after they were married, Robert asked an unexpected question, his first mention of her work. "What was the biggest order today?"

"I have no idea," she replies. "I never take any notice."

"Let's play a game. Tomorrow, I'll write down my guess, and you tell me what it was and who bought and sold. If I'm wrong, I'll treat you to dinner – a bet."

He had taken her out to dine, and the game continued, expanding until he was learning about the more significant trades. Then he was asking who had bought what, becoming familiar with the names of the most active and successful clients of Babcock, Williams & Evans. In her naiveté, Sara imagined that he was showing interest in her work, a husband's duty, she thought. In fact, as she discovered when his scheme came to light, he was using the information to buy and sell shares, on margin, through a rival stockbroker. For a number of years, his plan worked to his benefit, accumulating thousands of pounds, allowing him to follow the lifestyle of the rich without a job. Always believing that Robert had inherited his wealth, Sara never suspected his ill-gotten source of finances.

Life would have continued in the same fashion if it had not been for the collapse of the Baring Bank. Robert could no longer cover his margin position; his stockbroker demanded payment. The whole scheme was exposed, implicating Sara as much as Robert. Scotland Yard's investigation put the pieces together, leading to a charge of fraud and embezzlement.

"I find you, Robert Fielding, guilty," says the be-wigged judge at the Old Bailey. Ten years in Brixton was the sentence.

Good riddance, Sara says, for the umpteenth time, and hits the horn with her fist exactly the way the judge had struck the bench with his gavel. The sound makes her start, brings her attention back to the road just as it drops steeply into a valley. She reads WASKESIU RIVER as she careens over a bridge.

Forty minutes later, the scenery changes dramatically. The trees thin out and congregate into groves of aspen, a mosaic of green islands adrift in yellowing grainfields. Following a long downhill stretch, the land flattens, and a groundswell surges beneath an expanse of blue sky.

Sara crosses a wide river, the North Saskatchewan, and slows when she meets the traffic of Prince Albert. The jostling vehicles make her nervous. She pulls into the parking lot of a donut shop.

When she leaves the bustling town, Sara is pleased. She has not hit any other vehicle. At last, SASKATOON appears on a road sign, prompting an image of Peter impatiently waiting.

Another scenery change lifts her spirits. Her lungs savour pleasant aromas. Acres of bright yellow fields and occasionally a patch of blue, crops she does not know or recognise. Grain stretches to the horizon, fields of yellowing green, undulating gently, bending to the vagaries of the wind. The road cuts a cruel scar carrying speeding traffic. When Saskatoon appears on the skyline, she slows and opens the pencilled map. She passes malls, turns at traffic lights, crosses another river, and recollects Shorty's description of the greystone University as it slides by on her right. She turns into the grounds and finds the overhead parking at the rear of an impressive structure that looks more like government offices than a hospital.

She parks the truck well away from the bevy of immaculate cars. Her hands are visibly shaking when she pockets the keys. Emptiness gnaws at her stomach. To steady her nerves, she inhales deeply. The hot dry air laced with the smell of concrete and rubber is of no comfort.

Terrifying words weigh on her mind:

"I'm sorry, he didn't make it."

"Regretfully, he passed away two hours ago."

Leaning on the side of the truck box, Peter's paddle takes her eye. Impulsively, she grabs it.

"Peter's going to need you," she says out loud. "Give him hope; remind him of rapids to challenge."

With doubts corralled by gritting teeth, Sara follows signs leading to the entrance. An overhead walkway opens into a grand mezzanine with a cathedral ceiling, gift boutiques, and a central food court. Sara is reminded more of a railway station than a hospital. Uniformed workers criss-cross, stethoscopes hanging like halters, clipboards grasped to chests; the atmosphere holds memories – childhood visits at the end of a shift, her mother's cheerful greeting hiding a tired smile.

"I'm looking for Peter..." Sara has forgotten his surname. She tries desperately to recall that first introduction at Rock Trout. At her hesitation, the receptionist, an elderly lady, turns her attention to a bald man with two children standing beside Sara each clutching a handful of wilting flowers.

"Where can I buy flowers?" Sara asks when inquisitive eyes focus on her, no doubt puzzled by the paddle.

"Over there, to your right, past 'Admitting'."

Sara moves hesitantly in the direction of the woman's hand, wracking her memory, mouthing "Peter... Grimes, Gabriel. It was a country... like German."

She spins back in the direction of the Reception Desk. "Jordan!" she almost shouts out loud, her eyes wide.

"I've changed my mind. Too expensive. Peter Jordan, please."

The woman examines a list. "He's in ICU. Family visits only."

Small grey eyes bore into her, as if to say "Got you. Now take your paddle out of here."

"I'm his wife, Sara Jordan." The lie sounds... wonderful. Her spine tingles as goose bumps erupt. She stares defiantly at the woman, challenging her to doubt her word.

"Second floor. Elevators to your left. Ask the duty nurse for admission before you enter."

With utmost control, Sara doesn't run to the elevator. Squeezing into a melee of brightly clad visitors, she blushes at a question that evokes a burst of laughter, "Will you canoe me up *your* river?"

She's standing at the bottom of Peter's bed, suddenly uncomfortable, aware of the incongruity of the paddle. She watches the monitors – green traces that show the mysteries of the body's functions. Too many tubes – in his wrist, his neck, from under the sheet, into his nose.

"He's doing quite well," says a petite Chinese nurse, "under the circumstances. You can talk to him, he's awake. Are you Sara?"

Sara nods.

"He's mentioned you."

She edges to his side, leans forward, tentative.

"Peter? Peter."

Her heart leaps when a pale blue eye opens.

"Hello. I've brought your paddle."

"Thanks, Danika. I love you," he croaks. "What took you so long?"

With her foot hovering over the brake pedal, Sara drives the street crown, pressed by flaccid elms and parked cars, peering through the cracked windshield for number 954 – stucco with brown siding. She pulls to the curb beside a house that matches Peter's description; a bungalow with a manicured lawn, narrow beds of orange marigolds beside the house, and a driveway to a matching garage at the rear.

Sara approaches the side entrance, legs shaking like a door-to-door salesperson on her first call. Tugging open the aluminum screen door, she unlocks the half-glazed wood door. It grates on dried hinges. Quickly, Sara steps over the threshold. Frozen in subdued light, she stands on a small landing, listening to the silence, hearing only her heart pounding in her ears. She forces a short laugh, annoyed at her discomfort, angry that she still fears the unknown. Am I not the girl who challenges raging rapids? Sara scolds herself. For heaven's sake, control your imagination. This isn't a celluloid horror-farce. Sharply she slaps her thigh, takes several long, slow breaths, and forces herself to relax.

Two sets of stairs face her – down to the basement on her right, and up to the living room on her left. Deliberately she ascends, feeling her feet sink into deep pile. At the top, with her hand gripping a wrought iron railing, Sara waits for her eyes to adjust to the gloom. She senses Peter immediately; smells him in the still air, tastes his spirit. Loath to turn on a light or open a curtain, she creeps around the dark house, senses alert, absorbing its mysteries.

A fly buzzes angrily somewhere, beating against a window, then quits, exhausted. Sara stands in the middle of the living room. Compared to her own home, she thinks it opulent. Deep, dark lounge chairs, a bank of electronic equipment beside an enormous television, a well-stacked bookcase, Scrimshaw paintings of lakes and lightening, Hummel figurines, and, as she anticipated, a family photograph. Eagerly Sara picks up the frame from the end table and perches on the arm of the sofa. She peers closely at the group looking at her.

Peter is younger by maybe five to seven years – his hair is brown, flecked with ghosts of the future. Sara smiles; Peter is evidently uncomfortable in a suit, white shirt and tie, posing like a waxwork dummy. Eyebrows lowered in a scowl, his eyes are shooting daggers at the fastidious photographer. His wife and daughter, more compliant, are seated at an angle, their inside knees touching. Fingers, lightly clasped, nestle in their laps, partly hidden by the folds of full skirts. Peter's hands rest on the bare shoulders of each one. Sara's eyes gravitate to Danika, as the photographer had intended having recognised her fascinating aura. By posing Peter partly behind, Danika is the focus, she *makes* the photograph. The other two – insignificant sidekicks.

Sara is captivated by Danika's beauty; of darker complexion, soft brown eyes shine like mahogany beneath striking eyebrows. Graceful waves of dark brown hair fall to her shoulders. A wide mouth suggests passion. A single diamond gold necklace hangs against her breast, its fire accenting the low-cut black dress. Sara suddenly wishes she were still alive. She would love to have met her, to talk, women's chatter, discuss their lives, comparing her traditional class-oriented England with pioneering multi-ethnic Canada. Sara, though, does not miss the irony of her thinking, knowing that if Danika were alive, everything would be different. She wouldn't even be in Saskatoon.

Sara's eyes drift to the second woman, a girl in her teens, her namesake. There is a semblance to her mother's face, but less striking, a penumbra. The tight fitting dress shows off her petite body, a delicate fullness. Her eyes, however, are as blue as Peter's, sharp and decisive.

Replacing the frame, she gravitates to the bookcase. The books on the top two shelves are obviously Peter's. She recognised titles that feature the North, Peter Newman's *Company of Adventurers*, Farley Mowat's *Ordeal by Ice*, and Marjorie Campbell's *The North West Company*.

Canoe is the most conspicuous word on the spines of the second row of books. She extracts one at random, brown covered; *The Lonely Land*, by Sigurd F. Olson. Sara lets it fall open - to the middle. The page title, 'Lake of the Dead', shocks her, agitates her composure. The lake continues to haunt her, even though it's hundreds of miles away. Impulsively, she reads the first paragraph.

The valley was full of the sound of rushing water. A flock of mallards whispered by overhead on their way to some feeding ground above Trout Portage.

The words revive graphic images as she snaps the book shut: the wild ride, the shock of plunging into cold water, icy fingers grabbing her loins, the panic that immobilised her when she thought Peter had drowned.

Sara noses into the two bedrooms; the smaller at the rear with enough remnants indicates it's Sarah's, Peter's at the front.

In the kitchen, white with sepia accents, she finds Peter's gold watch sitting on the counter; its face tells her that the afternoon is almost gone. It's ten to four.

One thing eludes her; something that Peter had talked about hasn't yet come to light. Intuitively, she goes downstairs. In a low, narrow hallway, three doors face her. She tries the first – laundry room. The next, she enters into pitch black. She knows, from the lingering chalky aroma, before switching on the light, that she's in Peter's study. A desk, littered with papers, books, a tray of pens, faces the door, and above, as anticipated, Peter's picture. She leans against the desk, studying closely the familiar Rock Trout Rapids. There, on the left, where they had stood together, the old jack pine, and below, a canoe that is bursting through white waves. A thought strikes Sara. Leaning closer, her nose almost touching the glass, she examines the figure in the bow. Danika. Eyes wide, mouth open, Sara hears the scream, the joyful shout. In the stern? Peter, of course. And he had said that he took the photograph. Who then?

Suddenly, urgent knocking makes her jump, snaps the silence. Sara, guiltily, feels trapped, caught like a burglar. Again, a brisk rap and she hears the house door creaking open.

"Helloo… Anyone home? Peter?" calls a male voice.

Quickly, Sara switches off the light. From the bottom of the stairs she sees the man, dressed in jeans and a green Saskatchewan

Roughrider shirt.

"Hello," says Sara sharply, suddenly scared.

"Oh! Who are you? Where's Peter? I saw his truck outside. I thought he must be home."

"Peter's in the hospital, at the University. I'm... a friend. We met on the Churchill."

"I too am a friend, from across the street. Been looking after the place. May I come in? The name's Sam Urchenko." The tall man with receding sandy-coloured hair fills the landing. He pushes the door shut. "In hospital, did you say?"

"Yes. I'm Sara Sutcliffe," she replies, her confidence returning.

"You're English," a statement rather than a question. "Why's Peter in hospital?"

"I was about to make tea," Sara replies, hesitant to answer Sam's questions until her emotions are in control. "Would you like a cup?"

"Sure."

Sam slips off green-stained runners and leads the way to the kitchen. He fills the electric kettle and removes two mugs from a cupboard, setting them on the counter.

Uneasily, they sit at opposite ends of the table – one unwilling to announce bad news, the other apprehensive of its severity.

"Peter has cancer, colon cancer," Sara says quickly, springing the news into the open. She blinks rapidly, flicking away tears.

"Oh, no. Not him too. And retired less than a month. Shit! My wife will be devastated."

"He may be okay," Sara says with a false cheerfulness. "They operated last night, as soon as the air-ambulance arrived here. I left him an hour ago. He's his usual self," she adds, biting her lip.

"Here, I'll make the tea," Sam announces as the kettle begins to whistle. "I know where everything is, but there's no milk. I can pop home and get some," Sam adds.

"I drink it black, thanks."

With mugs of tea in front of them, Sara recounts her meeting Peter and how they had set off together on the Churchill River. As she skims details of their return after the fall, Sam keeps nodding, saying, "I know it well." And "I can just imagine him, the stubborn old coot. Running Trout! Geez!"

"You were lucky that pilot found you," says Sam. "Just before the storm. I've been on that lake in rough weather. Once we were windbound for three days."

"Have you canoed with Peter?" Sara asks. Intuition nudges her.

"Many times. At least once, sometimes twice, every summer for the last ten or twelve years," Sam replies.

"You took the photo. The one at Rock Trout?"

"Sure. *That's* why you were downstairs?" Sara nods, expecting him to go on. She can tell that Sam likes to talk, and imagines him leading conversation when canoeing with Peter.

"I took it when Peter and Danika, my wife and I, canoed what is known as the 'Six-Portage Route'. That was before Danika got the big C. Peter was in rough shape for a long time after she died. Didn't think he would ever get over it."

"He hasn't," Sara says quietly, remembering Peter's first words at the hospital, and his later apology.

"Are you going to stay here?" Sam asks. "You might as well. Saves hotel bills."

"That was Peter's idea."

"I'll bring your packs in for you," Sam says, rising and placing his empty mug in the sink. "You'll come over for supper, won't you? I'll tell Emily, my wife – gotta keep the little lady happy, you know. She likes to be part of everything going on. But you are more than welcome." Sam is already moving towards the door, not giving Sara any chance to protest, or offer thanks. Sam has taken charge. She has found yet another Canadian she can call 'Friend'.

Sam returns from the truck with Peter's Duluth bag. "I know this bag well enough. I was with Peter when he bought it, and I helped him build his wannigan. I'll take 'em downstairs."

Sam disappears into the basement. Coming back up, he tells Sara standing at the top landing, "You'll have to run through the whole story again for Emily. She won't be satisfied with me telling her."

In what seems to Sara like a whirlwind of motion, Sam quickly has the gear moved into the house – hers in the kitchen, Peter's somewhere downstairs.

"There you go, then. We'll expect you in, say, an hour. Make yourself at home."

"Which house?" Sara says quickly, before Sam leaves.

"Right! I almost forgot. That one over there," he says, pointing. "Number 947, the red one. Good job I cut the grass this afternoon. Didn't know Peter was having visitors -- from England, eh. See you in a while." And he's gone, striding purposefully across the street.

Sara closes the door, welcoming the serenity that returns, remembering her quiet tour before Sam's bursting upon the scene. A welcome 'burst', Sara adds mentally, not wanting to sound ungrateful even to herself.

She moves her backpack into the rear bedroom and pulls out some of the contents, searching for something to wear. With a pitifully small pile of creased clothes on the bed, she remembers that two-thirds of her wardrobe is cached on Black Bear Island Lake. She opens the closet door; it's full. The top drawer in a chest of drawers is filled with T-shirts. The first, sporting a picture of a sailing boat on blue water, says 'Lake Diefenbaker', and although Sara thought it too school-girlish, decides that it would look better than anything she can salvage from her crumpled pile. She pulls shampoo and wash bag from a side-pocket, undresses and pads into the bathroom. Within seconds, she appears ghostlike behind the shower door, then disappears in a cloud of steam.

On Friday, a grey day with a cool breeze from the north-east, Sara arrives at the hospital for her morning visit later than usual. She had overslept and has been playing catch-up ever since. The night before she had curled into a bulbous armchair with *The Lonely Land*. Words, flowing like a river, had carried her across Saskatchewan, from Ile-à-la-Crosse to Cumberland House, in the company of six middle-aged Americans, canoeing pioneers. After each chapter she cried "Bed!" but every time she made the mistake of reading the quotation opening the next episode, excerpts from the diaries of explorers the likes of David Thompson and Alexander Mackenzie. Shortly after two in the morning, she closed the back cover, the adventure complete. The last sentence was particularly poignant, its words keeping her dream alive: *Another year perhaps and the Lonely Land would claim us once again.* Sara knows in her heart that she'll be returning, but when? Hugging the book to her breast, with eyes closed, her mind recaptures scenes: a white pelican gliding inches above a serene lake; the desolate cry of a loon piercing the dusk of a dying day. Her nose puckers to the aroma of freshly caught fish baking over hot coals. An impatient current hurrying through a chaos of rocks, bouncing her over a parade of waves. Half asleep, her clothes drop in a heap at her feet. She slides into bed and the dream continues.

Her excitement bubbles when she wakes. She rushes her morning routine, singing as she butters toast, humming when tea scalds her throat. She's nearly running when she leaves the house, wanting to share her enthusiasm with Peter, to chat about *The Lonely Land* and, maybe, to consider their return to the Churchill River.

At the hospital, the elevator door whispers open. She enters, followed by a woman and her young son. They exit one level up, the ICU floor, and Sara silently wishes them well as she continues to the general ward. Cheerfully she greets the nurses at the control station and turns into Peter's four-bed ward. Sara stops abruptly. The sheets are pulled back. The bed's empty. Backing out, she checks the room number above the door. There's no mistake.

The old man in the opposite bed beckons with a wrinkled hand. "He's at the end of the hall," he says with difficulty, his sunken lips drawn over toothless gums.

Sara, turning in the direction from which she has just come, sees Peter in a green hospital-issue gown, legs bare, at the far end of the hallway, gazing out the window. An IV pole is parked beside him. She hurries past a line of wards, like cells, each with four inmates reclining in various positions of discomfort. As she nears, she slows, acutely aware of Peter's sagging posture. One hand clutches the pole, the other is thrust deep into a pocket.

"Hello, Peter," she says, her voice subdued, searching first his face then the view that's absorbing his attention. The South Saskatchewan River, black and cheerless, is below them. An arched bridge, which moments ago she had crossed, spans the river to her left.

Without turning his head, Peter says, "If you come this evening, bring me paper and a pen." His monotone is barely audible.

A dreadful premonition invades her.

"I can do that." She waits for an explanation, averse to prompt. She stares through the window, sees nothing. They stand, silent partners, their minds unknowingly in tune.

Sara slips her hand through Peter's arm and stares at his nebulous reflection. "Green doesn't suit you unless you're wearing a canoe," she ventures lightly, drawing close, resting her head on his shoulder.

"Peter, let's get out of here."

Peter turns. His grey face, sunken eyes – no longer stark blue, shock Sara.

"How about a drink, or outside for a walk?"

He nods, his face lightening slightly.

"Give me a minute. I'll find a wheelchair."

At the nurses' station, Sara speaks to the head nurse for a few minutes while an orderly brings a wheelchair and blanket.

"Can you hang on to the pole-thingy, or should I?"

Peter sinks into the chair. "You drive," he says huskily. "I'll push it."

"Left draw," Peter says, brighter, as they bounce into the elevator and eddy-turn to face the closing door.

At the first floor, the door opens and Sara moves aside for the same mother and child. Her face stony, eyes unseeing, she holds the boy close to her hip. His eyes, although dry, look ready to burst. In grim silence, the four sink to the ground.

At the self-service snack bar, Sara buys tea and a muffin, and juice for Peter.

"I'm still confused by your money," she says, as they wheel to a table, Peter cautiously balancing the tray and steering the IV pole through a tangle of tables and chairs.

"Last night I read *The Lonely Land*," Sara blurts as soon as she's seated. "That's why I was late. I slept in. I have no idea what time I went to bed. Peter, I want to take more trips."

"Where?"

"Oh, I don't know. Maybe… Tuk-whatd'yousay."

"Sara, you're crazy. You'll never make it that far." Peter laughs, pauses, and then looks serious. "I take that back. Yes you will, but you're still crazy."

"No crazier than you." She describes how she had read from cover to cover, recognising lakes, rapids and portages that they had travelled.

"Did you know that Alexander Mackenzie wrote about the rock paintings in his journal? And he talks about Silent Rapids."

Peter nods, smiling wistfully.

"The Indians used to leave their possessions as offerings, just like you left the tobacco..." Sara's voice tails off, suddenly aware that Peter's attention is in his cup, that he's no longer listening.

"Sorry," she whispers. "Sometimes I blab too much. I forget..." Sara swallows the lump in her throat. Peter's face frightens her.

Peter grabs her hand and smiles vaguely. She feels its icy coldness all the way to her heart.

"Finish your juice; let's go outside."

"I've had enough."

They find a tree-sheltered bench in front of a flowerbed brimming with white alyssum and orange marigolds. Sara snugs the blanket around Peter's legs.

For several moments Peter sits, hands gripping the armrests, his eyes closed, sucking in air.

"That poor little kid on the elevator – life's so unfair," Peter mutters. "I need clean air, clear skies... wood smoke. Not despair, a clouded future, and formaldehyde."

"You want to go back, don't you?"

Peter's eyes open. Tears glisten. "Yes."

"Will they let you?"

He shakes his head. "No. Soon as possible – next week. I saw what chemo did to Danika."

Chemotherapy? Sara's face blanches. Why chemo if the operation was successful?

"What can I do? I'm sure that Sam will help," Sara says, desperately suppressing her chilling thoughts.

"Sam has the food cache for Ile-à-la-Crosse. My plan was for him to drive there to meet me."

For the next half-hour, Peter tells Sara what she has to do, from buying food to assembling their gear.

"Fly-in? You're moving too fast for me. Where're we going?" she exclaims at one point.

"Black Bear Island Lake. The island where you left two hundred sweaters."

Sara laughs. "Where you insisted I leave them. Luckily, your daughter's clothes fit me."

Peter's eyes stare vacantly at the front of the T-shirt Sara's wearing.

"Sarah doesn't know," he says, slowly shaking his head. "I don't know how to tell her."

"Phone her. She'll want to see you."

"No!"

"Why not?"

"I don't want her to see me like this."

"But she's your daughter. If my Dad was sick, I would want to visit him, to tell him I love him."

Peter sits in silence, rubbing his palms back and forth on the armrests.

"I'll ask Sam to call her," he says at last, looking unsteadily at Sara. "After we leave."

Sara's mouth opens to reply, but she changes her mind, and it closes in a thin line. This is one matter that's too delicate, that breeds antagonism.

"Is that it? That's not too difficult. As long as Sam helps."

"He will. Phone Shorty for a canoe and book the flight."

"May I call my auntie. She's expecting me back this week."

"Sure."

"I'm going to cash in my return ticket home."

"That's a bit hasty, isn't it. You'll be going back – one day."

"I can use the money. I've decided to stay in Canada. With you."

"Whoa! Sara, I won't be here. Then what?"

There it is – out in the open. Until she heard it spoken, Peter's death was a possibility she had adeptly avoided. The sound of the traffic moving along College Avenue is suddenly deafening, filling her head with its monotonous snarl. Her dread, suppressed until now, rises in an angry swell, crashing against her reality, leaving her defenceless.

"The doc told me this morning. The cancer has spread and the only option is chemo. I don't want that, so I don't have much time…"

"How long?" Sara asks, her voice a throaty whisper.

"Two to four."

"Weeks…? Months?"

"Months."

The wave of panic ebbs and Sara's world falls silent. Traffic noise subsides, giving way to something quiet inside her. The sweet perfume of alyssum, out of place, lifts her, encourages her.

"Peter," she says earnestly, "we'll canoe every day. We'll play in Birch Rapids. We'll fish. I have to learn everything – everything you know."

"Why, for heaven's sake?"

Sara jumps up and leans over Peter, her hands on top of his, their faces close.

"You know why. You know what draws you every summer. On Black Bear we'll live. I can learn, you can teach. We'll live for the moment for as long as we're given. I promised you that we'd go back and, by George, I intend to keep my promise."

Peter laughs loudly. "Boy, there's no stopping you! But you're right; I know how you feel."

Later that afternoon Sara wheels Peter to his ward.

"I'm happy to see you smile again," she says as they ascend in the elevator. "You're like a diviner's willow – excited by the smell of water."

FIVE

Flying over Birch Rapids, Peter peers down on the two channels – the right, unnavigable with waterfalls; the left, a broken white torrent. Unlike at water level, from the air the route that he and Sara had followed is plain to see, he muses. The nose of the Cessna dips.

"There she is, Tom." His head aches from the engine's roar, and the angry stomach that he's suppressed up until now rises to his throat. He clenches his teeth. The journey from Saskatoon has been exhausting; all he can think of is land, set-up camp, and sleep. His mind has been bouncing around like a ball on a roulette wheel; into which slot will it drop? Will I die next month or not until October; before the leaves turn golden or after they fall; will the geese migrate before my last day or after? The only sure thing, red or black, odd or even, this is where my life will end, unless… Unless the doctor has excised every, *every*, diseased cell.

"I'll swing round and check for rocks." The floatplane veers sharp right, then banks steeply left. "Someone's beaten you to it."

"Ah, shit!" Peter mutters. "How many canoes?"

"I think… yes. Just one, and I see only one tent. Do you want to try another island?"

Peter swivels round and moves the microphone away from his mouth. "There's someone already here," he shouts to Sara in the rear of the aircraft. "Shall we go somewhere else?"

Sara, her face pasty white, shrugs as if to say, "I don't care. You decide, but be quick about it."

"Here, Tom," Peter says, jabbing downward with his index finger.

Tom completes the turn and heads back toward the rapids. The left wing drops suddenly as the plane turns again. Sara clamps a hand across her mouth, closes her eyes.

Out of the turn, Tom drops the nose sharply. The whole island fills the windshield, emblazoned by the late-August sun, like an emerald in a gold setting. Shaped like a thin letter B, the straight side runs east-west, the loops point north. In the bay, a strip of yellow, slim as a new crescent moon, is sandwiched between the water and dense bush. The island's elevation climbs from west to east to a bald headland. Standing at the point, two figures are watching the plane, their faces following it like sunflowers tracking the sun.

The Cessna drops onto the lake as gently as a pelican. White spray shoots sideways. Tom feathers the propeller and they quickly lose speed.

Sara sighs and sits back in her seat, wipes her face and rakes fingers through her hair. With a weak but triumphant smile, she returns the brown paper bag to the pocket on the cabin wall.

Peter turns in his seat, meets Sara's eyes knowingly. "Welcome to Black Bear Island Lake," he says, giving a long wink, a smile, and a pat on her knee.

"Next time, I sit up front," she says petulantly. "Last time was fine because I sat beside the pilot. Back here, it's squishier than a biscuit tin."

Tom, his landing routine completed, switches off the engine and hangs up his earphones. The sudden quiet is blissful, pressed only by the patter of waves lapping against the pontoons until they crunch lightly on the beach. Tom opens the door and steps out backwards, searching over the canoe until his feet catch the float's edge.

"Wait until I untie the boat," he suggests.

Peter wiggles over the control levers and squirms into the pilot's seat. When the canoe flops onto the lake, he clambers down, jumps into the knee-deep water and wades ashore, towing the canoe beside him.

In fifteen minutes, a pile of supplies sits on the shore – several bulging packs, paddles, fishing rods, food boxes, and the green wannigan.

"I'll run up and introduce myself," Peter says. "Hang on, Tom, just in case the squatters are hostile. Coming, Sara?"

Halfway up the steep climb, Peter has to rest for five minutes. Looking down to the lake, he gives Tom, sitting on the nose of a pontoon, a tired wave. The couple, following Peter and Sara's ascent, greets them.

"Hello," the man says.

"Hi! Do you mind if we camp here? We'll keep out of your hair."

"Not a problem. I am Harald, this is my girlfriend, Freia. Sorry, we not speak good English."

"This is Sara. I'm Peter Jordan. Your accent. It's Dutch, or German?"

"German. Ve're from Bremen. Come. Ve 'ave coffee going."

"Thanks," Peter replies, shaking hands. Peter notices that Freia's grip is the stronger, matching her Germanic appearance – blonde hair, healthily tanned, and high cheek-boned face. Harald, of slighter build, reminds Peter of Woody Allen except that his thick glasses are gold rimmed. Peter steps to the cliff edge and gives Tom a thumbs-up, who, in anticipation, has already drifted from shore. The engine coughs into life, propels the plane away from the island until it's pointing slightly south of the setting sun, then races. After the tail sinks momentarily, the Cessna is rapidly skimming across the surface, chased into the air by a rattling echo. It circles and heads towards them, gaining height. As it passes overhead, the wings rock. Four arms rise in unison. Peter stares after the disappearing plane, regretting its departure, feeling a void in his stomach.

"Come," Harald announces, "Ve 'ave some coffee and *biskuit* and then we carry up your baggage."

"Thanks," Peter says as they move to the fireplace where a blackened coffee-pot sits on a grate over glowing embers, "We've come here for our summer vacation, so I'm sorry if we've butted in."

"Dat's okay. Ve leave tomorrow." Freia rummages in a blue barrel and hands mugs to Peter and Sara.

"Do you have cups for yourselves?" Sara asks. Freia shakes her head and shrugs her shoulders.

"Freia does not vell understand, but no."

"You take this one," Sara says thrusting hers into Harald's hand. "I'll go and get ours."

Before any protests stop her, she's gone, loping down the cliff path.

"She loves to fetch things," Peter says, smiling. "Where have you canoed from?" he asks, watching the dark stream of coffee Freia is pouring into his cup. "Thanks," he says, smiling at the tall girl, intrigued by the sharp blue of her eyes. Trying not to, but admonishes the thought once it's there, he thinks of her as the perfect Aryan.

Her smile is polite, but her *"Wilkommen"* lacks sincerity. Peter suspects that, unlike hospitable Harald, she begrudges their intrusion.

Harald says, "Sorry. No sugar, no milk."

"I drink it black, thanks," Peter answers, clenching his back teeth, his insides in an involuntary twist.

"Ve start at Pinehouse and come down ze Churchill River. It is too wonderful. Better than ze Rhine."

"No doubt," Peter gibes. "No barges, no bridges, no traffic. And no pollution."

Sara returns panting, clasping her metal cup and Peter's yellow mug. "Phew! That's some climb. Saved a trip, though," she says, swinging a backpack off her shoulders. "I'll use this one," Sara says, raising Peter's mug. "You use mine," giving her cup to Freia who fills both before moving to Harald's side.

"*Prosti,*" Harald says, his cup raised.

"Yeah," Peter says ruefully. "Cheers."

"Ve will be leaving in ze morning. Ve must portage Birch Rapids."

"I hope you have lots of bug spray," Sara says.

"Sorry?" Harald looks baffled.

"For the mozzies," she replies. "Zzzeeee!" she adds, swatting make-believe mosquitoes around her head.

"Oh. *Yah!* Ze only thing ve no like. Ve got 'Off'" Harald says, wildly swinging his arm, his finger depressing an imaginary spray-can nozzle. Harald, Peter and Sara laugh; Freia smiles.

Draining her coffee, Sara says "You stay here, Peter. Harald and I can haul up our stuff."

"I can…" Peter starts.

"Do you mind helping? He recently left hospital," Sara asks Harald, "and he doesn't have his strength back."

"Sure. Ve do that. You rest, teach Freia some English."

Peter moves to the cliff and eases himself down, legs over the edge. He turns to beckon Freia, but she has disappeared into her tent. Looking straight down to the water thirty feet below, he remembers jumping from such heights, like a water bomb. To his left, stunted trees cling to bare rock, and beyond lies the path to the beach.

Peter hears the silence, grateful. Not even birdsong. Occasionally a breeze touches his cheek, lifting a few strands of his sparse hair. Hanging on to each puff of air, a whisper arrives from Birch Rapids. Alone, he realises, for the first time since leaving hospital. His mind flirts with the future, like a virgin's hand reaching to caress its first female breast. He butts-up against old dreams. He'll not see the Arctic as did Mackenzie, nor will caribou graze through his campsite. No longer can he anticipate inukshuks to guide him across the Barrens. All that he can hold onto is this fortress rock, his last home. His body slumps, his spirit crumples. Voices invade, but seem far away. His eyes rove right, then left. A cry pulls his head to the path.

Sara has fallen and the backpack is pinning her to the ground. Harald helps her regain her feet. Peter stares, as if frozen, his mind still adrift, not cognisant of her plight. Carefully, Sara plants each foot, and, with arms outstretched, resumes her climb. Harald, sandwiched between two packs, follows with a hand ready to prop Sara or give her a push.

"What've you got in here?" she shouts. "Enough to outfit an army?"

Peter retorts, "No! Just a platoon!" as he stands and approaches Sara. He laughs, the first time in days, remembering when their inside joke began. Helping Sara download, he resolves there and then to refrain from any more self-pity and, instead, soak in as much enjoyment as possible in the time he has left with this woman.

Chatting at the evening fire, Peter excuses himself early on and disappears into his tent.

"Peter, he look not good," Harald comments after several silent minutes.

Sara shakes her head. "He's had major surgery."

"Ahh. Dat is why he cannot lift things. Why he move so slow." More silence. "You are married?"

"Oh, no," Sara says, looking up, blushing uncomfortably.

"But are in love, yah?"

She doesn't reply. It's a reasonable assumption, but it leaves her momentarily tongue-tied. She stares into the blaze, comparing Peter's fiery temper at their first meeting with how much calmer he's become. During their drive north, between intervals of dozing while Sara drove, they had discussed how to spend his remaining days. His bitterness seemed to have mellowed. Anger-fuelled frustration had yielded to a quieter focus. He wished he could paint. Maybe write some poetry. Read a few must-read books. Only when Sara mentioned his daughter had his temper flared, and she hastily changed the subject, leaving her wondering what discontent had forged such a chasm between them.

"I don't know. I mean, it's not really like that," Sara says, knowing she's copping out, again. That morning, in Saskatoon, Emily had asked whether she and Sam would see Peter again. Although expecting the question, she couldn't answer it and responded unconvincingly.

"I haven't known him for long." Will knowing make any difference? She fingers her cheek where Peter had held her face in that ghastly cabin on Butterfly Island, then bleakly remembers that it was Danika who filled his hospital-induced coma, and how his words had innocently hurt.

"On dis island, you will soon know each other. This land will bring you together, close. It has changed Freia and me. She is beautiful, but I am not. But we love our canoeing together, and it has… tied us. It is good she no understand English, but I think she know I talk about us." Freia reaches out and takes Harald's hand.

Harald gives an embarrassed chuckle. "You'll excuse? I think it is time to sleep, yah," he says, throwing a sidelong glance at Freia. Freia smiles, and a flare from the fire flashes in her eyes.

"Some English she understand goodt. Goodnight, Sara. Until morning. Ve go early, so may not see you. If not, good luck. I vish you find 'appiness."

With childish envy, Sara watches them disappear into their tent. Her blue dome-tent is tucked into the trees, and she imagines Peter in it, asleep or lying awake. Waiting for her? *What made me shy away from Harald's probing? Am I a St. Peter? Denying my love until too late.* Quite unexpectedly, tears swell in her eyes. *Of course I want to love Peter,* but a nagging issue pesters her – how to cope with the heartbreak of losing him. *Surely we love each other, otherwise we wouldn't be here together. Would we?* But if it comes to light, Peter will feel guilty, even shame, for betraying Danika, and any love he has for me will sour. Sara lets the tears fall. She finds a tissue in a pocket and dabs her eyes.

Suddenly weary, she stands and kicks at the embers. Just a few sparks fly – no need to water the dying glow.

Kneeling at the tent door, she eases the zipper open. Ducking inside, Sara finds herself kneeling on her sleeping bag. He has laid it out for her. She listens to Peter's heavy breathing, punctuated by snores and groans. She slides into the bag, shivering momentarily from the cold nylon against her skin. Bunching her clothes into a pillow, Sara lies on her side, facing him. She strains to pierce the dark. In her mind, his face is visible – thinner, grey shadows under still piercingly blue eyes. She visualises his growing years: as a clean-faced boy, then a spotty teenager, as a clean-shaven young man, finally the teacher.

She's sinking, drifting into a dream. A still lake with rising mist. Two canoes, gliding beneath scattered clouds, a gentle wake that whispers onto a pebble shore. A cliff rises as they round a corner, white with red gashes spilling down its rough lines, spreading as they close the gap. She opens her mouth to say... Her canoe capsizes. Her legs kick, and startle her awake. She smiles to herself, realising she was in that soft place that hovers before sleep, where a dream can still thrust you back to consciousness.

"Good night." The whisper is like an echo in her dream, out of the darkness.

Fingers caress her face, then grip her hand.

"Sorry. I woke you?"

"I was waiting for you."

She moves her hand and their palms meet, fingers entwine.

"I'm glad we're here... together." A long silence. "G'd night, sleep tight."

Sara's smile splits her face. Deep inside she feels soft and warm and fuzzy. "I will..."

"...my love," she whispers in her head.

Peter awakens slowly. The plaintive whistles of a trio of grey jays flitting amongst the trees filters into his dream, coax him from sleep. A warbler's staccato rings a sweet-sounding alarm clock, an invitation to join the day. The small grey and yellow bird will soon be migrating with its mate to southern Mexico, to the hill-town of Oaxaca with its red-yellow adobe, tree-shaded *zocalo,* and ancient Monte Albàn.

One eye cracks open, enough to see shadows patterning the tent wall. In his dream a hand is mysteriously shoving an old fifty-dollar bill across a counter toward him. He has no idea who owns the hand.

His eyes suddenly open, blue irises focused beyond the tent wall to the source of voices. Male and female in an unfamiliar language, somewhere outside. Peter rolls on to his back, sees the back of Sara's head, and Harald and Freia flood into his memory. He visualises what they're doing from their garbled conversation. The voices fade. A canoe scrapes on rock and he realises that the Germans are leaving.

Peter, so as not to wake Sara, slowly unzips his sleeping bag, pulls his legs under him, opens the rear entrance, grabs his clothes, and crawls out on hands and knees. Standing naked a few steps into the trees he relieves himself. The sight of his hairless stomach shoves his memory back to seventh grade when Gary Sawatsky had told him that pubic hair, like mowed grass, grows faster when it's shaved. He borrowed a razor and, using face soap, scraped every hair from around his penis. For days, he surreptitiously scratched his navel. He never repeated the experiment nor did he again take Sawatsky's advice.

He slips into his clothes and, at the cliff edge, squints into the early morning sun for the Germans. A quarter of a mile away, a red canoe, loaded to the gunwales, inches towards Birch Portage. Paddles flash, Freia's blond hair shines from the stern. Peter smiles, shaking his head, not at all surprised that Harald is in the bow. Perhaps by instinct, Freia turns and waves her paddle. Peter raises his right arm and gives a single left to right salute.

He watches until the canoe disappears behind an island, then claps his hands and grins, turns away from the lake and checks when he sees a neat pile of wood by the fireplace, and on top, four *biscuits*. For the grey jays, he wonders, or us. Biting into one he knows, and waves to a pair of images unloading at the portage. "Thanks, and good luck. *Prost.*"

In twenty minutes, the campsite belongs to Peter – a fire burning, coffee brewing, his wannigan in place, and his cooking pots littering the ground. As soon as the perking stops, he pours a cup of coffee, stirs in a heap of sugar, and scalds his puckered lips with his first slurp.

He hears his mother's rebuke; "Peter! Drink quietly, not loik a gu'er-snipe."

"Yes, yerr majesty," he says, bowing and sticking out his pinkie for the next sip.

Cup in hand, he scrambles down the cliff wall to the lake. He drops his clothes in a heap. Naked, crouching by the water, he sucks in air, and stretches out in a shallow dive. An easy front crawl carries him away from the island. He floats onto his back and sculls backwards. His toes break the surface. His penis, resembling a piece of beaver-stripped aspen, floats limply against his abdomen. The skin-coloured dressing is barely visible. Looking up, he searches the blue expanse for an eagle. Empty.

He heads back on a lazy breaststroke. Ashore, he gulps down the remaining coffee, then lies spread-eagled on the rock, shivering as the water evaporates from his stippled torso.

"Well, t' be sure! Oim in luck. T' little people have answered me prayers and delivered a naked prince," pipes an Irish voice.

Peter's eyes fly open, and above him, at the top of the cliff, Sara's staring down at him.

"Well, you'd better come down and kiss his hand."

"Depends on whether ye're here t' take me on a magic carpet ride, away from t' banshees that scream all noit. Or will ye stay and be moi lover?"

Peter folds his arms over his chest, a finger rolls his bottom lip. "Hmmm. Tough questions. The first, not possible. The second option; *might* be fun."

He suddenly remembers he's lying naked, leaps up and, hopping from leg to leg, staggers into his shorts, his white buttocks gleaming at Sara as she skids down to his side.

"Good morning…" she says, smiling broadly, moving close and facing Peter. She places her hands on his backside. "…lover. Nice cheeks! It's become quite a habit of yours to flash them at me," she adds coquettishly, and slaps his butt with a cupped hand.

"It *was* 'good'," Peter says, acutely aware of the blush prickling his wet hair. "Until it was rudely interrupted by a peeping-Paddy."

Sara laughs and drops her head onto his chest, and snuggles into his body.

"You can't expect me to know when you're lying around in your birthday suit. Brrr! You're cold. I must warm you to stave off hypothermia," snuggling tighter.

"Not inside. The coffee was hot." He holds his hands inches from her back, wanting to pull her closer, to feel her body's contours, but drops them lightly onto her hips.

She leans back, searches for his eyes which flick aside. "Do you fancy another swim?"

"Why not? Sure."

Sara locks his eyes with hers, backs away one step and undresses, dropping her clothes beside Peter's shirt and hat. He slips off his shorts, tosses them on the pile. Taking her hand, he leads her to the water.

"Make a shallow dive," he warns. "Together?"

Both dive and surface instantly, treading water.

Sara shrieks. "Ooh! It's cold!"

"Only at first." Peter laughs. "Race you…"

He splashes off on his crawl while Sara follows with a leisurely breaststroke. He manages only a dozen strokes and stops, panting heavily. Sculling on the surface, he watches her approach, head up and hair slicked back. As she draws closer, her smile widens, she's looking beyond him. Within arm's reach, she chops water into his face, spins, and heads back as fast as she can, her laugh peeling like a silver bell.

"Grrr!" Peter splutters. "You've asked for trouble now, you little Irish vixen."

However, after only a few strokes, he has to switch to breaststroke. His head spins and he wants to vomit. Sara, close to shore, is standing on the bottom when he arrives.

"Oh, boy!" he gasps. "Must take it easy."

Seeing Peter's ashen face, Sara reaches out a hand. He grabs it and pulls himself to her.

"Sorry, that was mean. I can never resist temptation."

"I'll remember that," he says pointedly.

Clinging to each other as they balance on the slippery rocks, they gradually merge, her arms around his waist, Peter's over her shoulders.

He brings a hand to the side of her face; his fingers wipe her eyes, down her cheeks, linger on her lips. Cupping a hand behind her cold wet neck, he draws her mouth to his. Cool, wet, he's forgotten the way lips feel when they meet. Hers part slightly, and his tongue enters a warm mouth.

Suddenly, Peter's foot that's supporting his weight slips off its rock. In a tangle of arms and legs they submerge, thrashing water, and surface laughing wildly.

"You did that on purpose! Who do you think you are? John the Baptist?"

"Never! You, dear lady, were in the arms of Saint Peter of Golden Gate fame. I hear that you have sinned. You'll be punished with a ducking and a wet, sloppy kiss."

She answers with another barrage of splashing.

Peter lurches and grabs her arms. "Enough, enough!" He kisses her loudly on the lips. "No more. I'm pooped." He wades to shore, pulling Sara in tow. He helps her climb out. They grab clothes to their bodies and scramble up the cliff.

"I'll get a towel," says Sara, and steps awkwardly across the rough ground to the tent, wincing at every sharp stone or twig that cuts her feet.

Peter crouches at the fire. He tosses a couple of logs on and has to quickly back off as sparks shower his skin like bee-stings.

Sara returns, holding the towel in front of her body. "Turn round," she orders, and dries Peter's back, rubbing hard to erase the goose bumps. "Okay." Peter rotates and his front receives similar attention, but as she nears his dressing, she's gentle, dabbing with a bunched-up corner.

When she's done, she holds the damp cloth out for Peter. Their eyes meet, an invitation, approval. Unhurriedly, Sara turns and Peter wipes her back and legs, tenderly soaking up every bead of water. He scrubs her hair, leaving it spiked like a ragamuffin. A touch to the shoulder and she rotates, faces him, cheeks faintly flushed, the hint of a smile, eyes alive. Using both hands wrapped in the towel, beginning at her face, Peter softly dries her body; down her neck, cupping her breasts as if they're crystal glass, across her flat belly to her feet which he places in turn on his knee. Diamonds hang from her pubic hair, a dark patch against her white skin. He resists the desire to pluck each one with his lips, but instead touches lightly with the towel.

Peter stands up, hesitant, unsure of his next move, ashamed of his arousal. Sara takes the towel and tosses it onto the wannigan.

"Let's go warm up in the tent," she says, tugging his hand. For a moment, Peter hangs back, biting his lip. But Sara's eager face and naked invitation break his final fragment of resolve.

The fire dies. Coffee dregs cool in the percolator. The whiskey jacks clean the campsite of every crumb, enjoying the deserted landscape.

Sometime, about mid-morning, quiet words are spoken.

"I don't know if I can. And besides, what if... what if I leave you pregnant."

"Don't worry about that. Not now."

After making love, they lie exhausted, drifting in and out of sleep on rucked sleeping bags. From time to time, one of them glides a hand across a limb, down an arm, across a thigh, around a waist. Peter awakens first, sweating profusely. "It's too hot in here." Sara responds drowsily by snuggling closer and blowing into his ear.

"Another swim?" she asks.

"Tonight, maybe."

"Peter, I love you."

They stare at each other, their eyes inches apart.

"I've never said that to a man before. Well, except for my dad."

"I wish you didn't. It would be easier... for you," Peter replies, his frown a rift between his eyebrows.

"But it *will* be easier now. I wasn't really sure how you felt, you seem to change with the weather. I have to be careful with what I say. Don't want to poke that temper of yours.

"Peter, sweetheart, I don't want to keep talking in terms of 'our time together', or 'the end', or 'making the most of it'. From now on, please let's not dwell on your cancer and live as though you're not going to die."

"I've been through this. With Danika. It's ugly. You can't avoid that I'm dying."

"Why 'ugly'? Didn't your love for each other grow? Did you not find joy in just that?"

Peter contemplates for a while, and shakes his head. His eyes focus on a knot of Sara's hair standing comically on end, like an exclamation mark. He recalls how he had sat at Danika's bedside, recounting the events of that day or reminiscing about a particular countryside they had loved. For the most part, Danika was unresponsive, infrequently offering a murmur, or a weak smile, at times only a stronger grip from her hand. Yes, he had loved her to the very last minute, but he thought Danika had lost her will to live and to love. Her death had been a blessing. It had brought grief and heartache and loneliness that time had eased only a bit. And the dreams, those horrible dreams. At the thought, Peter realises he has not been tortured by any violent nightmares since his accident.

"I don't want you to be hurt, that's all. What say we go next week and get my canoe?" his mind jumping to cliffs and petrography.

"Do you think you shou..." Sara stops in mid-sentence. "We can take my tent and stay over-night somewhere on the way," she says brightly.

After lunch, a red tarp stretches between trees. The woodpile grows. Their small supply of perishable food – butter, apples, tomatoes, and lettuce – is stored in an old ammunition case and buried beneath a thick carpet of moss. A couple of low-to-the-ground chairs sit beside the fireplace. Sara retrieves her two packs, and now shirts, shorts and sweaters cling to bushes breathing fresh air.

Late in the afternoon, they jump into the canoe and paddle to the first waterfall of Birch Rapids. In fifteen minutes, Peter catches three pickerel and five jackfish. The latter are the luckier – they are released unharmed, allowed to return to their lairs beneath the waves.

That night, in a festive mood, they feast on pan-fried fish fillets washed down with white wine from a plastic pop-bottle 'decanter'.

As though a requisite ritual of love, they sit at the edge of the cliff, arms around each other, hastening the sun to set. The moment it disappears, they run laughing to the tent, pulses racing.

Kneeling on the two sleeping bags zippered together, they undress each other, recklessly at first but tantalisingly slowly at the last. They slide between the folds, clinging to each other passionately.

"At last," Peter murmurs. "I couldn't stop thinking about this all afternoon."

"Me too. I'm happy we found out on our first day. We might have been beating about the bush for weeks avoiding the truth."

"Sara, are you okay with just loving without the making? My sex drive is still in neutral, you might say."

In answer, Sara rolls Peter on to his back, and with his face cradled in her hands, kisses his whole body, then covers his lips with hers, seemingly for hours. When they finally sleep, they are like babes in the wood, and the wicked witch that night is far away in Hudson Bay.

A week passes and the days grow noticeably shorter. A grey blanket covers the sky and a fine drizzle drifts in a north-east breeze. Loons are calling, their liquid ululation echoing through the velvet mist.

Peter stirs first, leaves the warmth of the sleeping bag and dresses. Once clear of the tent, he slips into rain pants and jacket. With his head hooded, Peter tilts his face to the sky. The cool rain bathes his tangled beard, moistens his skin, washes out the facial creases. He inhales deeply, relishing the complex aroma – a harmony of fermenting fruit-wine and fresh pencil shavings. Peter briskly rubs his face and eyes, wipes away traces of sleep.

He feels good. No, he feels wonderful.

He loves weather like this, when the elements close in like kid-leather gloves, with the air soft and smelling sweet from decaying vegetation. Even his body moves differently, unhurried, pliant.

He brews a pot of Earl Grey, delicately flavoured tea, compared to the bite of coffee, befitting the mood of the morning. As he had for Danika on many occasions, he takes a cup to Sara.

Kneeling at the entrance, he reaches into the tent.

"Wake up, sleepy head," he says quietly. "It's a beautiful day."

"Wow! Morning tea. Thank you," Sara says dreamily. "Such royal treatment."

Resting on an elbow, her shoulders bare, Sara sips the fragrant liquid. "It's cloudy, isn't it? Is it raining?"

"Yes, and yes. A fine drizzle."

"I don't like rain. It reminds me of London."

"I can understand that, but here it's different. The air smells clean, not of concrete and exhaust fumes. Hot oatmeal in about ten minutes, followed by warm bannock," Peter says, leaving Sara to dress.

During breakfast, sitting beneath the tarp, Peter suggests that they go for his canoe now that he's been recuperating for more than a week.

"In the rain?" Sara questions.

"Why should rain stop us? When it's gentle, mist-like, it can be quite soporific."

"But cold and uncomfortable."

"Dress for it. Besides, any weather condition is part of the wilderness experience. There're two kinds of weather – good, and not so good. I hate wind, but today the little that there is will be behind us."

Sara shrugs and spoons the last of her food into her mouth and eats disconsolately.

Taking Sara's empty dish, Peter suggests firmly, "Take your

smallest pack, two changes of clothing, including your poly-underwear. We'll take enough food for two days, and your tent."

"Can't we wait until tomorrow?"

"No! It'll be wetter, and the wind will change."

"Peter, you don't know that. You can't forecast the weather – without a radio," she protests.

"Remember the day we met?" he replies testily, "Was my prediction correct?"

Sara's face is blank, her lips pouting.

"Did you notice the ring around the sun yesterday? That's a sure sign the weather is going to change. Also, the loons were calling this morning, not last night."

"Oh, come on. There's a limit to what I'll believe. I suppose you believe in red sky at night, sailors' delight, red sky in the morn…"

"Sometimes! It's shepherds', not sailors'. Stay if you want. I'll go by myself," Peter explodes. "Do what you damn well please. I don't need you! When Tom comes by, why don't you go back with him!" Peter storms from the shelter, yanking the hood over his head. At the fireplace, he flings the dishes and spoons into the dirt and stomps down to the beach.

She calls after him. "At least he likes me, and he's not going to…" Sara clamps her hand over her mouth, drops her head, aghast at what she almost blurted from her lips. She runs to the top of the footpath. Her knuckles are pinched white. Her face is hot, but surprisingly, her eyes are dry. She holds her head in two hands, sinks to the ground. Peter has the canoe upright, half into the water. He's already heading back up the slope.

Peter enters the tent, gathers his sleeping bag and clothes and packs them into the Duluth bag. Sara's tent, still in its bag, is added. He strides to the fireplace and pots and bowls and cups and cutlery clatter into the wannigan. White faced, lips in a thin line, eyes focused on packing, he never gives Sara a glance.

He slings the wannigan onto his back. "I'll wait five minutes," he spits, standing at her side. "If you're not at the canoe with the Duluth in that time, I'll come and get it and assume you're staying." He disappears down the path.

Peter drops the box into the canoe and pushes it further into the water. He sits on the sand, legs bent, hands clasped round his knees.

By God, he's serious. Sara shakes her head, growls. What if I bluff him out, let him go by himself. He'll soon turn back. But he's so pig-headed, he won't. And kill himself. She envisions his body lying at the rock paintings, a picture that's still fresh in her mind. Guilt hits her.

Peter stands up. "Damn him!" Sara cusses. She runs to the tent and drags the Duluth bag by its straps to the path. Swinging it round, she sniggers as it rolls down the hill, coming to rest halfway against a rock. Back at the tent, she shoves her clothes into her smallest pack, closes the flap, and stomps down the path.

"Don't say a thing," she blurts. "I don't want to hear a peep out of you. For all intents and purposes, I'm not with you. Just going for the ride to see the paintings again." She plonks herself in the bow.

Peter snorts quietly, covering his mouth. "Here!" he snaps, smiling behind Sara's back. "You'll need this," and hands her a paddle.

"Thank you!" A pause. "What are we waiting for? Are we going to sit here all day?"

Sara is almost jerked off her seat when Peter shoves off. Both paddle furiously, unwilling to cool down, to forgive. They head north, their faces into the breeze, past densely foliated islands, then swing west around a peninsula. The wind, which has freshened, is now on their right beam, helping them as they head into a wide-open stretch of water. The rain on their backs is almost unnoticeable.

Damn him, damn him, Sara says to herself. Why, why? Tender in making love yet stinging in anger. Magically elastic in a canoe yet mulish by nature. Why did I expect a change? Did I think he would be more tolerant? Suppose I was about to die, would I behave differently?

Maybe we rushed things, remembering Peter's initial reluctance to follow her to the tent? Did I seduce him? She catches her breath – me, Sara Sutcliffe, a seductress! That's not me. More like someone I've read in a novel. Sara smirks.

But there's so little time... Her mind peers bleakly into a well, a well that's almost dry, that's dark, full of foreboding.

All morning they travel in angry silence. Sara starts humming tunes, singing the lyrics quietly to herself if and when they come to mind. She sings the first bars of every rain song she can remember. She wants to turn to look at Peter, but stubbornly resists.

Peter suddenly speaks. "Sara, I want to explain."

Sara stops, leaves her paddle in the water, stares at her feet. There's a lull in the wind; drifting, they hear only the rain's whisper.

"When Danika was in hospital, she expected *our* Sarah every day, waiting for her to come through the door," Peter says, his voice grim. "I phoned, left messages, but she never replied, never visited.

"Heart-broken, Danika gave up, lost interest in everything, just wanted to die. She was drugged heavily for the pain, and I began to think that I should pull the plug and let her go, or slip her an overdose. It took weeks. I didn't know or understand how she felt. I realised I had been keeping her alive for myself, not for her. Not until the final days did she even know I was there. But by then, all she could do was smile, nod, or squeeze my hand.

"I don't want to go like Danika. This morning I was feeling better, ready for anything. When you balked, you got in my way, became an obstacle. That angered me. I'm very sorry, you didn't deserve that - especially after caring for me the way you have, and... after last night.

"Sara, I don't want my life to drag on. When the pain gets unbearable, which, believe me, will happen, please end it for me quickly. A little extra morphine will do it..." Peter tails off.

Sara stares at the lake through glazed eyes, unable to see where the water ends and the sky begins. Her mind skits, bouncing between the past and the present, and now into the future. She wants to look at Peter, but is afraid. Fingers of dread tighten her throat. Surely, he doesn't mean I should kill...

Peter's paddle slices into the water; half-heartedly, she picks up the stroke. Tears begin running down her cheeks.

Two canoes pass by heading east, the occupants grimly bent into the weather, acknowledging Peter and Sara with waves. Sara is thankful that they didn't stop, knowing she can't face anyone at the moment.

"I'm hungry!" Sara announces.

Tucked into a lee shore, they lunch on cheese and bannock, bannock, Sara remembers, that was meant for breakfast.

"We'll be at the paintings in a couple of hours," Peter advises as they resume their journey. "We've made good time, thanks to the wind."

Uncomfortable with memories, they don't linger at the petrograph site, departing as soon as Peter's canoe is retrieved and the packs evenly distributed, heading back in search of an island camp site.

Alone in the canoe, her mind tangled in a web of dismay, Sara mutters a prayer. She thanks the spirits she senses spinning around her – she and Peter have indeed been saved, and have returned.

She hears the croak of a raven, and looking up, spots it circling, a black cross against the sky. The rain, still with them, washes her face, clings to her eyelashes. The bird swoops low and soars into a tall aspen. It has disappeared but she hears it cackling, laughing at her. Or, is it an invitation?

Sara smells smoke and hears a baritone voice. Glancing over her shoulder, the thickset person, dwarfed by a large red pack on his back, surprises her. He holds out a hand, blue veined, grime beneath the fingernails. Unable to resist, she places her hand in his, her long fingers disappearing in his grasp. He nods at her as if to say "All is ordered." The tender hold he has on her is unnerving, melting her like butter left too close to the fire. She senses trust, a confidence swelling unlike anything before. Then a change. The grip suddenly scorches. She pulls back. But her arm is trapped, she cannot move. Panic strikes, and she yanks hard. Her hand bursts from fire, a crackling fire, snapping, making no sense, but she feels her body stinging, recoiling from angry jets of hot air. Turning away, she collides with an Indian. She observes features that are strangely familiar – hair long and black, skin like old leather, half-clothed in deerskin breeches. Red wavy lines highlight his cheeks; more coiled on his naked chest, fangs poised above his heart. Before she sees his hand, she knows what to expect – three fingers. The cry of a wolf sends a shiver up her spine, wails aimed at the heart, squeezing lifeblood, leaving a stone that crumbles to dust, that floats away on a swirl of water.

"Sara. Helloooo…"

Sara's head jerks backward, a knot across her chest. Her eyes slowly focus, in time to see Peter broadside in the water, watching her intensely.

"Huh." Sara digs in her paddle, comes to rest.

"You look lost in a dream."

"I think so." She nods sluggishly, looking beyond him. "Yes… I was."

*   *   *

After a short distance, they find an island with an easy approach and a flat, grassy ledge overlooking the water. They erect the tent together, but it's Sara that makes a fire and boils water for tea.

Standing at the water's edge, gazing towards the western horizon, hands in pockets, Peter says, "We could have made it, you know." Sara frowns.

"To Tuktoyaktuk," he continues, crossing to the fire. "Silent Rapids is only an hour or two from here. I would like to take you there. Another day, maybe. But I'm exhausted. And I wasn't exactly pleasant company today. I'm sorry. I hope tomorrow will be better."

"Go and lie down now? I'll cook supper and bring it to you when it's ready."

Peter ducks into the tent, and when Sara delivers a bowl of soup, she finds him asleep, his tea untouched, cold.

Under the tall pines and with the overcast sky, night comes early. Before total darkness falls, Sara cleans up and crawls into bed. Lying close to Peter, she yearns for sleep, but her thoughts, like an annoying mosquito, keep it at bay. Eventually, she sleeps restlessly.

Outside, the rain stops and the clouds draw back, like curtains opening on a star-studded stage. A sliver of a new moon rises in the east, dimly illuminating the water that undulates like a breathing giant. The wind has died, yet latent waves continue to surge, gurgling into holes and crannies beneath black shadows. The air chills. Raindrops hanging onto leaves freeze, a crusting like sugar candy.

Winter's first frost lays its white hand on the land, galvanising food gathering for residents; bears, beaver, muskrats; sanctions departure for migrants flying south, and curtails the flow of sap in a million leaves. Beneath a steel sky, with a biting north-west wind behind them, Peter and Sara journey through a landscape that overnight has been daubed by an artist's yellow brush, crossing waters that reflect the pageant of summer's demise. In sheltered bays, King Midas has touched lime-green cattails and reeds. Wild rice begs harvesting, but the Indians with their airboats are far away, denied access by impassable rapids. Coniferous trees, steadfastly dark green, shelter a carpet of cardinal, russet and sienna; bunchberry, yarrow and wild lilies of the valley.

A Churchill River autumn is short, just a few days that stretch into September, and is acutely sweet. Blueberries swollen to bursting, bright red cranberries and ruby buffalo berries compete to be picked, entrusting birds, bears or man to spread their seed. The air is aromatic from Nature's last gasp, vibrant before winter's white cloak stifles growth for seven frigid months. For many, their hours of life are numbered. The cold's bounty will be grasped without compromise. Only the strongest and the prepared will survive, strengthening their species by handing on unique patterns of amino acids.

When Peter and Sara arrive back at their island roost, they are cognisant that this may well be their last homecoming. Peter knows the future does not promise many more overnight trips, if any. He enjoys the sense of home the island brings, its permanence. Sara, on the other hand, considers it temporary, a stepping stone to further camps, to future ventures. She is determined to fill their time together, not only with love, but also absorbing his knowledge, learning his skills so that she might remain in this land.

That night, they make love. Like a honeymoon couple, they discover in each other nuances that had gone unnoticed, missed in their rushed joining. Places where a caress draws a gasp, others that trigger a giggle. They explore with tongues and lips and noses. Peter fingers a small scar under Sara's chin – "I fell off my bicycle" – then guides her hand to his wounds – a slice from his improperly sheathed knife, the mark where his appendix had been cut out. Peter, at last, whispers in her ear, "I love you." Sara catches her breath as emotion washes over her like a warm shower. Never in her thirty-seven years has she felt this way – loved, wanted, needed.

Sara wakes suddenly. It's still dark. Peter's hand, clammy and cold, is clutching her shoulder, shaking.

"What is it?" she asks nervously as she rummages for the flashlight.

By the light's glow, she's shocked by Peter's drawn, pinched face.

"Give me a painkiller, Sara," he demands through clenched teeth. Ready for such an emergency, she digs the vial from the tent pocket near her head. An icy chill fingers her spine. She hands Peter a capsule, followed by the water bottle. Peter swallows and falls back. Sara grabs the bottle before it spills. She pulls the cover up to his neck. Caressing his head, she studies his face, her stomach in knots, until finally he sleeps. Sara holds him, an arm lightly across his chest.

Sara worries the rest of the night away, dozing fitfully. Not until the tent walls lighten does she sleep soundly, to be woken in what seemed like five minutes later, by Peter rolling over with a groan. Outside, birds are singing, her signal to rise and dress. Leaving the tent that morning, Sara is tired and her nerves are raw. She's conscious of the weight of responsibility on her shoulders – her nursing and wilderness skills are about to be tested.

The sun, well clear of the treeline across the water, lights-up her face. Her eyes sparkle and her skin glows, but her inside is ditch water, a quagmire of apprehension. With coffee perking, she lopes down to the lake, undresses, and dives in. The cold jolts her; she didn't expect the drop in temperature in so few days. Afterwards, scampering naked for a towel, she's electrified, her mind cleansed, her confidence restored. Her first thought in the water was "Never again," but now, with coffee delivering warmth, she resolves to begin each day the same way. How I've changed, she ponders, shaking her head, how I've changed. For a brief moment, her mind harks back to a railway carriage, huddled in a corner, a lonely soul on its daily commute.

*　*　*

Peter and Sara quickly establish a revised routine. With the pain dulled by analgesics, Peter refuses to submit to the cancer raging through his body. He rebuffs Sara's admonitions, determined to carry on as if nothing has changed. They take day or half-day trips, returning with a pickerel or two for the frypan. On lazy days, they bask in Indian summer sunshine, lounging in their chairs at the cliff-edge, chatting or reading. Sara breezes through several Grisham's and Danielle Steele's; Peter plunges into Joyce's *Ulysses*, claiming that he should at least read the infamous novel before he dies. Every day, after a few pages, he comments, "I just don't get it. I don't even understand what the guy is writing about. I need a dictionary for every second word. My brain, I suppose, is too mathematical. But there's a strange poetry in his words."

One day, idyllically breathless and warm, they take the Old Town canoe to the top of Birch Rapids and play – surf riding and perfecting different turns. Sara is thrilled when they execute a successful front ferry, crossing the sixty-yards a few feet above a ledge. They finish off the day by running the rapids and return to camp by 'Pesky Portage', mercifully bug-free from frost.

Depending on his schedule, Tom flies over every two to three days. One evening, Peter, hearing the approaching Cessna, waves a red flag tied to a tree limb, indicating that their food supply is low. The next morning, the plane returns and lands in the bay.

"I hope you brought Coke," Sara shouts to Tom as the aircraft drifts towards her. Wading into the water, she grabs Tom's rope and pulls the plane onto the sand.

"Here," Tom says, taking a can from his jacket pocket. "How's life?"

"Wonderful," she replies enthusiastically, gulping Coke. "You brought one for Peter, didn't you?"

"Of course. A dozen. And some beer. I must say you look

extremely well," remarks Tom, smiling. "How's Pete?"

"Coping. He's hurting, though. He's ready to kill for a Coke," she says, laughing.

Sara leads the climb to the campsite.

"Hi, Pete," Tom calls out before they reach the top. "Coke or beer?"

"Tom! Good to see you. Beer, of course."

Tom takes a blue can from his other pocket and hands it to Peter. "Great – I'll drink this Coke. My prediction was right, fortunately, otherwise I'd be going back down to get one."

They stand, urgently drinking, like rescued castaways.

"So. How you doing, Pete? You're looking well. Better than when I dropped you off."

"Can't complain," Peter answers, but knows Tom is being generous, remembering his frowning eyes as he breasted the climb. Peter raises his arm to Sara, and intuitively she moves into his side, an arm around Peter's waist.

"Do I sense something between you two?"

Sara blushes. "You could say. It's love, if that's what you've noticed."

"Super! When will we hear wedding bells?" Tom asks.

"I don't think you will, Tom. There's no need." Peter says quickly, aware of Tom's reddening face beneath his tan, "Let's get that plane unloaded. We're dying for fresh food."

"Not literally, I hope," chivvies Sara, kissing Peter on his cheek.

Together they unload and carry boxes of food up to camp.

"I brought more fresh than you ordered," Tom says when he drops the last box on the pile next to the fireplace. "With the cooler nights, I thought it would keep okay. I'll be back with more in seven days, or sooner if you signal."

"Thanks, Tom. We appreciate your help. Say 'hi' to Shorty and Sandy when you get back to Missinipe."

"Sure thing. By the way, the Roughriders are leading the West. They play the Eskies on Friday."

"Who's winning the East?"

"Allouettes and the Tiger-cats."

"What's today?" asks Sara, her face dead-pan, mystified by the men's discussion. "I've completely lost track."

"Wednesday. The sixteenth. Well, so long, Pete," Tom says, shaking hands. "Sara, I need you to push me off?"

Peter watches the two lope down to the beach, strangely resentful as they talk. Unnoticed, his grip has crumpled the beer can. Spinning on his heel, he moves to the boxes, opening each in turn until he finds the carton of chocolate bars.

"He looks drawn," Tom says to Sara as they prepare to cast off, "and his colour is a tinge yellow. He's lost weight, but otherwise not bad," he adds encouragingly.

"I don't notice. Not when I see him every day."

"Do you think he could get better?"

Sara shrugs. "Miracles happen, but no. He's taking painkillers daily. It's already two months, and the doctor gave him two to three. We actually pray every day. It keeps him feeling hopeful, although the last time, he says, God didn't help."

"In another month it will be too cold to stay here," Tom says as he hops onto the pontoon. "Give us a push. What will you do then? Could even have a foot of snow next week. Just a minute." Tom climbs into the cockpit and re-emerges.

"Take this," says Tom, glancing up to the campsite. "Best not tell Pete, though. It's Shorty's sat-phone. His idea. The number's on the back if there's a need."

"Thanks, Tom. I'll hide it somewhere."

Once Tom is in the cockpit, Sara gives the plane a mighty shove. She tucks the phone beneath a rock in the trees, and realises guiltily it's her first act taken without Peter's knowledge.

"What took you so long?" Peter asks, regretting the edge in his voice.

"Were we long? We were just chatting," replies Sara, avoiding Peter's look by moving to the boxes.

Peter nods. "Piece of chocolate?"

"Mmm. Thank you. We've lots of unpacking to do."

For the first time in nearly three weeks they eat fresh meat, feasting on a thick steak and vegetable stew.

"We've been so busy, I'd forgotten about good food," Peter says, wiping his bowl with his last piece of bread.

"Sara, I've decided. I want you to have my canoe."

"Really?"

"Yes. Who else can I give it to? Tomorrow, you're going to take it down the rapids."

"Oh, Peter. Thank you, thank you so much," says Sara quietly. "I wish I had something to give... in return."

"You already have; say no more. You were *chef coeur d'un bleu* tonight; I'll be chief bottle-washer." Peter grabs a pot and heads down to the lake.

"Do you want to share a chocolate bar for desert?" Sara calls after him. A raised arm, thumb up, tells her.

Sara shuffles the dishes and pots together and tosses a log onto the fire. Sparks fly into the dusky air. The days are short, and darkness draws in quickly after sunset. A Coleman lantern gives them some extra hours at the end of the day, hours for sharing memories and stories. However, night's chill sends them early to the tent, where warmth of love soon brings on slumber.

Two days later, after two days of solo canoeing in the rapids, Peter asks Sara, thinly disguising his sadness, for morphine. Later that night, when Sara takes him into her arms and caresses his head lying on her chest, she inwardly cries. She blinks rapidly so that no tear wets her cheeks. Unwillingly, she numbers the days that they have left and feels hollow, her inside chewed out by misery. Her thoughts tempt her to make a phone-call, sensing her inability to cope. But alone she must remain, as Peter had wished, and love him intensely.

Leaving Bloom peering into a butcher's shop in Joyce's Dublin, Peter's eyes drift off the page. Diverted by a smudge of yellow, they stare at the lichen-covered rock under his foot. Symbiosis is easy to understand, that complex bond between algae and fungus. But *Ulysses*? Huh! For every sentence comprehended, five remain a mystery, the words rattling around in his brain.

Peter's eyelids droop. His fist relaxes and the book slips to the ground, remains open.

Slumped in the chair, he dozes. A girl's laughter, his daughter's; she's running in the shade of elms, pirouetting. Her thirteenth birthday. A day alive with expectation, the day she wore her first adult dress, his gift. Velvet blue that matches her eyes, a simple but elegant cut, capped sleeves, and a full skirt that accentuates her slim waist. A silk sash drapes her hips. "Daddy, it's beautiful. Thank you, thank you. I love you."

A cumulus cloud blots out the sun. The air chills. A shadow pewters Peter's face, but the ghost of a smile lingers.

*   *   *

After the bush pilot's visit, the days merge into each other. Sitting over the fire, or staring at Black Bear Island Lake, Peter whiles away the hours. With each succeeding day, movement becomes more painful, necessitating additional morphine. Sara knows, however, that he's content. She sees small events that give him joy; grey jays feeding from his hand; loons calling morning or night; a 'Woolly Bear', a black and gold hairy caterpillar, searching for a winter nook beneath rotting leaves.

But there are numerous times when his creased forehead tells her his mind is elsewhere. He stares for hours at the wide expanse of sky; usually blue, often broken by scattered cumulus or high cirrus, occasionally a grey blanket. Vapour trails, ephemeral scars, for Sara's amusement are tagged according to their perceived destination: "Winnipeg." "Toronto, from Edmonton."

Then one clear morning, with the sun glinting off rippled water, Peter gives a long "Ahhh," followed by an excited shout. "Here at last!"

Sara interrupts her reading to scan the lake. "Who?"

"The geese, silly. Can't you hear them honking?"

Peter points north. "There. High up." Sara follows his hand and catches sight of a white wrinkle approaching as high as the wispy cirrus. A commotion, carried on a breeze, reaches them, suggesting a troop of hilarious clowns bursting upon a circus ring. A wide-flung vee across the sky is heading southward. Five minutes later, another wave, this one a long diagonal black thread, a perforated line. Sara counts out loud as might a child, reaching thirty-six before a gasp for breath. The front dozen or so birds break away, square dance indecisively, and then cobble together in formation, like Spitfires patrolling against the German invader. The birds remaining in line, unaccustomed to a new leader, waver momentarily, protest loudly, and continue to squabble until they, too, disappear to the south.

213

"Those were Canada geese," says Peter. "The first skein was snow geese. Heading for the prairies. They'll rest there for a week or two, feeding on grain much to the farmers' chagrin, before going on to Texas or Arizona."

Peter, noticeably relieved, returns to his reading, glancing skywards whenever heralded by new calls.

"A wonderful day," Peter exclaims after supper, as, with fingers entwined, they huddle close to blazing logs beneath a sky that's also on fire. "I didn't want to miss the migration. I always find it exciting; one of life's incredible mysteries."

He stares into the flames, captivated by the dancing colours."I don't have many more days, Sara," he says bleakly. "But I'm not really upset anymore. I've kinda gotten used to the idea, actually. It's losing touch with this land, this nature, which I regret. Not life itself. I've had enough of so-called civilisation. You can keep it for all I care – your pop culture, T.V. and radio, computers and high-tech cars. I can't abide it. Too noisy and shallow. The *audible grime of society*, someone once said. What I care for and love is out there. Look at that," he says with a sweeping gesture, encompassing the land beyond their island roost, "look at those colours – the reds, golden hues, the yellows, orange... An artist may try but will never adequately capture nature's design, its balance, the tension and contrast, the harmony and discord. Soak it in, my love, fill your soul – the trees, the lake, the weather, the aromas, and that sky. Have you ever seen such a sky? We are a part of this, you and me. Mother Nature cradles us in her arms. Nope, I don't regret dying; what I regret is being separated from what Goethe called '*the living, visible garment of God*'. This I will truly miss."

They stare in awe as the colours change. Peter turns to Sara with eyes that seem to be withdrawing into his skull, and says, "When I die, I want you to do something for me. It's something to which I have given much thought and will be difficult for you. But you must promise me."

Sara nods pensively. "If I can."

He tells her, and why. She sits aghast, ringing her hands.

"Peter, I can't. Impossible."

"You will, you must, for me." He grips her hands in his. "It has to be. Will you promise?"

Sara sits for several minutes, staring wide-eyed into the fire. She recalls her premonition at the petrographs, its meaning now shockingly clear, and shivers.

Finally she nods slowly, stony-faced. "Alright," she breathes.

Peter gently pulls her close with a hand around her back, her head resting inside his shoulder. In silence, they sit, their minds adrift, whisked skyward in the fire's updraft. Not until a bed of red coals glows in the hearth do they move. Peter stands, pushing himself upright by his knees. He holds out his arms. Sara moves into them. "Let's go to bed," he says softly.

For a few more days the geese traverse the sky. On the fifth day, overcast with a north-east wind, they pass directly over the campsite, having followed the length of Trout Lake, and, swinging right, the twisting course of Birch Rapids. They are low enough for Peter and Sara to see the white-chinned, black heads turning, and can pick out the geese that are honking.

"Watch," Peter says, after the first two flights. "When they see Besnard Lake, they'll veer to the south."

Sara gapes in amazement as each skein follows Peter's prediction, as if maps are etched in their brains.

All night they hear the geese overhead. No sooner has silence returned than the next flight announces its approach from the east.

Sara asks how they can possibly see their way.

"By moonlight – shining off the lakes. The direction of the wind,"

Peter answers softly. "They know their way. They feel it."

Sara sleeps fitfully, wing feathers constantly whispering in her dreams. For the first time, cold lances her flesh and she wishes for extra clothes. Thankful when daylight eventually throws back the shadows, she lies on her back and soon realises something's different, something is amiss. It's all too quiet. Ten minutes pass and still she has not heard a sound. The geese!

"Peter," she whispers. He doesn't stir. "Peter," a little louder, "the geese have gone." Gently, she shakes his shoulder. It's rigid. Her hand slides to his neck. Cold, dry.

"Oh, no," she whispers to no one but herself. She's alone. The geese have gone and so has Peter. Perhaps he hung on just long enough to journey with them.

Sara eases out of the sleeping bag, scared to nudge him. She dresses quickly, including her red sweater under her anorak. Marching on the double back and forth across the campsite, she begins to feel warmth flowing into her fingers and toes.

Her promise to Peter storms through her muddled head. I can't do it. It's not like he'd know. Or would he? She wrings her hands. She bends for stones, sharp and angular, and throws them far into the lake, trying to jettison Peter's imposition.

Coffee, that's what I need. Then I'll decide.

Fortified by caffeine and the fire's vigour, Sara resolves to comply with Peter's wish despite the consequences.

She grabs the Swede saw and plunges into the forest. The first fallen tree succumbs to the bite of her cut. Bucked to manageable length, she drags it to the tip of the island.

She lays the first element, the foundation of Peter's funeral pyre.

All morning it grows, a great mound of dead logs and branches bearing tanned needles. Scurrying for alternate habitat, insects –

beetles, ants, woodborers – fall to the ground, their laboriously chewed tunnels abandoned.

As she works, Sara remembers the bonfires she and her father had built back home for Guy Fawkes' night.

Remember, remember, the fifth of November.

The familiar rhyme pounds in her head. With hundreds of fires throughout London, the glow would light up the sky, a ghastly remembrance, not of the traitor Fawkes, but of the Blitz. Rockets and Roman candles would streak and sparkle like tracer. She stops in horror when she realises that it's to be Peter's body rather than the traditional 'Guy' effigy that she has to lift onto the top. Her will to fulfil Peter's request evaporates. I can't, she argues, visualising flames licking at his legs, singeing his white hair, scorching his flesh into a blackened mess. And the smell. It will be abhorrent! I can't, I can't. Tears begin to brim, hot tears of horror, sadness and loss.

Desperately, she rushes down the cliff to their swimming place. She collapses to the ground, arms wrapped around her legs, her chin on her knees. Eyes clamp shut, tears squeeze out and trickle hotly down her cheeks. Silently she weeps, her body shaking uncontrollably.

Memories surface – swimming together, drying each other's bodies, where they had first kissed. For an hour she sits, petrified. Not even the pair of loons nearby, their desolate cries permeating the air, breaks Sara's trance.

It's pain that eventually moves her. A numbing pain slides up her spine, reaching her brain. Awkwardly, she stands, unfolding her stiffened limbs, and trudges up the cliff. Without glancing at the bier, she goes resolutely to the tent and enters. Her eyes won't focus, seeing only a blur of green as she grabs the corner of the sleeping bag and drags it outside with Peter's body still wrapped in it.

Should he be dressed, she suddenly thinks, or left naked. She rolls him onto his back. His eyes are closed. Her's focus unwillingly.

Little by little, the tightness across her chest eases and her breathing returns to normal. Sara is startled – Peter's face has changed, is softer, smoother. No longer pinched. Yes, pallid, but more like the Peter I first met. Really only two and half months ago? Such a short time, yet I know him better than I've known any man. Sara stretches out a hand, strokes his cheek, ignoring the coldness of the skin, and traces its hollow curve into his jaw. She fingers his lips, and before she can stop herself, she bends over and kisses his mouth.

"Now, Peter, I think I can do it. As usual, you've bolstered my courage."

She half rises, pulls back the sleeping bag, slips her arms under his naked waist and legs, and stands up. Sara is shocked by its lightness. She compares now with that day at the rock paintings when she had carried him down from the cliff. Straight backed, she carries the body to the bier. Placing it on to the shoulder-high table of logs, she straightens his legs and sets his arms across his chest. She raises his head and slips a log under his neck. Standing back, she wonders if she should pray, or say the few words she remembers from funerals she has attended. But something is missing. Then, turning, she flies down the cliff path to the beach, flips over Peter's canoe, and grabs his whitewater paddle. She runs, arriving breathless.

"Peter, you'll need this. I'm sure there's whitewater in heaven," she gasps. Carefully, she lays the paddle lengthways on the body and folds his fingers around the shaft.

Again she steps back, but this time her composure disintegrates. Is he really dead? He looks like he's sleeping. Dreaming of rivers, tree-lined shores. The fateful moment has arrived. She cannot change her mind. Or might she? Again, tears flood down her cheeks. Quickly, she crosses to the wannigan and clumsily grabs the box of matches. Several spill to the ground. Through misty eyes, she finds one. It breaks as she strikes it against the side of the box. The next one, the same. The third one burns. She tastes its sulphurous aroma sharply in the back of her throat. Hands shaking, she holds it to a piece of birch bark. It spits into flame, black smoke billowing. She plunges it through a gap in the logs. The dry needles burst, crackling orange and red, smelling sweetly of pine, a spicy incense. Sara's heart hangs in suspense. What if the fire goes out, she thinks fearfully, I'll never be able to do this again. Oh, dear God, please burn.

The flames, tentative at first, spread rapidly, growing hungrily, consuming the dead branches, licking at the body. She falls back, the heat intense. She gags at the smell of burning hair.

"Peter," Sara moans, "I'm sorry. I can't stay here any longer. Goodbye, my love. God bless and keep you."

She runs. Down the path she plunges. Grabbing Peter's canoe, she shoves it into the water. Seizing his bent paddle, she jumps in.

Driving the blade into the water, she leaves the island. At first, unable to steer, her path is erratic, but gradually, the water gives her its rhythm, its calming music easing her mind. Faster and faster she paddles, the light canoe surging, flying across the lake. She casts the cremation out of her mind. She heads into the bay above Birch Rapids, where Peter and she had gone – on their second day together heading for Tuktoyaktok; to fetch the canoe at the rock paintings; on a day trip just last week.

The thunder of Birch Rapids, to her right, burns into her brain. On an impulse she turns the canoe. In front of her, a hundred yards away, white horses leap skyward. At the spot where she and Peter had previously landed, Sara feels the water is alive, carrying her along. It's too late to turn back, just as it had been when she plunged the flaming birch into the pyre; she remembers the island she must circumvent, or use to bail out, an escape hatch. The current grips the canoe, swings it into the curved channel. Now is the time; now is the last opportunity to cede defeat, or confront the challenge. Inexplicably, Sara keeps going, maintains her course.

The island is behind her. Confidence swells as she jiggles the canoe through the chute near the shore. Into the main stream. With the water taking hold, pitching the canoe from side to side, she's ecstatic. Her mind and body suddenly burst free.

"Oh yes, Peter," she shouts. "I feel you. In my veins. I hear you in my heart."

Cold water soaks her within seconds. The canoe races down the wild river. Sara sees the mountainous waves approaching, remembers them, and rides them like a rodeo bull-rider.

All at once, the water slackens. Sara lets the canoe drift, turning in slow circles. She looks back up the torrent; a wide smile saturates her face. "Thank you, Peter," she hollers, waving the paddle.

For an hour, Sara plays at the foot of the rapids. Ferrying to a large eddy on river-right, she uses it to track upstream, to where the first standing waves form. She rejoins the current and rides the big upsurges. Time and time again, she repeats the circle, each time daring the waves to capsize her, a perverse desire to join Peter in death.

Eventually she tires. A weak sun warms her face, but sodden clothes soon chill her. Sara shivers.

She paddles to 'Pesky Portage'; surprises herself by lifting the canoe easily onto her shoulders. She slops along the trail, generating a little desperately needed warmth, but her soggy attire keeps her in an icy glove.

Reluctantly she approaches the island. A thin wisp of smoke drifts up from the point, but the flames have died. Relieved, she increases her pace, arrives at the beach.

She runs up the slope and with eyes avoiding the burning remnants, strips and drapes herself in Peter's sleeping bag. From her pack in the tent vestibule, she takes Shorty's phone.

"He's dead," she says, breathlessly, as soon as the phone clicks.

"Sara, is that you?" Sara recognises Shorty's voice.

"Yes. Tell Tom. Don't let anyone come with him."

Shorty pauses. "Sure. Whatever you say. He's at the base. Give him twenty to thirty minutes. Sara, I'm sorry. Peter was a good friend."

"I know." Sara abruptly switches off the phone.

Apprehension and a shortage of breath wrack Tom's heart when he reaches the campsite and finds Sara glued to where he'd first seen her from the air. Sitting at the cliff-edge, a sleeping bag draped over her shoulders, she seems to have been petrified. She's oblivious to Tom's arrival. He stands uncomfortably shuffling his feet, hands thrust in his flying-jacket pockets.

"I'm sorry..." Tom says after several seconds. His voice catches in his throat.

"Where's his body?" Tom ventures, "In the tent?"

Sara shakes her head slightly. Tom frowns, eyes scanning the site.

Tom bends to one knee at Sara's side. "Where then?"

"Gone. Cremated."

"Jesus! What did you say...?"

"Cremated."

He turns and the pile of ashes that he had seen from the air as a grey smudge now tells him its tale.

Sara nods. "He wanted... to be..." she mutters. "...on the island. Out here." She looks at Tom, her face a white mask. "He wrote a letter. Tucked into *Ulysses*, I think."

Tom wavers, then walks to the point. He breathes through pursed lips, thankful that no charred limbs remain. He's horrified that he'd see scorched legs, or fingers, a blackened skull. The sweet smell in his throat is stronger, now unmistakable. Heat radiating from the rocks tells Tom how big the fire had been.

"How did you…?" Tom says, back at Sara's side. Her bleak look stops him cold.

"I can't go over there," she says, nodding with her head. "Has everything burned?"

"I think so."

"I have to take his ashes," she whispers hoarsely. "I can't stay here, Tom. I have to leave as soon as possible."

"That figures."

"Would you pack everything for me?"

"Sure. I'll fly you to Mis…"

"No! I'll go by canoe… take his ashes. I know where he wants to go."

Tom nods, understanding.

"What do you need? I'll pack it for you. And I'll clean up the site once you've gone."

Within the hour, Sara flees the island in Peter's canoe. Anticipating she'd take the portage, Tom is surprised to see her head for Birch Rapids, eventually disappearing down the far side. Shaking his head, Tom starts packing, haphazardly stuffing the tent, gear and remaining food into packs and boxes. Eager to leave himself, he hurries down the slope, slings the bags into the cabin and lashes the 'Old Town' canoe to the wing-struts. He can't dispel the notion that Sara has purposely had a mishap and drowned.

Once out into the bay, Tom shortens his preparation, opens the throttle and takes off into the sun. Banking away from the island he stays low and heads east. Flying beside Birch Rapids, he searches for signs of Sara and breathes easier when he finds none. Swinging to port, he sees the second rapids, and then beyond, a narrow island. On shore, at a break in the willows, he spots the hull of Peter's canoe. Sara runs from the trees and waves. Heaving a sigh of relief, Tom rocks the plane, soars into the darkening sky and heads for Missinipe.

Early next morning, as the sun rises over Trout Lake, burning-off fingers of fog clinging to treetops, Sara sets out, steadfast in her promise to fulfil Peter's last wish. She portages Trout Falls, runs the next two rapids, and by early afternoon, she's crossing Stack Lake. Vivid memories shadow her, and on rounding her 'corner of conflict', as she's named it, the rumble of Rocktrout Rapids greets her with a standing ovation.

Sara lands in the all-familiar bay, and before erecting her tent, wanders around the site until all the ghosts have been exorcised. She soon has a fire burning. From where Tom has stored it in the wannigan, Sara removes Peter's billy. The lid slips from her hand when she pries it loose, exposing the grey dust.

Sara grabs another pot and walks purposefully down to the river. Beneath a golden sky, the valley, deep in shadow and rising mist, feels as solemn as a cathedral in lent. If a Gregorian Chant reverberated in the trees, Sara imagines, it wouldn't surprise me.

With bated breath, she probes the air for nighthawks. Her face drops. She realises they, too, have gone.

Sara feels acutely alone, a forgotten beach chair after summer's tourists have gone home. Clutching the billy to her breast, she fingers the ashes. Soft as talc, Sara stirs them. She rubs a pinch between her thumb and forefingers, and into her palm. Her skin colours dusty-grey.

Smiling, she says, "Your atoms are part of me now, Peter. In my memory. In my flesh. And possibly – I have an uncanny feeling – there's a new life inside me."

Nearing the river, fine dew clings to every tiny hair on her face. "Sorry the casket isn't much to write home about, Peter, but it kinda suits your style. You don't mind, do you? Being in your billy? You must admit, it's somewhat ironic, befitting." Sara laughs. "Day's end, your favourite time. Time for tea. Sorry, my love, I shouldn't joke. Yesterday, God, was I miserable, but today, here in your place, your *Shangri-la*, I'm joyful. I'm happy for you because you found life, and for me because I found you, or you found me, whatever. Do you remember? You must. I'll never forget. Scared me out of my wits, you did. And now, my sweet, it's time... back to the world you love." Sara lobs the billy into the waves. The thump as it disappears into the foam is like a heart-throb.

For ten minutes she stands, a hand on her stomach, her eyes staring into the foam, watching the waves' rise and fall, advance and retreat.

Filling the second pot, she returns to the fire, throws on branches and, when the water boils, makes tea. She strolls to the canyon's edge.

Easing herself down beside the old jackpine, she relishes its scaly bark digging into her back. As she drinks, her mind drifts, mingling with the mist.

At first, she thinks it a trick of the light. A movement beside the river gives her a start. An otter or a beaver, she assumes, or a deer taking its evening drink. Concentrating furiously, she sees a body bend low, scooping a billy in the water.

Sara shakes her head. To see better, she slides until her legs drape over the edge, gripping the rocks beneath her. No, that's impossible, it can't be. The figure is wearing a red shirt and a crumpled Tilly hat. Standing, it turns and searches the sky.

"Peter?" she whispers. "How is this happening?" Sara gets up quickly, her fingers visibly shaking. The figure appears to be in conversation with another, sinister in a black frock coat and a white frilled shirt. The willows part, pushed aside by something, or someone. How can this be? There's no wind. The shadow heads up the slope.

Picking her way through the trees, Sara cautiously approaches the campfire. Somehow, she's expecting what she sees, is even excited. There on the green box sits Peter, warming himself, watching water heating on the fire. As Sara creeps closer, he looks up, smiles, and pats the box beside him. With knees knocking, Sara sits.

"It was a fun day," she begins nervously, afraid to scare off the apparition. "Ran some whitewater, then a wonderful sunset."

Sara senses his body move as he nods.

"No, I didn't run Trout Falls – once is enough – but I did Birch yesterday, twice in fact," she says, answering the imagined question. Tea made; the ghost drinks from a yellow mug with heaps of sugar.

She describes the rest of the day, sharing her fascination of the changing scenery, the mosaic of colours. Time slips by, measured by the flare of the fire as she tosses on more logs. Above, a heaven of stars glitters with icy coldness.

"Now, Peter, I'm deliciously tired. You know? Limbs heavy like lead. My eyelids need toothpicks to keep them open. Look after the fire for me, make sure it stays safe."

She slips into the tent, removes only her outer clothes, and snuggles into her sleeping bag. She lies for a while, fingering shards of memories, crystal blue eyes and a precious smile. Before she sleeps, she promises herself that she will return every year. In her heart she knows she'll find him here, waiting for her stories and sharing her adventures.

The next morning, she wakes with a start. She has overslept, and knows, before she leaves the tent, that the sun is high in the sky.

She packs quickly, bagging her few items, and portages her pack to the end of the trail. Without a second thought, she zippers into her lifejacket and shoves off in the empty canoe. Turning quickly into the current, she hugs the shoreline. The keel hits bottom as she runs the ledge. Swinging hard right, she kisses the rooster tail, and floats to the bottom of the canyon. She lands and loads the canoe.

Sara checks the map after nearly taking the wrong channel into Mountney Lake, and makes good time to Nipew, blissfully running the rapids. Turning onto Nipew from the sheltered Churchill River, a cold wind punches her face. She pulls over to the right, lands on the peninsula that projects into the lake and walks the few yards through open trees to the windward shore. She searches the sky – a cold blue, a hint of winter's approach. She senses *The Lonely Land* – summer's hiatus is history; canoeists and fishermen have returned to their cities, birds have migrated, rodents are deep in their nests. Bleak. The air sharp. She braces herself in the wind, hands deep in pockets, hair flattened. She waits, constantly moving. Far out is the island she remembers, the battleship-shaped one. Again, it draws her and she wonders why. Next year, she says to herself, I have to go to it, discover its secret. A couple of times, she turns into the woods and runs around for warmth, then returns to her spot.

At last, a speck appears on the horizon. From mosquito to raptor in seconds, the plane approaches. Twice it circles before landing on the lee side, choosing to set down on the estuary rather than the open lake. Cautiously, it taxies closer.

Tom gestures to Sara to paddle out to the plane. "We'll have to load here because of the wind and rocks."

Within minutes the plane is loaded and they're skimming across the water, lifting off just before the river flows into the lake. As they climb, Sara peers down. *Nipew* quickly recedes. She's overjoyed to leave, flying free from its icy grip, its grim history. She knows in her heart, however, that next year it will claim her again.

"Will you go home to England now?" Tom asks politely, once they have levelled off and are heading for Missinipe.

"I don't want to but there's lots to sort out with the police and immigration. Maybe I won't be allowed to stay."

"You will," Tom responds assuredly. "Peter's letter should help.

You'll not have any trouble."

"I hope you're right. I want to live in Missinipe."

Tom glances at her. "I like *that* idea."

EPILOGUE

The lone wolf, partly hidden by yellowing hazel and river alder, hungrily watches the woman depart from the other side of the river. Its belly growls.

She disappears down the rapids. The gaunt animal slinks to the water, briefly laps. It scales the rocks overlooking Rocktrout Rapids, reaching the edge in time to see the canoe turn the corner. Human scent, sweet like spring flowers, hangs in the air, drifting on the damp breeze. The wolf's tongue drools.

Caution abandoned, the animal lopes along the riverbank to the end of the canyon. The sight of Sara on the other shore sends it into a frenzy. It trots to another vantage-point, but is again stymied by water.

The animal lifts its right hind leg, a reflex action to ease the perpetual soreness of infection.

The woman pushes off. If she had glanced to her left, she would have seen the animal not ten yards away. However, her attention is focused on a map. Ahead an island splits the river into two channels. To the right flows the main course. But the map fails to show the hidden constriction that almost blocks the left passage.

Sara noses left. Gingerly she stands up, steadying the canoe like an aerialist. Frowning, she sits and re-examines the map – it shows an opening. Sara, two strokes; the wolf, four strides. Sara shakes her head and back-paddles. The stern, swinging through a half-circle, approaches the shore. The wolf stands a yard or two away. It crouches, its head tense, ears pointing. A few more feet. Closer.

Inches before the canoe strikes bottom, Sara commits herself. With a pull, the boat moves forward, points to the right-hand passage.

The animal races, desperately leaps the stream, and with the last of its strength darts through the island's underbrush, reaching the far side just in time to see Sara glide by, her paddle trailing in the current.

Panting heavily, the wolf watches its salvation disappear. Turning, its energy spent, it drags itself back up the canyon to the rapids. In the last month it has eaten little; two voles and a deer mouse. Unable to keep up with the pack, it is now alone, its ambition to lead long forgotten. Finding food, any food, fills its mind, its sole ambition.

At the ledge, it collapses, its head resting on ragged paws. Looking across the torrent, it eyes a squirrel that scampers up the old jackpine. Tail twitching, the squirrel balances on a branch over-hanging the river. With no reaction from the canine, it descends and scuttles off to a winter cache.

The wolf remembers better days: loping through miles and miles of forest, an organised attack that brought down a doe and its fawn and nourished the pack for a week, playful nipping of ears of an attractive bitch, foreplay to regurgitation, and singing to the stars. The wolf pushes itself onto straight front legs and wails; from deep within its chest, a cry of pain, loneliness, and hunger. The howl, sailing upstream, competes with the thunderous torrent and dies meeting its echo in the forest. Relatively few creatures hear the call, but those that do recognise a death rattle. Unafraid, they continue with their hunting and gathering. The animal bays several more times until, exhausted, the howls turn to cries of anguish. The wolf drops onto its side, its ribs shuddering, one eye skyward.

The growl of the water crashing over the rapids dulls the wolf's senses, cloaks the flap of a raven's wings as it lands behind the wolf's vision. The bird, black as a night sky, advances one tentative step towards the prostrate animal. Head cocked, it searches for life signs. Two more strides and the raven's beside the trembling ears.

It waits. Like lightening, the head strikes. The huge black beak clamps onto the eyelid, shakes it like a jackhammer, and when the raven pulls back, a piercing green eye is lodged in its mouth.

The wolf's head shoots up with a yelp, a sobbing cry that shrinks to a whimper when it falls back. The raven walks fearlessly to the front. The second eye, a delicacy unsurpassed, bulges against the ground. The bird skews its head nearly horizontal. Strike – but misses. Bared fangs snap, cling to feathers, but the massive bird is already airborne. The wolf growls at the raven, oblivious of the trickle of blood oozing down its cheek.

That growl is its last in defiance, its final clutch on life. Collapsing, the wolf's head strikes granite and its last breath expires through flared nostrils. The raven returns, shifts the skull with its talons, and yanks the eye from its socket.

The bird gurgles, releases a cackle, and family members, sentinels in nearby trees, glide to the rock. Within minutes, eight ravens are tugging, digging, and gulping down hunks of red meat. In their midst, their leader balances on fur-coated ribs, its head plunging rhythmically into a gaping wound, into the warm heart of the timber wolf.

Canis borealis est mort.